HUNG OUT TO DIE

A CRIME NOVEL

GREG MORE

Best wishes Carol from author.

Morebooks

G M More

GREG MORE
the Author

'Hung Out to Die' is Greg More's début crime novel and was primarily inspired by his study of theology in New Zealand and Rome, this led to him imagining sitting in church at Eastertime with all the statues and crosses covered in purple shrouds which when removed during the *Gloria of Resurrection Mass* revealed a cross with a dead body on it.

Greg has always had an interest in crime novels and a desire to write one. After attending a talk by Portsmouth novelist, Pauline Rowson, he decided that it was time to write his own.

Born in New Zealand in 1947 Greg More moved to England in 1990 and now lives with his partner in Portchester in the south of England.

He is currently working on a further crime novel with the young detective featured in this book, playing a key role in solving yet another gripping crime.

CHAPTER ONE

The Church of the Holy Virgin was in darkness, total darkness, not even a flickering candle to indicate the presence of the Eucharist in the church. The church was locked, therefore there was no-one to see the figure of a man crucified on the make-shift Easter Cross by the main altar, covered in a purple shroud.

Chapter Two

Although it was a Saturday, Reverend Sean MacAleese woke up just before the alarm went off, at his usual time of 6.00am, and leaned across his wife to cancel it so that it would not wake her. Today would be very busy, because tonight's midnight service would have to be perfect, as the Easter celebration is the most important in the church's liturgical calendar.

Before he had found sleep, he had been going over in his mind all the things that still needed to be done before he was ready to light the Paschal Fire which marked the beginning of the celebration of Christ's resurrection. He got up, showered, and then went downstairs to make coffee and leave a cup on his wife's bedside table. He was anxious to get to the church to check that the organist had made the changes to the order of hymns that he had requested, along with a thousand other things to do.

He let himself in by the side door of the new room extension, which was built in 1977 for Sunday School services and as a tearoom. He dropped off his bag on a table in the tearoom, filled and turned on the hot water heater and then made his way into the church. On turning on the lights, he looked around the twelfth century Norman church built from Isle of Wight stone, and then moved to the west door to unlock it.

He turned back and started walking towards the altar, passing the font carved from Caen limestone, and then passing the large plaque on the North Wall that commemorated a grant of £400 from Queen Anne in 1710 to repair the church after its misuse by Dutch prisoners of war from the 1660's. Further on he stopped in front of the two World War memorials that commemorated the military deaths of local residents, and made a silent prayer for the repose of their souls as he always did, and then glad to see that all seemed to be in order, he knelt in front of the altar and prayed that The Holy Spirit would guide him through the coming religious celebrations, and that there would be no untoward occurrences that could shift the focus from Jesus's death and resurrection.

The statues and crucifixes were all covered in the purple shrouds as a sign of Jesus's passion and death. These shrouds would be removed during Midnight Mass as the triumphant notes of the organ sounding the 'Gloria' reverberated throughout the church. A sign that the resurrection of Jesus was upon us. Sean inspected each one in turn as he recalled one year when the release pull failed to operate, and a ladder had to be brought in to uncover the statue. A distraction that he did not want repeated. On close examination, he noticed that the covering over the makeshift cross that had been used in the previous day's Good Friday procession did not seem to be hanging properly. He decided to release the shroud and reposition it.

On pulling the cord, he was stunned to see a body on the Cross and immediately checked whether it was alive or dead. He found no pulse, presumed death, and immediately blessed himself. He knew enough about this type of situation not to touch anything. He then looked hard at the face of the body and suddenly realised that he knew the man. Josh Christopher. Not only was he a parishioner, but he was the actor who had played Jesus carrying the cross during the Good Friday service the previous afternoon. Whoever had done this had tried to

3

imitate Jesus's crucifixion with rope instead of nails, and white sports shorts instead of a loin cloth. There was even a slash in the right side of the body obviously intended to replicate the Roman centurion who thrust a spear into Jesus's side rather than break his legs as ordered, in order to ensure that death occurred before the Sabbath.

Sean took out his mobile phone and dialled 999. The operator patched him through to the police and Sean could tell from the tone and manner of the duty officer that answered that he would have preferred to have been at home with his family on this holiday weekend, rather than taking early calls from a no doubt drunken nutter who had lost his cat! His manner quickly changed when Sean said that he would like to report a mysterious death that was probably a murder. Once assured that some action would be taken, Sean put his phone back in his cassock pocket, and examined Josh's body on the cross more closely.

He could not see any blood or water stains on the floor at the foot of the cross, so he concluded that if that is how he had been killed, then at least the deed was not done in the church. This meant that the perpetrator had to carry a dead body into the church and suspend it on to the cross. Some feat. Further examination of the body showed some bruising around Josh's neck so maybe he had died by strangulation? Sean was just thankful that he had discovered this when he did rather than be faced with it during the triumphant opening chords of the 'Gloria'. That did not bear thinking about. Sean made a mental note to himself to tell the police that they had to be done and dusted by about 9.00pm tonight so Midnight Mass could go ahead as scheduled.

This was not how Sean had planned to start this day!!

CHAPTER THREE

Detective Constable Jo Fletcher had drawn the short straw for the Easter Holiday weekend duty, and so it was she who took the message at 8:05am from the police duty officer. She finished her Latte that she had bought at the *Freshcos* supermarket coffee shop across the road, grabbed her coat and Dictaphone and set off to the compound to draw a police pool car, a good old reliable Vauxhall Astra. Having lived locally for all her life, Jo knew the route to the castle and church without the need for satnav or a map. Only half the castle grey door would be open, so she parked in the small car park and walked down the drive to the church. She noted the security camera opposite the entrance to the *English Heritage* run castle keep and thought that that might be useful later.

On entering the church, she could immediately see the body on the cross, and the vicar standing beside it. She walked quickly up the aisle and introduced herself to the vicar.

'Not really the Easter celebration that you were planning reverend, I bet,' she said.

'No, lucky I discovered it now and not during the Easter Mass tonight,' he replied.

'Yes, we would have had to close you down and send everyone home. How long have we got?'

'Well, the congregation will start arriving about 11.00 tonight, so if you could be done and dusted by about 10pm that would be

5

good, in case the choir and organist come in for some practice.'

Jo peered at the body. 'I know that man,' she said.

'Josh Christopher!' they both said together.

'Yes,' said Sean, 'he is a parishioner, and ironically the actor who played the role of Jesus and carried the cross to where it is now, in our Good Friday service, yesterday.'

'He is also plays fly-half for the England rugby team and he would have been a vital player against the All Blacks when they tour in the Autumn internationals in November,' said Jo. 'Reverend, this story will be big, when it gets out. Unless we act now, your church will be overrun by the press. I would suggest you keep the outer gates and doors closed so the TV outside broadcast trucks cannot get in, and the church door locked until we have concluded our investigations.'

'What about Josh's family,' said Sean, 'they will have been missing him since last night, I presume?'

'Obviously, we need to tell them, but I will organise that as I want to impress on them the need to keep this secret for a while. I will also need to talk with you later reverend, but I now need to call this in and get the Scenes of Crime team and our photographer to attend. Can you please close the doors to stop wanderers coming in for a few hours? I will get some police tape put around and get some community constables in to protect the crime scene.' said Jo.

'I'll lock the doors now,' said Sean 'as I do not want anyone seeing this either.'

At that Sean went down the aisle while Jo took out her phone and rang through to the sergeant in charge of the Scenes of Crime Officers, known just as the SOCO team. 'It's the church in the castle grounds, Church of the Holy Virgin, sergeant,' she said 'and you have got about twelve hours max, before the

6

congregation starts arriving for the Easter services.'

'I'll mobilise the unit,' said Sergeant Munden. 'Be there in fifteen minutes, tops.'

'That's great, Sarg,' replied Jo. She then dialled her boss.

'Sorry to disturb your Easter break, sir,' she said when Detective Inspector Spencer Bligh answered his phone, 'there has been an unusual death down at the church in the castle grounds and I think that you had better come down. If it's not a murder, then it is something very suspicious,' said Jo.

'I have called in the SOCO team and the photographer, Graham Clare, is on his way as well. We will have to be finished by 10pm this evening for the Easter Vigil Mass, so time is of the essence,' finished Jo.

'We will finish when we are finished,' replied the DI, 'but I am on my way.'

'Ring me when you are near, as I need to let you in as I have secured the crime scene,' said Jo, 'and I have got some Community Support Officers to come down and put up the ribbon barriers.'

'Good work Jo,' said the DI, 'see you shortly.'

Jo went back to view the body, because she knew that as soon as the SOCO team arrived, there wouldn't be any further opportunity to get a good look at the victim in the flesh, as it were. She could see that Josh looked to be a fit young man, probably in his mid-twenties, she thought. He had a full head of black, wavy hair, strong facial features, but with a nose that had obviously been in the wars, which she put down to his rugby playing. His chest muscles indicated that he worked out in the gym, and she estimated his height to be just slightly less than six feet. She could not help thinking that his death was a total waste of a life prematurely cut short. Inwardly she vowed to bring the perpetrator of this evil deed to justice.

She noted that the body was tied to the cross bar with the rope going around his wrists. At least the perpetrator did not nail him to the cross, she thought, but as she examined the rope, something started niggling at her about the rope and the knots. She dismissed the niggles as something she could ponder on later. She then looked more closely at the victim's head, and then his shoulders, and there was some evidence of bruising around the neck and each shoulder, about three inches from the armpits. Perhaps the victim had been strangled and then dragged along by his arms, or maybe that was how he was lifted onto the cross. She then turned to examine the wound on the right side of the body, which was below the rib cage and appeared to be going upwards. It was probably some sort of knife, but she could not tell whether that was the cause of death, or administered for effect, to maintain the theme that this was a religiously motivated death.

Jo knew enough about Christianity to know that Jesus was crucified on a cross, and that his side was pierced by a soldier's lance instead of having his legs broken, which was the customary way of speeding up the death of victims so they could not raise their bodies to breathe. The soldier had realised that Jesus was already dead. As there was no blood or other fluid at the base of the cross, Jo deduced that the victim would have been dead before being hoisted up onto the cross. She also knew that it would be up to the forensic pathologist to determine the cause of death. That reminded her to get Peter Good down to view the body *in situ* and organise its removal to his laboratory in the morgue after the SOCO team were finished.

Just then Jo's phone rang, and the opening strains of Beethoven's Fifth Symphony reverberated around the church. She could see by the display that it was her DI. She started walking down to the church font door, as she answered the call saying, 'I'll open the front door for you sir.' As she opened the door to let him in, she could see Sergeant Arthur Munden and the SOCO team wheeling their equipment down the castle path. 'The body is up by the altar, sir,' she said. 'I will just wait here to let the SOCO team in and then I need to ring the pathologist, so I will be with you in a few minutes.'

Peter Good answered his phone after the second ring, as though he had been expecting a call, and after Jo explained the situation, he said that he would come down straight away.

Jo then waited for Sergeant Munden, and as he entered the church she said, 'Hi Arthur, thanks for your quick response. The victim was found by the vicar and he is up there by the altar on the cross.

A couple of things, please, there is a midnight vigil service this evening that will bring some people in from around 10.00pm onwards, so we really need to be done by then, and the victim is very well known, at least in rugby circles, so you and your team need to keep stum otherwise you will be fighting off the media, who would not hesitate to contaminate the crime scene to get the scoop of their careers.'

'Who is the victim, Jo?' asked Munden,

'Josh Christopher,' said Jo.

'You mean the England and Lions fly-half?' replied Munden. Jo nodded.

'That will be heartening for the All Blacks,' said Munden, 'one less for them to worry about,' he finished.

'I'd like to think that there are others who could take his place,' said Jo, 'but Josh will be a hard act to follow.'

Glancing out of the church door again, Jo noticed Peter's distinctive red Ford Ka just entering the car park at the top of the castle path. Peter walked down the path, and as he passed through the lych gate, he brushed back his hair with his hand, and came towards Jo.

'Hi Jo,' he said, 'thanks for calling me out, as I was with all my family and could really do with some relief,' he quipped.

'Well, this should occupy you for a few hours,' said Jo, 'a bit different as we have not had a suspicious death around here for some time.'

'Great,' said Peter, 'are SOCO here yet?'

'Yes, they have only been here for about ten minutes, so you should have a clear run.'

'Right, I will get on with it.' He was carrying a traditional type medical bag and he stepped through the door into the church. Jo closed and locked the door behind him, and then followed him up to the altar.

By this time, Detective Inspector Bligh had reconnoitred the crime scene, and he was standing in front of the cross, as Jo and Peter came up.

'Thank you for coming in, Peter,' he said, 'our first suspicious death in a long time.'

'Yes, boss,' he said.

'What do we know about this, then?' he asked.

'Nothing much yet,' replied Jo, 'until I get a chance to talk to the vicar. All we know is that the victim is Josh Christopher and yesterday afternoon he was involved in a church pageant, where he carried the cross into the church, and the vicar found him here at around 8:00am this morning.

Just then, a loud banging on the church door resounded through the quietness of the church. Jo hastened down the aisle, opening the door, hoping it was not the media already, and saw that it was Graham, the police photographer.

'Thanks Gray for coming out so quickly,' said Jo, 'after your

10

interior shots, can you see outside if there is any evidence of how the body might have got into the church. I haven't spoken to the pathologist yet, but from the lack of evidence around the body, I think that the victim was dead before he was brought here.'

'Right-ho,' replied Graham, 'where's the body?'

'Up by the altar,' said Jo, walking back up the aisle.

Inspector Bligh moved to the centre of the church he bellowed in his rather stentorian voice, 'Colleagues, can we gather round for a moment, please. As you can see,' he started, 'we have our first suspicious death for some weeks, so polish your detecting skills and let us see if we can move quickly on this one and resolve it. You all know that the first few hours are critical, so please let Peter do his work and give Sergeant Munden and his team any assistance they require. I do not want anything done that will contaminate the crime scene, and that includes outside the church, as the body had to be brought here somehow.

Once SOCO have given the all-clear, then we can roam around more freely. Remember we must be out of here by about 9.00pm tonight at the latest, and also be very circumspect whom you talk to as this victim's death is going to be big news and not just in the world of rugby. If I hear that any of you have compromised this case by an off chance remark, then the words 'guts' and 'garters' come to mind.

First we need to get some background material, so Jo could you talk to the vicar please, if that is alright Reverend? Remember, colleagues', he added, 'this is a House of God, with a Eucharistic presence, not a museum, and so please show some respect.'

'Yes, of course, inspector,' said Sean. 'We can go into the tearoom where there is some quiet, away from all this.'

Jo's mobile phone started playing Beethoven again and Jo

11

quickly answered it and turned away while she took the call.

'Shit!' she muttered and then turned around and looked at Spence.

'What is it?' DI Bligh queried.

'The victim's parents have just been at Fareham police station reporting him as a missing person and as the duty officer knows I am here, he is asking what we want to do?'

'I'll go and see the parents,' said Spence, 'and impress on them the need to keep this secret for now. If you find anything that I should know, any of you, then ring my mobile.'

At that he left the church.

Jo turned to the vicar and said: 'Ready Reverend?'

Chapter Four

They both entered the tea room together and Sean went behind the servery and called back over his shoulder to Jo, 'would you like a cup of tea?'

'Yes, please,' she said, 'just milk will be fine.'

Jo went and sat at one of the small tables and took out her tape-recorder and set it up in the middle of the table. She switched it on, spoke a few words and then played them back to check that it was recording.

On the table were some pamphlets about the church and Jo picked up one on its history and popped it into her bag. As Sean was coming over with a tray, she announced, 'Interview with Reverend Sean MacAleese, timed at nine twenty-five, Saturday 15 April at the Church of the Holy Virgin.'

Sean placed the tray on the table and sat down. Jo poured out two teas, and as she did so she started the interview.

'May I call you Sean, or would you prefer Reverend or Vicar?'

'Sean is just fine, detective constable.'

'Jo, please'

'Fine Jo.'

'How long have you been vicar here, Sean?'

'Well, this will be my third Easter Celebration,' replied Sean.

'Could we start please with an account of what happened yesterday,' asked Jo.

'Well, this was our first time at staging a Good Friday event, and it arose from a suggestion made at one of our Pastoral

Council meetings, as an alternative to the rather long-winded prayers, hymns and readings that we usually have on Good Friday afternoon, usually timed to be about when Christ died. Josh's father owns Christopher Builders and he offered to build the cross and he said that he would get his son to carry it.

The procession was to re-enact the route that Christ walked along the Via Dolorosa in Jerusalem, but for us it would start from outside the castle pub via castle path and into the church.

Josh wanted to do it properly, so we included him falling three times, and we also got another man to help him carry the cross, as Simon did for Jesus.'

'Who was this other man, Sean?' interjected Jo.

'It was a friend of Josh's, Simon Cheyney. I think he is also a rugby colleague of his. They both attended White Hart Lane College together. I believe they also both played in the school first fifteen.' replied Sean.

'Cheyney?' said Jo, 'I have heard of him. He plays for the Harlequins. Does he also live locally?' asked Jo.

'Yes and no', replied Sean. 'He mostly lives in London but often returns here and stays with his parents. I think I have his address somewhere, so I will send it to you later.'

'So, Josh and Simon carried the cross right into the church, I presume, and did you then tie him to the cross?' asked Jo.

'Goodness no', Sean uttered, 'when we got to the altar, we just stood the cross up beside the altar, in the base that your saw and covered it in purple at the same time we covered the other statues.

We then sang a few hymns, said some prayers and I gave a blessing. Then everyone left. Finally, I made sure the church was empty and then I locked up and left.'

'Sean, do you know if anyone took any photos of the

procession, please?' asked Jo.

'Well, actually I did, as a matter of fact.'

'Could I have some copies please?'

'Yes, they are still on my phone. I could email them to you, if you like.'

'Brilliant,' said Jo, and immediately handed Sean her business card.

'Can we go back to after the service', asked Jo, 'somebody must have got in before you locked up, so are you sure that you locked all the doors, Sean?' Jo asked.

'Absolutely, and I left through the main door, and locked it securely. That would have been about 6:30pm.'

'Could anybody have stayed back and hidden themselves away while you locked up, do you think?' asked Jo.

'Well, there are lots of cupboards and curtained off areas, I suppose,' said Sean, 'and I don't usually look in every nook and cranny before I leave, but I think that I would have seen somebody if they had stayed back. I remember that Josh and Simon were among the last to leave, as I spoke to both to thank them for their part in the service, and I actually invited them back to the vicarage for a drink, but they were both going to go and do some kicking practice, while there was still some daylight.'

'Does anybody else have keys to the church?'

'Only the parish secretary and she is away over the Easter break with her daughter in London. She is meticulous about safe-guarding the keys, so I can guarantee that she would not have left them out for anyone else to find,' replied Sean.

'Can you tell me a bit more about Josh, please Sean, as I only really know of him as a rugby player. Do you think that he has any enemies?'

'Enemies? I don't think so, but I have to say that some of the parishioners were a bit concerned at some of his theological utterances.

Josh was a member of our Theological Reflection Group and on one occasion he spoke about hell, saying that he did not believe that hell exist and on another occasion he pronounced that it did not matter whether Jesus was born of a virgin or not. What mattered was that he was someone special right from birth. I believe that those views upset a couple of the group members.'

'What did you think, Sean?' asked Jo,

'Well I did not think that it was anything new, what Josh was arguing was just redefining the old, but for some of the others, they thought that it might affect some of the younger parishioners, if you started saying that hell did not exist and so evil would not be punished.

I can certainly identify with Josh's thoughts. Both of us have studied theology, I, in the seminary, and Josh at university. I originally began studying for the Catholic priesthood in Dublin, Ireland, as I felt that I had a calling to have a career in the church, but I could not handle the celibacy issue, mainly because at the end of my first year I met a young lady, we fell in love, and now she is my wife.

I then decided to continue my studies in an anglican college, and so I came over to England and got sponsored by the Bishop of Portchester. I then studied at Sarum Theological College in Salisbury.

Josh is, or should I say was, along with his rugby interests, studying for a BA in theology and religious studies at Chichester University. I had offered him a work placement here, during his non rugby-playing times.

Members of the Theological Reflection Group knew this and one of them approached me with concerns that if Josh could preach then he could confuse the congregation with some of his views.

But the view that really got the group members worked up was when Josh declared that re-incarnation was a possibility.

One of the members then formally complained to me and I promised to talk to Josh.

'Who was the person who complained to you?'

'Well, co-incidentally it was Simon's father who was concerned. I reassured him that I would speak to Josh and that I would be monitoring everything Josh did as part of his placement here and just because he raised some thoughts in the Reflection Group, which is why the group was set up in the first place, it did not mean that he would start promulgating them from the pulpit!'

'Did that satisfy Mr. Cheyney?' asked Jo.

'Well, he has not mentioned anything to me since,' replied Sean.

'Did you speak to Josh, Sean?'

'Yes, I did, and I received an undertaking from him not to make any more controversial pronouncements without checking with me first. I have to say that Josh did redeem himself when he delivered a particularly good sermon at last Christmas's Midnight Mass.'

'So, Josh returned to the parishioners' good books?'

'Yes,' replied Sean, 'at least I hope so and I haven't had any more complaints.'

'How old would you say Mr Cheyney is please?' asked Jo.

'Aaaah, I would say about sixtyish. I think he has recently retired, and he is a great help around the church. I wouldn't think, that he would be strong enough to lift a body on to the cross, if that is what you are thinking, Jo,' replied Sean.

'But his son could,' interjected Jo.

'I really doubt that,' said Sean, 'They have been firm friends since school, and they still train together. In fact, as I told you, they were both going off to do some kicking practice together after yesterday's service.'

Jo immediately thought that that would give Simon opportunity, but she didn't share that thought with Sean.

'Well, that's probably all I need from you for now, thanks Sean,' Jo continued. 'OH, just one more thing, Sean, 'How did you find out the body was on the cross?'

'I was checking the purple Lenten covers and when I took it down to check it, the body was under it,'replied Sean.

Switching off her Dictaphone, Jo said, 'I'll go out and see how the team are getting along and find out when we can leave you to get on with your preparation for tonight.'

Jo then got up, shook Sean's hand, and made her way out of the tearoom and back into the church.

By this time, Peter was organising for the body to be taken down from the cross, he had also called in his mortuary attendant, Nick Davies, as he had a gurney ready with a large, thick black plastic zip-up bag spread out on it. Some of Sergeant Munden's SOCO team members had untied the ropes holding Josh's arms and were gently lowering the body.

Peter came over to Jo and said, 'I have managed a preliminary examination of the body, while it was *in situ*, but I will need to do a more thorough examination back at the mortuary before I can be truly certain as to the cause of death. As you will have noticed, there was bruising around the neck, as well as an obvious wound on the right side. I will need to determine whether death was by strangulation or exsanguination. I also found bruising on the abdomen, just below the ribcage, probably caused by a blunt

18

object thrust upwards, but I cannot determine the extent of injuries here, or which one actually caused the death.

I will try and get a report ready for you ASAP. I would like to take the cross back with me to the laboratory, as I have noticed some marks on it, which I want to examine further. If that is okay, Jo?'

'Hang on Peter, I will just confirm that,' replied Jo.

'Arthur,' Jo called, 'are you finished with the cross, yet, as Peter would like to get it back to the lab.'

'Yeah, Jo, that's fine.' Sergeant Munden replied.

Jo then turned to Sean, 'Do you have any objections to our taking the cross away, vicar?'

'No, Jo. I think that would be good as I don't particularly want it near me during the liturgy tonight, in view of what it has been used for,' replied Reverend MacAleese.

Peter nodded to his assistant and said, 'can you look after getting the cross back to my lab, please Nick?'

'Sure, Pete,' replied the mortuary assistant, 'I should be able to fit it into the wagon as well as the gurney.'

Jo then went to see Sergeant Munden to find out how they were progressing.

'Well, we have finished with the area around the cross, but didn't find anything illuminating, no footprints to work from, or pieces of material, or blood, just a few rope fibres, which we have bagged up to take back for testing.

I would like to now have a look around the rest of the church, and the tea-room, now that you have finished with it, as I want to work out the killer's mode of entry and to see whether he stayed back after the service or got in some way. If he stayed back, then at least that reduces the number of suspects to the number of people who attended the service. Rev. Sean should be able to

19

help us put an initial list together. By starting with the known attendees and interviewing them and asking them to tell us who else they knew attended.

I also want to have a look outside as the body had to be carried from somewhere. I noticed that there is a camera above the pathway opposite the entrance to the castle, so that might also tell us something.'

'Yes,' said Jo, 'I also noticed that on my way in this morning, so I will get some constables onto that and any other CCTV that might be helpful. Trouble with this bank holiday weekend, we will not be able to get going properly until Tuesday.' said Jo.

Graham Clare, the forensic photographer, came over to Jo and reported, 'I have taken photos of the victim on the cross, and the position of the cross in relation to the altar and now I want to get some outside photos. Is there anything in particular you would like me to photograph, Jo?' he asked.

'Could you get one of the vicar, please? We can then put it on the crime scene board back at the station'

'I have already got one of him, when he was not looking, as he just came into shot while I was photographing something else. I'll go outside now, and then I will be off, but I will check in with you before I go.'

'Thanks, Gray. That is much appreciated,' said Jo.

Just then Jo's mobile rang, Jo quickly answered it. She could see from the phone display that it was her boss, DI Bligh.

'Yes, boss,' she answered, and on hearing her boss's request she called out to her team to gather around.

'Colleagues, can you come over, as the DI wants to talk to us all.'

She switched her handset to speaker phone and held it up, moving into the middle of the circle.

'Hi, everyone, thanks again for coming in this morning. I have just been speaking with the victim's family, and obviously they are very distressed at losing their son in this way. They do not want any grief from the media, just as we do not so they have agreed to keep quiet for now. They did ask if they could tell Josh's rugby coach, as he will need to make other plans, and I have allowed that as long as they impress upon him to also keep the news quiet. I would like you all to come into the station's major incident room, number one, on Tuesday at 8.00am so we can really get started on this. Jo, feel free to let the team return home for Easter, as you see fit. Happy Easter!'

Jo could just imagine the smirk on DI Bligh's face as he said that, as they all knew that this Easter would not be happy. Murders have a way of upsetting everybody, and it was always a race to see if they could solve it before the evidence got away. No good copper can sleep easily when they know that there is a killer out there who needs to be caught.

Jo then went into the tearoom and Arthur came up to her and reported, 'I think that the killer brought the body in through that fire door, as there are some marks outside the door consistent with dragging something heavy through it.'

'But that only opens from the inside,' said Jo,

'Exactly,' said Arthur, 'so the killer I think stayed back after the service and then let himself out of this door, probably wedged it open, as it would not be seen around the back here and came back later with the body. Probably after dark.'

'Well, we need to establish what Josh did after leaving the church and his parents becoming concerned at his not returning home. Somewhere along that timeline, he was killed, and probably hidden until the killer was able to return to bring his body here,' mused Jo. 'I'll just go and see how Gray is getting on.

I think he is working outside now.'

'Right you are, Jo. We are just about done here, and so I will move my team out. I will upload my report to HOLMES so that you can check it through. You can tell the vicar that he can have his church back!' said Arthur, and walked away.

Jo went out to find Gray, and she was a bit taken a-back to see him with a remote in his hand and a drone flying overhead. Gray was looking at the images on his laptop that the camera drone was filming.

'Are you becoming all hi-tech now, Gray?' she asked.

'Yeah, but no thanks to the police, I had to pay for this myself, but it is definitely worth it, come and have a look at this.'

Gray motioned for Jo to look at his laptop as he guided the drone to provide a birds-eye view of the grass that went from the front door of the church and around the south side towards the east wall of the tearoom extension to the fire door where Josh's body may have been moved.

'See those tracks along the grass, I think that they are tracks of the vehicle that the killer used to transport the body here. You can see the outline, it looks like two tracks following each other, and another one to the right. I am just trying to work out what type of vehicle it is.' said Gray.

'How about a motorbike and side-car?' suggested Jo. 'That would fit the tracks and be a way of bringing Josh's body here without raising any concerns. The body could have been in the side-car, with a crash helmet, so nobody could see who it was, and that vehicle would fit easily along the castle paths and between the gravestones here.'

'Yes, Jo, I think that you're right. We will need to view CCTV coverage of the roads and paths, to see if we can pick that up and confirm.'

'I'll get somebody on to it straight away,' replied Jo. 'Have you finished now, Gray?' she asked.

'Yeah, I think so, I may come back later for another look around. If we are right, then there will hopefully be more tracks that we can pick up if we can work out where he was killed.'

'Right, Gray,' said Jo, ' I'll see you soon.'

Outside the Church the three PCSOs that Jo had called in to protect the crime scene were still there, standing in front of the blue and white crime scene tape, and Jo went up to them.

'Thanks guys, for coming out. Any problems?' she added, 'We seem, to be finished here now, so you can wrap up your tape and get off home and try and enjoy your Easter. If your other duties allow, I would be grateful if you could help with further inquiries into the major incident, when needed?'

'Bye DC Fletcher,' they said in unison.

As Jo went back into the church through the main door, Peter was just about to come through with the gurney and the body encased in the plastic bag. Behind her two SOCO members were carrying the cross. Jo looked back outside to make sure that there were no members of the public around and then motioned the team out. They moved quickly to the mortuary car and managed to fit the cross inside on top of the body. Fortunately the vehicle had obsured windows, as it was not a very dignified way of transporting a body.

Peter then had a quick word with his assistant Nick, as he closed the tailgate and got into the driving seat, waved goodbye to Jo, and walked back up the path to his car.

Jo returned to the church, to have a final word with the remaining members of the team who were also getting ready to leave, and then she looked for the vicar, to say goodbye and hand the church back to him.

The vicar was in the tearoom, and he had a prayer book open in front of him, and Jo could see that he was praying. She stopped beside him, and said quietly, 'We will get him, Sean, and I promise to keep you informed.' she said.

The vicar raised his face and Jo thought that he had been crying, so she added, 'My D.I. has told Josh's parents and they have agreed to keep it to themselves until we release a statement, so you could go and see them if you think it is appropriate, also, would you have contact details for Simon, please?'

'Yes, of course,' said Sean, and he took out a card and wrote the address on it.

Jo thanked him, and said 'Well, we are finished here now, so it's all yours.' Looking at her watch, she continued, 'at least you still have about five hours until your service starts, so I hope it goes well for you. Goodbye for now, Sean.'

'Goodbye Jo,' said Sean and went back to his prayers.

Jo walked back down the path towards the small car park. She looked at her watch and decided that it was still early enough to call on Simon and at least tell him that Josh was dead.

She was technically still on duty and on call, so she thought she should make use of the time, rather than return to the station and just sit around to pass the time. She was also aware, that Simon was a possible suspect, although his long-standing friendship with Josh would probably contradict that.

The address that Sean had given her, took her to a neat brick built bungalow in a cul-de-sac half-way up Portsdown Hill above the crematorium. The house was set back slightly from the road, and the front lawn was beautifully manicured and the border garden alive with spring flowers. It would have been an estate agent's dream if it were on the market.

Jo knocked on the front door and it was opened by a strapping

24

lad in his early twenties. He looked out beyond Jo at the police car, and immediately said, 'You must be here about Josh.'

'Yes, do you know already? Simon, isn't it?'

'Yes' to both, answered Simon. 'Josh's Mum came round, she has only just left.'

'Are you up to answering a few questions, Simon?' asked Jo.

'Yes, anything I can do to help catch the bastard who did this,' he replied.

'Well, I am Detective Constable Jo Fletcher, and part of the Fareham Constabulary Crime Team. Reverend MacAleese called me out this morning, when he discovered Josh.

'You had better come in, detective, and meet my parents and then we can go and talk.'

With that Simon turned around and Jo followed him into a large sitting room with a feature wall and ornate fireplace that dominated it. After introducing her to his parents, he went into the kitchen and motioned Jo to sit at the table. He then said, 'Would you like a drink?'

'No thanks, Simon,' replied Jo, 'I just need to ask you a few questions and then get on, if that is okay?'

'Sure, ask away.'

Jo then took out her Dictaphone, and asked, 'Do you mind if I record this, as it is important that I get your answers accurately, please Simon?'

'No, recording this interview is fine,' replied Simon.

'I understand that you were in the pageant with Josh on Friday afternoon?'

'Yes, the vicar thought that for a change this Easter he would re-enact Jesus carrying his cross. Josh's father was quite chuffed as he had suggested this liturgy as an alternative to the usual boring Good Friday service, and my Dad helped Josh's Dad build the cross, and I played the part of Simon of Cyrene who was forced by the Romans to help carry the cross. The procession started outside the pub, and moved down the road towards the castle wall. I joined it as we went through the main gate, and we both carried the cross right into the Church and up to the altar.'

'Was it very heavy?' intervened Jo.

'No not really as although it looked like solid wood it was actually made from plywood, so was really just two long boxes crossed and fitted together. It was not expected to hold any weight, and so I am surprised that it took Josh's weight.'

'What happened after the ceremony?' Simon.

'Well, after the final hymn we all started leaving the church and Josh and I went home to change as we had already agreed to meet up on the school rugby field for some kicking practice, while there was still some light. Josh is or should I say was, an excellent kicker. He had the skill to kick start the game with the right amount of distance and height to enable his forwards to be under the ball before the opposition so that possession was not kicked away to the other side.

This is a skill that the All Blacks are particularly good at and Josh knew that if England was to have any chance of beating the Blacks in the Autumn Internationals then we would need to practice this too. Josh had agreed to teach me how to do this. We both met up about 5.00pm at the school and practised for about an hour. I remember arriving home about 6:15pm as the national news was still on the TV.'

'Wouldn't the grounds be locked over this weekend?' asked Jo.

'As we are revered Old Boys', sniggered Simon, 'we have been given keys to the Sunningdale Road entrance so we can practice any time.'

'Can you tell me what Josh was wearing please, on the field?'

26

asked Jo.

'He was wearing his old Portchester club shirt with the black and white hoops, white shorts, and his new rugby boots. He was immensely proud of those. They were Addidas and cost about £140. He said that if he was going to kick the All Blacks into history then he needed a quality pair of boots to do it. He said that he was only wearing them to get used to them and break them in,' recounted Simon. 'Was that what he was wearing when you found him?'

'No.' replied Jo. 'He was only in his shorts.

'That means that his boots and shirt must be somewhere, perhaps still on the rugby field. Those boots would be a good find for someone.'

Jo briefly wondered whether she should organise a search of Simon's house for the shirt and boots but decided against it.

'Good point, Simon. I will get my team to search the area.' said Jo. 'Was Josh still practising when you left to come home?'

'Yes, he said that he wanted to practise some long place kicks and do some running up and down the field. You see, The All Blacks are well known for being able to stay on the pitch, running all the time for the full eighty minutes, and Josh was determined to be so fit that he could last the full two, forty minute playing periods. Our coach has taught us to run with one kilo dumbbells in each hand to strengthen our shoulder and forearm muscles. Josh wanted to do that. I had to get home for dinner, as Mum and Dad don't like to be kept waiting, so I will do my practice on Monday.'

'Were there any other people about while you were practising, perhaps walking along the public footpaths that are just outside the playing fields?' asked Jo.

'Not that I saw,' replied Simon. 'It is usually very quiet at that time of day, especially when we practise at weekends.'

'How did you and Josh get on, Simon, after all from what I understand you are possible rivals for the Number ten shirt? queried Jo.

'I have always played second fiddle to Josh, right from school days. In the school first fifteen, we both usually played together, Josh was fly-half, the number ten and I was inside centre, the number twelve. We did well as we worked out some good plays together that were quite successful. Josh was the much better kicker, though, as well as his kick starts, his goal kicking was very impressive and accurate.

We both joined the Portchester Rugby Club on leaving school, and then news must have got around as Josh was approached by London Irish, and I by Harlequins. So, we both ended up playing for different London clubs, and on occasions we would be playing against each other. They were fun games, as we could read each other's moves, and thwart each other's play. We both trialled for the England squad and Josh was selected for the main number ten, but I usually get to join the match in the last twenty minutes or so.'

'Does Josh's death mean that you will now be the main number ten?' Jo asked, watching Simon very closely, as she knew that this was the crunch question as to a possible motive for Simon.

'I suppose it does, really. You know, with all that has been going on, I had not considered that until you mentioned it just now,' replied Simon, and Jo thought that he was probably telling the truth.

'Who would you think, will be your replacement, if you move to becoming an opener?' asked Jo.

'Probably Raymond Salter,' said Simon, 'he plays fly-half for Bath. He is good and so if I do move up then he will keep me on my mettle,' laughed Simon. 'He is also a bloody good kicker, so I will have to get in more practice.

'What about sponsorship?' asked Jo. 'Did Josh sign up for any marketing deals?'

'I don't think so 'said Simon. I know that a company called 'Quality Sportswear' were trying to do a deal with the RFU, involving sponsored strip and boots, advertising around the ground and on the pitch, and they were even prepared to pay a small fortune to get naming rights to Twickenham, but that part fell through as it's 'Twickers' now and forever. I think that Josh might have been in the frame for some of that sponsorship.'

'Well, will some of that come to you now then?' asked Jo.

'Well, I would definitely consider it, if it does,' said Simon.

'Do you know of anyone who might have it in for Josh, Simon? I hear that your Dad was not too impressed with some of his theological outbursts.' asked Jo.

'No, no one,' Simon said. 'Dad was a bit concerned, but he spoke to the vicar and was happy with his assurance that he would, in future, monitor Josh's public outpourings. Anyway, he did not think it a life and death situation, just a need for caution.' replied Simon.

'What about girlfriends? Did Josh have a girlfriend?' asked Jo.

'Not in any serious way, that I know of. Funnily enough, at college, there was one girl, Stacey Myers, who went out with both of us. I think that Josh was quite keen on her, but she did not want to settle down with any specific person. She was quite an attractive, tall girl, with long blond hair. Her parents were professional, Dad a solicitor and Mum a local G.P. Stacey was a bright girl and she is now at the University of Southampton studying medicine. I went out with her on a couple of occasions, but she only went out with me when Josh was unavailable.'

29

'Do you know if they have had any recent contact?' asked Jo.

'Not that I am aware of. With her being in Southampton and Josh in Chichester and then London it's not geographically easy for them to link up.

Neither of us have had much to do with girls as we spend so much time in training, therefore we don't have much of a social life outside of our team mates.'

'If Stacey is that attractive, there must be other guys in her life. Do you know anything about them?' asked Jo.

'Well, at college, there was one guy who was really keen on her and he used to try and be with her all the time and get her to walk home with him, continuously asking her out.

Stacey was not that interested in him, and when she went out with either of us, this chap used to get angry. On one occasion when Stacey and Josh were going to the College Ball this guy approached Josh and offered to pay him if he would cancel his date with her and not go to the ball so that he could partner her. Josh, of course, told him to get lost and he also told Stacey. Apparently she remonstrated with him as well.'

'Do you remember this guy's name, Simon?'

'Yes, it's Billy Gore.'

'Is he local?'

'I think he lives somewhere in Roman Grove.'

'Thank you for that information, Simon, it might be relevant.'

'How has Josh's death affected you, Simon? Would you like the opportunity to talk with our family liaison officer?' asked Jo.

'Well, I am devastated, really. We went to school together and have done so much as friends since. I think that I should be okay, without the need of your liaison officer, but thanks anyway for your offer.' replied Simon.

'Well that's probably all for now, Simon. I would appreciate it if you could let me know your whereabouts if you have to leave Portchester in case there are more questions. Is there anything that you want to ask me?' queried Jo.

'Just, I suppose it is too early for you to have any leads yet?' he asked.

'Yes, Simon, far too early. Our crime team will be working over Easter but there is not much likelihood of anything cropping up soon. Please feel free to contact me at Fareham Police Station if you can think of anything further that might be relevant,' replied Jo handing Simon her card.

At that Jo switched off her recorder, put it back into her pocket and got up. Simon showed her to the door and as she passed his parents, Jo suddenly decided that while she was there, she would interview Simon's father as well.

Jo turned to him and said, 'Mr. Cheyney, could we have a quick word please?'

'Of course detective,' he replied, 'let us go into the kitchen.'

'Thank you for this, sir. Do you mind if I record this conversation, as I find it the best way to be accurate, and preferable to scribbling down things in front of you?'

'No, that's fine, record away.'

'Your son seems to be coping well at the moment, but it may hit him hard, later, so if you feel that he needs to talk to someone, then please ring me, as we have a family liaison officer on call who could visit.'

'Thank you for that,' replied Mr. Cheyney. 'Obviously, we will keep an eye on him, as he and Josh were very close.'

'Can you tell me what time your son came in yesterday evening after his rugby practice, please?' asked Jo.

'About six fifteen. The news was on the television, and we

were just about to sit down for dinner.'

'Simon said that you helped to build the cross?' asked Jo.

'Yes, I gave Josh's Dad a hand. We made it out of plywood, so in effect it was two long narrow boxes crossed together. Although Josh is quite strong and fit, we did not see the need to use solid wood. I doubt anybody was any the wiser.'

'Well, it was obviously strong enough to support Josh's weight,' said Jo.

'Oh, yes,' said Mr. Cheyney, 'box structures are extraordinarily strong. The physics behind it are all about dissipation of load. The principle was discovered by an architect who absent-mindedly placed a heavy tome on top of a light birdcage and was amazed at the strength of the structure. Most skyscrapers are built on that principle.' replied Mr. Cheyney.

'Just one more question, please, if I may?'

'Yes, of course.'

'The vicar told me that you had some expressed some theological concerns about Josh's placement in the parish. How serious were your concerns?' asked Jo.

'Oh my God, am I a suspect?' blurted out Mr. Cheyney.

'At this stage of the enquiry, everybody is a suspect,' replied Jo.

'Yes, of course,' said Mr. Cheyney. 'I suppose even Simon is.'

'Well, yes and he does have a possible motive.' said Jo.

'I don't think so,' said Mr. Cheyney, quite forcibly.

'Well, he stands to take Josh's place in the opening line up, rather than being brought on as a replacement and he could now also get a major sponsorship deal. Simon tells me that a company called *Quality Sportswear* are interested,' said Jo.

'Yes, when you look at it that way, I suppose that you are right.' he acknowledged. 'However, that's never really been an issue between them. They have always got on really well together and as you know they play for different clubs?'

'Yes, Simon told me. Now, what were your concerns about Josh, please?'

'Well Josh and I both attend the monthly Theological Reflection Group and during a couple of meetings he came out with some rather non-traditional views regarding Hell, the Virgin Birth and Re-incarnation. Now, within the group, it is okay to expound different views, but my concern was that Josh will probably be encouraged to preach as part of his placement in the parish and if he starts voicing these views from the pulpit, he would be leading people astray. The parish is not ready for such open theological debate. The ordinary parishioners believe that whatever comes out of the pulpit as 'Gospel' not the speaker's conjecture, and I just wanted to express my concern to the vicar.'

'And did you?' asked Jo.

'Yes, and the vicar assured me that his role was to closely monitor Josh's placement, and that he would ensure that nothing untoward was said, especially from the pulpit.'

'And did the vicar reassure you'?

'Absolutely'.

'Did you discuss your concerns with Josh, at any time, Mr. Cheyney?'

'Not outside the Theological Group but at the time he put his views, I said that he should be careful what he said publicly outside the group, as the parishioners were not ready for any 'off the wall theories'. He wasn't happy with my calling them that and he argued that there were several German theologians who had similar theories. He did however concede that there was a time and place for that type of dialogue. That is how we left it, as we have not had any meetings since.'

'And now, of course it is no longer relevant,' said Jo.

'Quite so, but I will miss him, as he was a bright lad and I enjoy a good discussion, that is why I joined the group,' continue Mr. Cheyney, 'also his sermon last Christmas was very good and traditional.'

'Yes, the vicar told me about it. I think that is all,' said Jo, switching off her Dictaphone, and putting it into her pocket.

They both got up and Jo walked towards the door. Simon was there before her, and he opened the door for her. Jo called out thanks and goodbye, went out through the door and off to her car. As she got into the police car, she looked at her watch, and realising that her shift was now over, she took out her mobile, and rang the station.

'Hi, it's me, I am going off duty now, is there anything that I need to know?' she asked,

'No Jo,' came the reply. 'Have a good evening if you can?' said the duty sergeant.

'I will be on my mobile if you need me,' said Jo, 'otherwise I will be in tomorrow. I will take the car home and leave mine at the station. Don't worry I will garage the police car so it will be off road and out of sight.' Jo then rang off and set off home.

Tomorrow and Monday, she knew, would be busy writing up her interviews, and setting up the crime scene boards, in Major Incident Room no 1, in preparation for the team meeting on Tuesday. She called in at the BP garage/Marks and Spencer shop to buy a pizza and salad for dinner and added a bottle of Italian red as an afterthought and within minutes she was pulling into her driveway in The Thicket.

The house was a single story 1950's three-bedroomed brick bungalow with a room in the roof, that had been built by her father when he bought the house in the late eighties. He was

34

interested in renewable energy and was the first in the street to have photo-voltaic panels installed. There was a small lawn in the front, and one out the back. At the end of the back garden the bank supported the main south coast railway line and she had now grown used to the rumble of the trains that went on day and night. Jo entered the house, went into the kitchen, to prepare her dinner.

She put her meal on a tray and went into the lounge. She sat in the sofa opposite the open fire. She liked this room, with the grand piano, plasma TV on the wall and the walnut cocktail cabinet. She only had wine in it now, not the large range of drinks that her father used to keep. She looked around the room, and her eyes fell on the photograph of her detective school classmates. Two of the guys had tried to date her, but she had a rule that she would not become involved with a policeman, so they never got a look in. As they both played rugby, she did consent to watch them play at the local rugby club, but she preferred the ladie's rugby and most of her social network revolved around the North Hampshire Ladies rugby club.

Her eyes then caught the photograph of her Dad above the mantelpiece, and it immediately brought back her memories of her father and the house. This house was her family home. Her parents moved into it in the late 1980's and Jo's mother was pregnant with her at the time they moved. Jo was born two months later.

Growing up, she remembered her father building the patios and the terraced back lawn and garden. Her parents were both now dead. Her mother died of early onset dementia, which necessitated her going into a care home. Fortunately, her Dad managed to get her into a local care home which was just past the end of her road, so she could be visited every day.

Her Dad had worked for the local borough council in the Civic Offices and was the Senior Planning Officer at the time of his death. As Jo, was an only child, she inherited the house, and she knew that on paper, at least, she was worth nearly half a million pounds!

Memories then of her father's death came flooding back. It had been some time since she had reflected on her Dad's death, and so these memories were possibly brought on by the current investigation into Josh's murder. Her father had been murdered, but at first it was thought that he had died naturally from a massive heart attack. The pathologist had argued that it was due to stress and high blood pressure. Jo had not accepted that as she knew that her Dad had been no more stressed than usual, and he had been meticulous about checking his blood pressure and taking his Valsartan tablets, morning, and evening. He had his own blood pressure monitor, an Omron M5-1 which was the same type as his doctor had, and Jo had checked his last fifteen readings which were all in the normal range. Because her father had talked to her about possible corruption over a planning permission, Jo believed that her father may have been murdered as he was advising the Council to not to approve the application.

The applicant was a large multi-million pound house building company and they wanted to build in the Green Belt, which her father argued was contrary to the Borough Local Plan. Jo knew that her father's boss, the Director of Planning was in favour of the application and her father believed that his boss was in the pocket of the applicant but because of the pathologist's report, the police would not involve themselves.

Jo had been researching the internet as to possible causes of cardiac arrests and there was one possible cause that caught her eye – an air embolism, where an amount of air injected into a vein could cause an obstruction of the right ventricular outflow tract, leading to a cardiac arrest.

Jo then decided to take the matter into her own hands and see if she could find any evidence on her father of needle tracks. At that time, her father was lying in state at home, and the funeral was not for a couple of days. Then he would be cremated and all possible trace of murder would be erased.

Jo decided to extensively examine her father's body and after a couple of hours she was convinced that she had found something unusual under both his armpits. She knew that she would have to get that confirmed.

Jo had first met the current forensic pathologist, Peter Good, when she was at Portchester University. Although they were both doing different degrees, they had a series of criminology lectures in common. They had hit it off straight away, and so she turned to confirm her findings about her father.

Peter was hesitant at first as he had only recently been appointed as an assistant pathologist to the Portchester NHS and he did not want to step on the toes of the most revered Doctor Michaels who had carried out the post-mortem on Jo's father.

He did however examine Jo's father and was convinced that Jo was right. Peter considered that a twenty-millimetre needle had been used, which was similar to that used by diabetics to inject insulin. Jo then remembered that her father's boss was a diabetic, as he had had a hypo attack during a staff social function and had to be given sugar to bring him around.

Jo then knew that she had to find evidence of a needle. The next day, she went to the site of the planning dispute and looked around the area where her father was deemed to have collapsed, and after some time in a nearby bush, she found a syringe.

Eventually, that syringe was traced to a pack that the Director of Planning had had prescribed for him, and he was arrested, and confessed.

That episode, emotional as it was for Jo, was the reason she decided to join the police and become a detective. She managed to gain a place on the Hampshire Police Specialist Entry Detective Programme as a detective constable, having initially joined as a student police officer. Her first appointment was with the Fareham Division with her first appraisal stating that 'she was exceptionally good at her job and a major contributor to the crime team.'

CHAPTER FIVE

Jo was the first to arrive in MIR 1 on the Tuesday and she looked over the weekend's reports. She had placed the lectern by the main crime board which included photos of the victim on the cross, the church, and the surrounding area, together with photos of the procession that Sean had e-mailed over to her. She also had photos of the college rugby field that she had taken on her way to work on Sunday, despite peering over the fences surrounding the field she could not see any evidence of anything.

That would be a task later today, she thought, to get SOCO to do a thorough search of the area before it became contaminated by the school kids. She had written up the names and addresses of the main people involved, and placed her interview notes in a manilla folder on the lectern for her SIO, D.I. Spencer Bligh to refer to. She looked at her watch and decided that she had time enough to pop over the road for a coffee before Spencer was due to arrive.

Jo lived on cappuccinos and the occasional croissant. Despite that, she was not overweight. She was an attractive twenty-something, with a smallish face, long black hair with a centre parting. She had a small mouth, with pretty, red lips and she wore black glasses, which gave her an air of authority.

She kept herself fit by playing rugby for the Alton Ladies Rugby Team as one of the backs. While at *Freshcos* Jo purchased a couple of packets of Digestive biscuits to take to the meeting, and when she returned to the station, she organised the tea and coffee pump pots which she knew would be in great demand once everyone arrived.

Once back in MIR 1, she did not have to wait long before the team started to arrive. Spencer was first, and as he walked in he looked around and turned to Jo and commented,

'I presume that this is your doing. It is particularly good, thank you, Jo.'

'That's fine, Sunday was quiet, and so I thought that I would make a start,' replied Jo.

Just then, Sergeant Munden arrived with one of his team, and directly behind him, came Gray, the photographer. Gray had his laptop with him and he immediately started setting it up to project on to the large screen that took up most of the end wall of MIR 1. Detective Sergeant Matthew Oliver was next, a large man, who brooked no nonsense. He went straight to the crime boards and digested them thoroughly.

Peter, the pathologist, then arrived and Jo went up to him and thanked him personally for coming in.

'Fine,' said Peter, 'I have a preliminary report so I can speak if you would like me to.'

'Well, that will be down to Spence, but I will tell him and I'm sure he'll want to hear from you, Peter.'

Spence then called the meeting to order, introduced everybody, and thanked everybody for attending.

'This is the first crime scene meeting of what I have decided to call 'Operation Golgotha' after the Hill where Jesus was crucified at the time of the first Easter,' began Spencer, 'It is some time since we have had a murder in our patch and this is tragic as well as unusual. Tragic in that a young man has been killed in the prime of his life and his death is a loss to the rugby world as

40

well as to his family and friends. It is not public yet, but I have scheduled a press conference after this meeting, and Jo, I would like you to attend as well please.'

Jo nodded and Spencer continued, 'It is unusual in that had the vicar not discovered the body under the purple cover then this whole episode could have been unveiled in a very public and horrific way, which would have been deeply upsetting for everybody, and cause a media frenzy. The resulting crime scene contamination does not bear thinking about. This morning, I would like to hear from Detective Constable Fletcher, Sergeant Munden, Gray, and Peter. Then we will allocate duties and get the ball rolling. Jo could you start please.'

'Right, boss,' she said as she moved to the lectern. 'The call from The Reverend Sean MacAleese, came through at about eight o'clock on Saturday morning, and as you know all of us here responded and commenced the investigation. I interviewed the vicar, and he reported that Josh, the victim, was the actor in the Good Friday re-enactment of Jesus carrying the cross from his place of condemnation before Pontius Pilate to Golgotha, (Calvary?) where He was crucified.

Josh wanted to be true to the story, so he fell three times on the way from the oak tree outside the Castle Pub to the church. As in the story, Simon Cheyney who was a close friend of Josh's and also a fellow England Rugby player helped him carry the cross in the same way that Simon of Cyrene did for Jesus. I have also interviewed Simon, but more of that later.

After the service, both Josh and Simon went to the rugby ground at White Hart Lane College, to practice their ball kicking skills. They are both former pupils of the school and are held in high esteem. This allows them to have keys to the Sunningdale Road gate to allow them access to the rugby pitch.

41

Prior to being selected for Premiership Rugby, Josh was studying theology at Selsey University and he was currently on a placement for six weeks while he was on holiday from the rugby.

The vicar is, or now was, his placement supervisor. As part of that pastoral work Josh was attending the Theological Reflection Group which met monthly and he had already built up a reputation for having some 'different' theological views, shall we say.'

As Jo said the word 'different' she made parentheses marks with her two index fingers. 'One group member took exception to his denial that Hell exists, and his statement that whether Jesus was born of a Virgin or not did not matter or alter his being the Son of God. This person, who happens to be Simon's Dad, expressed his concern to the vicar, in case as part of his placement he started preaching to the congregation.

The vicar assures me that he put Mr. Cheyney's mind at ease when he said that he would be monitoring everything that Josh said and did and would ensure that nothing was said or done that could be construed as controversial. This was also re-iterated by Simon about his Dad when I interviewed him. It does mean, however, that Simon could be a suspect, if he were carrying out his father's wishes, as the old man himself could not have lifted Josh's body on to the cross, with or without pulleys.

I did comment on this to the vicar, but he thought it very unlikely that Simon was involved as the two were very close friends and had been since their early school days. Also, Simon wanted the England Rugby team to beat the All Blacks during their forthcoming tour, just as much as anybody, and he knows only too well that Josh was their front gunner in defeating them. Ironically, now with Josh dead, Simon will probably pick up the number 10 shirt and so it will be down to him. So if you are looking for a personal motive for Simon, that would be it. Both Simon and Josh left the church after the service and went off to the school.

We will come to SOCO in a moment, but I understand that a preliminary finding is that it is probable that the killer remained in the church after the service and hid himself while the Vicar locked up at around 6:30pm. That would rule Simon out, as he was by then home with his parents, having left Josh on the rugby field. Simon confirmed these details and told me that Josh was wearing his old rugby shirt, with white and black hoops, white shorts, which I presume were the ones he was wearing on the cross, and a new pair of Adidas rugby boots. As the body did not have these on it, I presume they could be somewhere near where he was killed, or the killer took them with him or her. The only other thing to add, is that while at college, both Josh and Simon went out with a girl named Stacey Myers, but in Simon's view, she preferred Josh to Simon. Stacey was not serious about any of the college guys as she seemed to have been focused on becoming a doctor and is currently studying at University of Southampton.

I only mention this as it could provide another motive for Simon to remove Josh as a competitor, if Simon is lying about the strength of his feelings for Stacey.

According to Simon, there was another guy on the scene at college who was keen on Stacey and at one point tried to pay Josh to not go out with her. He is a local lad, by the name of Willie Gore. It may be necessary to talk to him at some stage. There are copies of my interview with the vicar and with Simon on the back table if you want to read them. That is probably all for now,' ended Jo.

'Thanks for that Jo,' said DI Bligh, as he turned to Sergeant Munden, 'What can SOCO tell us so far, Arthur?'

43

Sergeant Munden walked up to the lectern, took out some papers from his inside jacket, spread them out and stated, 'Well, this is the first crucifixion that I have attended and I think that Easter will always be a bit different for me from now on. We did not find any clues near the body, or the cross, but, as Jo said, we think that the killer hid inside the church after the service, waiting for the vicar to lock up and leave. There are spaces at the back of the church with curtains across them and a row of cupboards in the New Room (I think this is what it is called) any of these could hide the killer. Also, in the north transept there is an outside door with a curtain on the inside, but there is enough space between the curtain and the door for a person to stand.

Unless the vicar made a point of looking in every nook and cranny before he locked up, the chances of the killer's hideout being discovered would be negligible.

Once the killer was alone there are several ways, he could have left the church and left a door unlocked so he or she could return later. The main outside door from the New Room has two turnkey deadlocks, which do not need a key to open from the inside, also there is a fire-door in the tearoom which could have been used as an exit and left propped open. That door is hidden from the front of the church as it is in the east wall or seaside wall of the New Room.

We did find some tracks and disturbed ground outside that door. Therefore it is our belief that was the way the killer exited the church and re-entered later with the body.

I think our next phase is to go to the college rugby ground, as that is probably the last place that Josh was before he was killed and the probable murder scene. I think I will now hand over to Gray for the photographic evidence.' Sergeant Munden then returned to his seat.

As Gray was getting out of his chair, Spence stood up and said 'My thanks to SOCO for coming out on their day off, not that anyone has a day off when there is an ongoing murder investigation, and yes, Gray, if you please.'

Gray moved to the laptop, brought it to life, and immediately a picture of the outside of the New Room fire door was projected onto the screen.

'I can confirm that we have found tracks around the outside of the New Room to the fire-door and as you can see from this picture, the tracks are two in line and one single track to the right. Jo and I both agree that they were probably made by a motor bike and side-car, which would be an ideal way to transport a dead body inconspicuously with the body concealed in the side-car with a helmet to hide the head and the vehicle narrow enough to manoeuvre around the tomb stones to the fire-door. Hopefully, we can find this vehicle from the number plate recognition cameras around the area, if the killer was stupid enough to pass under one. Please feel free to browse through my photos on the laptop after this briefing.'

'Thanks, Gray,' said Spencer.

'Peter, thanks for coming along this morning, is your report ready yet?' asked Spence.

'Yes, sir,' replied Peter as he got up from his chair.

'I have some preliminary findings, but I cannot complete my report until the toxicology results are returned. However, I don't expect any surprises there. As you now all know, the victim was tied to the makeshift cross with white rope and there was of course bruising to the wrists and rope fibres in the skin. There was bruising around the neck, but the neck was not broken, and so the victim did not die from hanging but possibly strangulation. There was a large bruise to the solar plexus with contusions going upwards, which would indicate a heavy blow to the stomach and that would have been sufficient to bring the victim down to his knees. I believe that the body was then dragged by the neck along grass as there were grass stains and vegetative material around his ankles. This would mean that his footwear was probably not removed until he was at his final resting place before being brought to the church. There was vegetation around his torso, and some in his hair, which would indicate that the body was covered in probably leaves and grass, to conceal it. A two-inch-wide knife wound on the left side of the abdomen travelled upwards through the lung into the heart. The aorta was severed and so death by exsanguination would be quick. The body on average contains about five litres of blood and it only has to lose between two and three litres to drain the brain and then the body would die in three minutes. There would be quite a pool of blood as all five litres would drain out.'

Turning to Sergeant Munden, Peter reported, 'SOCO should find some evidence of that somewhere.'

He continued, 'Until the toxicology results come in, I don't know whether any poison or drugs were administered but they would not have been be necessary. Now, I also examined the cross. It is not a solid wood cross but made with construction ply in two boxed sections forming the cross. Although light, it was sturdy and well able to support the body of a man. There were markings near to where the horizontal section joined to the vertical section and I have deduced that they are compatible with a type of clamp that could hold a pulley which would have enabled the perpetrator to haul the body up the cross while the wrists were tied.

My reasoning for the pulley system is that the position corresponds with the bruising around the victim's arms and if the body had been pulled up by ropes then there would be deeper bruising wounds around the arms and there would be markings of rope burn around the wooden cross. I do not think that the cross was lowered, and the body laid on it, tied, and then hoisted back in place as there would be some evidence of hoisting the cross upright, and it would have been heavy. The victim weighed 90 kilos. Any questions?'

Jo stood up 'Peter, rugby players often train by running the length of a field carrying dumbbells to strengthen their arms. They are not very heavy about one and a half kilos each. Would that be consistent with your findings?'

'Yes, definitely,' replied Peter, 'I have considered that it would be something like that or the perpetrator had a rock in his hand. My conclusion is that the victim was running and his attacker was also running towards him with a heavy object and as they passed the victim was hit hard in the solar plexus, which would have stopped him in his tracks. Then while he was in that state, he was strangled by some ligature being wound around his neck, until he suffocated. He was then dragged into some bushes where he was stabbed in the right side of his body and hidden in leaves and other vegetation until he was transported to the church and hoisted onto the cross. If I am right, then we should find some disturbed pile of vegetation with plenty of blood around. That is all for the moment, Detective Inspector.'

'Thank you, Peter. A very thorough report at short notice. I am grateful to you. Now we need to plan our next move.'

As if on cue, there was a loud knock on the door, and in came the Duty Sergeant holding out a portable phone in his right hand.

'Sorry to disturb sir, but I have the caretaker of White Hart Lane College on the line and he says that it is most urgent that he

47

speaks with you, now.' He handed the phone to Spence.

'Yes, D.I. Bligh here. What! Right, we will come straight away. So, do you know who it is? An old pupil. Simon Cheyney? Can you please keep people away from the scene? Are there many children around, we don't want them to see this, Inset day. Teachers only. Well, that's a stroke of luck. You will leave the Sunningdale Road gate open. Right. See you very shortly. Bye and thanks.'

Spence handed the phone back to the Duty Sergeant, and then turned towards the group. Sorry, but we will have to put allocation of duties on hold. Well, you have probably got the gist of that phone call. The caretaker had just arrived at the school, and the body of Simon is hanging from the cross bar of the north end rugby goal posts. I want you all over there immediately. Arthur, Gray, Peter? Is that okay?'

'Yes,' they all replied in unison.

'Sergeant Oliver, can you organise the minibus, out in front under the arch, ready to go in five minutes?'

'Yes, boss.'

'Okay, people, five minutes. It's the Sunningdale Road entrance. You can drive straight onto the field and go to the North West corner. I will get some constables to join us for crowd control. See you all downstairs.'

'Well, that's put paid to the theory that Simon killed Josh,' muttered Sergeant Oliver.

'Not if this one is a suicide' returned Jo, as they all made for the stairs.

The minibus was soon on its way to the college. As Matthew sped around the edge of Portchester Precinct and into Jubilee Avenue towards the 'Home Zone' set up by Alison Quant, the borough landscape architect, he narrowly missed one of the

48

wooden garden edges.

Jo called out, 'Careful Sarg, we are going to an incident, we don't want to become one!' This caused a laugh, but everyone was soon serious again as the bus drove through the open school gates at the end of Sunningdale Road and travelled across the playing field and the body was now visible hanging from the crossbar of the rugby posts.

As they drew nearer, Sergeant Munden called out to Sergeant Oliver to stop so as not to get too close and possibly contaminate the scene. He then told everyone to get into their protective clothing and just be mindful of what they were doing. As they got out of the bus they could see that D.I. Bligh was already there, dressed in his white protective overalls and latex gloves examining the body.

 For Jo it was easy to recognise Simon as the victim, after all she had been with him only a couple of days earlier. He was hanging at the end of a short rope like a rag doll from the left-hand end of the cross bar, with his head bowed, touching his chest. He was still wearing his football gear, jersey, shorts, and even his boots. Beside him, on its side was a set of small kitchen steps, as you would find in any type of homeware catalogue.

The question then was, is this suicide or a murder made to look like suicide. There was the typical noose or slip knot around his neck and a short length of rope just long enough to suspend the body without Simon's feet touching the ground.

Peter went over to the body and took some photos. He ascertained the length of drop was sufficient for Simon to have dropped enough to be classed as a complete hanging as opposed to an incomplete one where some of the body weight is taken by the feet still touching the ground. If this was a case of death by hanging, then Peter would expect to find that there was virtual decapitation, with the distraction of the head from the neck and torso, and fracture of the upper cervical spine which is medically known as typical traumatic spondylolisthesis of C2 in the classic hangman fracture and transection of the spinal cord.

To ascertain this, Peter needed to examine the body once it had been brought down from the rugby posts. He then requested that SOCO bring the body down so he could examine it more closely. Sergeant Munden and his team did this and then he searched the clothing and held up a small amount of money contained in one of those plastic bags which the banks hand out for depositing coins. He opened it out and tipped the contents onto a cloth. They were 50 pence coins. 'I bet that there are thirty of them,' Jo said, to no-one in particular.

'Yes, you are right, Jo,' said Sergeant Munden. 'How did you guess?'

'Judas,' she said. 'Judas betrayed Jesus for thirty pieces of silver, and then in remorse, went out and hung himself. If this is murder and not suicide, then the murderer wants us to believe that Simon killed Josh and then in remorse went out and hanged himself.'

'Peter, we need to know as a matter of urgency whether Simon took his own life or was murdered.'

'Yes, of course, Jo,' said Peter, 'I should know soon enough.' Now that the body was on the ground, Peter examined it starting at the head and confirmed that there were the typical signs of the 'hangman's fracture'. He then lifted up the jersey and examined the stomach. It was clear of any bruising. There were no wounds suggestive of someone hitting the body in the solar plexus as was present in Josh Christopher's death, and so this case was more suicide than murder. Peter then examined the neck. He concluded that this was suicide. Turning to D.I. Bligh, he looked up and said, 'This seems to be a typical hangman's fracture and there are no signs of any other cause of death or dragging of the body from somewhere in the field to these posts,' said Peter.

Turning to Peter, Jo asked, 'Thanks, do you have a time of death?'

Peter thought for a moment and replied, 'I would say more than twelve hours ago, probably about fifteen hours. That would make it about six p.m. yesterday evening.'

'That would be his usual time of coming down here for practice,' said Jo.

'Okay, men,' shouted Sergeant Munden, 'you heard Peter, we are dealing with a suicide, but I want a search of the whole area in case anything is found that compromises a verdict of death by suicide.'

Just then, Gray came over to Spencer and Jo with his laptop open. 'I have found some tracks, similar to those that we saw around the church,' reported Gray. 'I would surmise that this is where Josh was killed. The tracks seem to lead towards those electricity transformers over there in the far corner. I have been over there, and there is a break in the chain fencing where the fencing could have been rolled back to allow the motorcycle and side-car to come onto the field and take Josh's body away and down to the church. These deaths are linked. It may be that Simon killed Josh, and then in remorse, committed suicide. Either way, there should be blood around here, so I will keep the drone searching to see if I can locate it.

'Sergeant Munden's team should find it if it is nearby,' said Jo.

Just then, Jo's mobile phone rang and she could see from the display that it was the Duty Officer at Fareham.

'D.C. Fletcher,' she said into the mouthpiece, then continued, 'tell them that I will meet them at the Sunningdale Road entrance. Yes, I will tell Spence, and thanks for this, it is helpful,

She then went over to Spence, and said, 'I have just had a call from the Duty Officer and a lady has come in with her son, and a very bloodstained pair of sports shorts. Apparently, her son and a friend were playing about on this field and he ended up getting blood all over his shorts. His mother is bringing him down now so he can show us where he was playing. This hopefully will lead to where Josh was killed.

'That's handy, go and meet them, and try and prevent them from seeing Simon's body.'

As Jo walked off towards the gate, a red Kia Picanto was slowly arriving through the open gate. Jo beckoned them towards her, and when the car reached her it stopped and a woman and a boy got out. The woman was holding a plastic bag which she handed over to Jo as soon as they met.

'I am Mary Curruthers, and this is my son Roger.' She then turned to her son and said, 'Show the policewoman where you were playing, Roger.'

'Shall I walk over to it, Miss?' asked Roger.

'Yes, take me there please.'

Turning to Mary Curruthers, Jo said, 'Thanks so much for coming. This will be helpful. I am D.C. Fletcher.'

They set off with Roger leading the way across the playing fields and as they neared the goal posts, Sergeant Munden joined them. The boy took them into the trees behind the posts towards the northern boundary fence of the school. The land was overgrown with thick undergrowth amid a copse of trees. It was an excellent place to hide a body, thought Jo. Not even Gray's drone would pick anything up here.

'What type of games do you play here, Roger?' asked Jo.

'We just play rolly-poly in the leaves, and throw handfuls of leaves at each other,' replied Roger.

'So that's how you get your clothes all dirty!' scolded his mother.

'Well, its lucky for us he does,' laughed Jo. At this, Roger stopped and then pointed to a pile of leaves about three yards in front of them. 'That's where I got blood over my shorts,' he pointed.

Sergeant Munden went towards the pile, bent down to examine it.

'Yes, definitely blood here,' he said, 'you better go and get Peter over here to estimate just how much, Jo.'

Jo went off and soon returned with the pathologist. When Peter arrived, Jo introduced him to Mrs. Caruthers and Roger, and they gave Peter the bag with the bloodied shorts in it.

Peter said, 'Many thanks for this, we will test the blood to see if it belongs to Josh.'

'Why Josh, has he been wounded?'asked Mary.

Realising that Mary Curruthers would not have heard about Josh's death, Jo took her aside and explained what had happened and told her that it was essential that she kept quiet until the police released the story to the press.

Jo then asked Roger, 'When were you playing here, when you found the blood Roger?'

Roger hung his head and looked up at his mother.

'Answer the policewoman, Roger,' she said.

'Well, I know that it is wrong, Miss,' he said, 'but we sometimes climb over the fence and play here on the weekends. I was down here yesterday afternoon; Will I get into trouble?'

'I think that we can overlook it this time,' said Jo, 'but don't do it again Roger, as it is trespassing and the school could make a formal complaint to the police which would not be good for you now or later in life to have a police record,' said Jo.

Jo then asked Mary to take her son and leave, asking her again to say nothing to anybody until the press statement is released.

Meanwhile, Peter, SOCO and Gray had taken samples of the bloodied leaves, photographed them and documented their position in relation to the rest of the crime scene. Peter had called out his colleague, Nick, who had already brought the mortuary car to pick up Simon's body.

Gray was able to establish the wheel tracks from the pile to the boundary fence and Peter established the trail from the rugby field to the pile, reinforcing the proof that Josh's body had been dragged from the point of impact in the field to the pile of leaves where it had been stabbed, bled to death and hidden until it was transported to the church.

D.I. Bligh came over, and they all huddled together exchanging views until they agreed that they now had all the evidence that they needed from the school playing fields and they could close the crime scene and return it to the school authorities.

'Well,' said Spencer, 'I think that we can conclude that this is a case of murder and suicide, and so we just need to tie up a few loose ends such as find the motor bike and side-car, which I presume will belong to Simon, and I presume that Simon somehow transported himself here and so his car must be close. We need to find out what type of vehicle he drove and locate it. Sergeant Munden, did you find any keys on Simon's body?'

'No sir,' replied Sergeant Munden.

Jo suddenly had a thought and turned to Peter, 'Peter, did you take a sample of the rope that bound Josh to the cross?'

'Yes, Jo. I have it in my lab.'

'And have you got the rope tying Simon to the crossbar,

please?'

'Yes, I have got that as well as I intend to see if the two samples match.'

'Just what I was thinking,' said Jo, 'if they do match, then there should be more rope somewhere in Simon's possession.'

Jo then turned to Spencer and said, 'It is a wonder that since Simon probably died about 6.00pm yesterday evening that we have not heard from Simon's parents. Perhaps I should pay them a visit before they hear anything from anybody else.'

'Sure, Jo, take my car and go now, I will get a ride back in the van and I will see you back at the station,' replied Spencer, handing Jo his car keys.

As SOCO could not find any of Josh's rugby boots or top, they concluded that Simon must have taken them with him. Jo went off to talk to the Cheyney's and on the way she passed the caretaker, who had been standing around and said that they were handing the scene back to him. She then asked him if he could somehow dispose of the bloodied pile of leaves so that other children did not find them. He agreed to transport them to his compost heap and keep them well covered.

D.I. Bligh then loudly announced that he wanted everybody to return to the Fareham Police incident room after lunch to allocate tasks.

Sergeant Oliver went off to bring up the minibus, and then gradually they all left the school playing fields and the caretaker closed and locked the gates behind them.

CHAPTER SIX

Whilst driving back to the station in Spencer's car, Jo answered the in-car phone when it rang.

The display said it was the Fareham office. 'D.C. Fletcher here, Duty Sergeant.'

'Hi Jo, I have a message for you all, Roland Marley from *The News* is here for his appointment with D.I. Bligh.

He has been waiting for nearly half an hour now and is concerned about his copy deadline for the final edition. Do you know when Spence will be back?'

'He is on his way now in the van with Sergeant Oliver and so he should be nearly there. Pacify Roland by saying his waiting is worth it as there are now two suspicious deaths, not just one. I am on my way to visit the Cheyneys so I will join you in an hour or so. Can you get the conference room ready for the press release and could you organise in some lunch as Spencer will not have had time to get anything?'

'Fine, Jo. Leave it with me, I will sort it. Bye.'

Jo switched off the hands-free phone and turned into Dore Avenue. Within a minute she was outside the Cheyney's house with its manicured garden and feeling sad at the devastation she was about to unload on the Cheyney family. To lose a son by suicide and who is now also considered to be a murderer is as devastating as it can get for any parents, and Jo was not looking forward to conveying this type of news.

This was compounded for Jo, because deep down she was uneasy about the verdict of suicide. She understood the medical pathology, but she could not bring herself to believe that Simon was capable of murder and of taking his own life. She thought that she would have had some inclination of this when she spoke to Simon on Saturday but he came across as totally honest in his compassion for Josh and his sincere sympathy at his death.

Her question to herself was should she express these doubts to the Cheyneys at his time? One thing for sure, she decided, was that his case was not closed for her, not at all. She knew though that she could not voice these thoughts to Spencer, as he was an 'open and shut case' sort of guy, more concerned with crime clear up rates and appeasing his boss, Detective Chief Inspector Abbottsford than thorough investigations. He was of the school of 'swings and roundabouts' where if some injustice was done in some cases, then it was balanced by other cases where actual *baddies* got let off more lightly than they should.

Jo could not bear the fact that there might be a chance that there was still a murderer out there and it was not fair that the Cheyneys could be vilified for a murder that was not of their son's doing. What Jo did know was that any further investigations she carried out would have to be in her own time and as discreetly as possible. She knew that Sergeant Oliver would not countenance going against Spencer as he would never jeopardise his job, and would not rock the boat, but would officially support the verdict of murder and suicide with the case closed.

Jo decided that she would not express any of her reservations to the Cheyneys until she had investigated further and had something concrete to give them hope of re-instating the family name that would certainly be damaged by the revelation that their son was a murderer and had commited suicide.

Mr Cheyney opened the door almost before Jo had rung the bell and ushered her in saying, 'I saw you pulling up. have you got some news already?'

'Yes, but not the news that you will want,' blurted out Jo before she could stop herself. She walked past Mr. Cheyney into the lounge and said, 'I am terribly sorry, Mr. Cheyney but I have some bad news for you. Is your wife here as I need to speak with both of you?'

'Yes, I'll just get her,' replied Mr. Cheyney as he went out of the lounge. They both returned, and Jo said: 'I think that you both better sit down. I am afraid that Simon is dead. His body was found this morning hanging from the rugby goal posts at the school. There is no sign of any injury other than what you would expect to occur when someone dies as a result of hanging.

The pathologist has not found any evidence of any foul play, and so, at this stage, we can only assume that Simon took his own life. I am really deeply sorry for you both.'

Mrs. Cheyney then burst into tears with a loud wailing and Jo just waited while Mr. Cheyney comforted his wife. She then looked at Mr. Cheyney, and as though he understood, he extricated himself from his wife's embrace, got up and beckoned Jo to follow him into the kitchen.

'She will be better, soon, if left on her own for a while and I suppose that you will want me to come and identify Simon?'

'For the official record, yes, but there is no question that it is your son, as remember, I only saw him on the weekend and the school caretaker who knew him in his school days found him this morning. The pathologist believes that he died about 6.00pm yesterday evening and so I am surprised that he was not reported as missing,' continued Jo.

'Well, we weren't expecting him home last night. He left here around 4.00pm saying he was going to do some practice down at the school and then he was to return to London to his flat for rugby practice this week.

We were a bit surprised that he did not ring us to say that he had arrived in London safely but he was not always the best at keeping in touch with us, unless of course, he wanted something!' said Mr. Cheyney at a desperate attempt at a bit of humour.

'Do you know whether he was going to meet anybody at the school, or was he just practising on his own?' asked Jo.

'On his own, I think. He usually went on his own unless he was with Josh,' replied Mr. Cheyney.

'How did he get there, Mr. Cheyney?' asked Jo, surprised that she had not thought about how Simon had gone to the playing fields the previous evening.

'Oh, he took his car. He usually drives himself if he is staying with us for holidays, but if it is just a day or so he will take the train. His car should be down near the school.'

'Could you describe his car please?'

'It is a green Peugeot 205 five door saloon, registration KY62 XNP. I bought it for him when he moved to London with the Harlequins. God, somebody will have to tell them and the England coach. He will be livid, losing two good players in the year of an All Black tour. I wonder if this is a New Zealand conspiracy to reduce our team's effectiveness?'

'I doubt they would sink that low, but it is a theory to consider,' replied Jo. 'Do you have a spare set of keys for Simon's car, as there were no keys found on his body?'

'Yes, I do. I will get them for you. Simon usually parks in Sunningdale Road and then lets himself onto the rugby pitch through the nearest school gates. You should find it there.

'I have to tell you, Mr. Cheyney, that the theory that my boss is working on, is that Simon was somehow involved in Josh's death, and then in remorse he took his own life. Simon did not

59

appear to be jealous of Josh when I spoke with him on Friday, did he ever express any negative feelings to you at all?'

'No. never,' replied Mr. Cheyney, 'right from his school days he knew that he was a good rugby player, but he accepted that Josh was better, especially as a kicker. Simon used to say that it spurred him on to try and overtake Josh. I am struggling to believe that he would ever do it this way, detective.'

'You will obviously get some flak from people once this all gets out, I suggest that you work out some strategy to deal with it. Some professional advice might help, perhaps a lawyer who can issue a statement on your behalf. Dealing with Josh's parents will be difficult, I presume, but remember this appears to be so out of character. You could also do well to contact Reverend Sean.'

'Thank you, detective. I will get some advice and talking to Sean would be good for my wife also. You will let me know if there are any developments, won't you?'

'Of course, Mr. Cheyney. I am so sorry for your loss and England's loss. Please say goodbye to your wife for me and I will let myself out.'

Once in Spence's car she rang the Fareham office and gave the details about Simon's car to the duty sergeant, insisting that it was imperative that it be located to establish whether it contained any items relating to either death.

Josh's boots were still missing and the clamps that Peter said were used to hoist Josh's body onto the cross. If they are in the car then that would underpin the theory that Simon was responsible for both deaths. Then again, thought Jo, if Simon were murdered and it was not suicide, the killer could plant the evidence pertaining to Josh's death in Simon's car. It was imperative to find the car before any evidence in it was contaminated.

CHAPTER SEVEN

Media briefings are always fraught with dangers, especially with murders, as the reporters always act as though you are not telling them everything. You can easily be caught out and the reporters will give the story a unique slant allowing them to claim outstanding journalistic prowess.

Fortunately, the Fareham police had a good relationship with *The News*, and this was demonstrated by the fact that DI Bligh had singled out Alex to publish the story, rather than release it to the nationals, like the *Daily Mail*. They would, in turn, pick the story up from *The News*. Alex would appreciate this and so would co-operate fully with the police.

Just before Jo and Spencer went to meet Alex, Jo pulled Spencer aside and said, 'I suggest, sir, that we do not mention the use of the dumbbell to stun the victims as this is information we can use to screen out the time wasters and attention seekers that any public request will bring out. Also, it will help identify any persons wishing to confess to the murders.'

'Good, thinking, Jo,' Spencer replied.

'Yes, we will leave out that detail and I must pass that on to the team at our next briefing meeting.'

Spencer started his media release by pointing to Jo saying that she was the lead in this investigation as she was on duty when the original call came in and so she was best placed to state the facts.

Jo then outlined the story from the beginning and Roland wrote feverishly to keep up. When Jo mentioned the names of the victims, Alex visibly shuddered as he realised the importance of what had happened and its effect on the rugby world. He knew that he had a cutting edge news story and could hardly wait to get it in tomorrow's edition. He would be a day ahead of the national dailies and that should increase the paper's circulation, especially the on-line customers.

When Jo had outlined all the relevant facts as they were known to date, including the motorcycle and side-car and Simon's car, Spencer turned to Alex and said, 'Could we ask two favours, please Alex, to help us in our investigation?'

'Sure, if I can, I will,' replied Roland.

'Well, we need to find out if anybody saw or heard anything unusual around White Hart Lane College, at or around 6.15pm on Saturday evening, or again around 6.pm yesterday. Also, we would like everybody who has CCTV between the college and the Church of the Holy Virgin to look at their footage, especially when it was dark to see if they can spot a motorcycle with side-car travelling either on roads or paths. As Jo said, we believe that Josh's body was transported in the motorcycle side-car probably around midnight or later.

We need people to come forward who heard a motorcycle engine around that time. We are also looking for Simon Cheyney's car, which is a green Peugeot 205 five door saloon, registration KY62 XNP.'

Roland promised that he would include all these requests in his article. Jo then turned to Roland, and without checking with her boss, she said, 'Can I ask that you go easy on the Cheyneys, as they are devastated, that a son of theirs could murder his closest friend from school days and put an England rugby win in jeopardy. I have just returned from speaking with them, and they are not a young couple and are going to have an exceedingly difficult time dealing with all of this. I have suggested to them that they speak through an intermediary'.

'Of course, I will have to speak with them and with Josh's parents, but I take your point, detective constable, and I will be sympathetic.'

Roland realised though the sooner he spoke to the Cheyneys the better before they had time to engage a lawyer who would only issue sanitised brief statements.

D.I. Bligh asked Roland if he had any questions.

'Firstly,' he asked, 'has the English coach been told?'

'Yes, he probably has by now,' replied Jo, 'Josh's parents have spoken to him, and the Cheyneys were going to ring him as I left their house about an hour ago.'

Roland nodded, and then asked, 'Do you have any photos of the crime scenes that I could use, please. Especially one of the victims carrying the cross?'

'We cannot give permission to use them in the media, Alex, as they are not our pictures but were taken by the vicar. You could always ask him for copies? The vicarage is in Castle Street.' said Jo.

'Yes, I will do. I need to speak with him anyway. Well, I better get off, as there is a lot of background work to do before the deadline for tomorrow's paper. Many thanks for only releasing this to *The News*. I do appreciate it,' Roland said, as he got up to leave.

The media briefing ended and Roland hurried away to write his copy.

Once in his car, he rang his editor and yelled into the phone 'Hold tomorrow's front page, as I have a story that will blow your socks off! I will be there in five minutes. Call a meeting with the art department and the sports editors. I have some interesting work for them this time!'

He then broke every speed limit to get back as soon as soon as he could to *The News* offices by the old IBM building. He reckoned that with this story, the paper would not mind paying for a speeding ticket, although as he would be doing a favour for the police, he thought that they would probably let him off anyway!

As he negotiated his way along the A27 past *Freshcos*, towards Lakeside, North Harbour, he was running possible headlines through his head. He thought that he would suggest 'Hung out to Die' to his editor, with 'Portchester's Story of Easter' as the sub-heading. He wondered if the art department would be able to create an image of a body on a makeshift cross or hanging from rugby goal posts. He also thought that a photo of the church, preferably showing the altar and a photo of the rugby posts at the college could also illustrate the story.

Anyway, that was the editor's prerogative to design the front page. Alex knew that he was up against deadlines to get his story written and tomorrow he would be occupied with the follow-up stories from interviewing the Christopher and Cheyney families, and staff at the college, especially the caretaker who found Simon's body hanging from the goal posts. There would be a lot of human interest in this story, which should boost circulation.

Jo and Spencer returned to the incident room, where the team were deep in discussion and waiting for the next tasks to be assigned.

Spencer went to the podium and announced, 'This is the resumption of the first meeting of Operation Golgotha. Well, today's events seem to indicate that we now have the killer of Josh Christopher and the possible cause of Simon Cheney's death, suicide. Well, we have certainly opened the flood gates, with our press release to *The News*.

Although we have a good relationship with *The News*

reporters, please still be on your guard against any utterances to them. Especially, do not mention to anyone the use of the dumbbell to stun Josh as this is information we can retain to use to screen out the time wasters and attention seekers that any public request may bring out. Also, it will help verify any persons wishing to confess to causing the deaths, although I doubt that there will be many, if any, since it will be seen as a murder out of jealousy and a suicide out of remorse.

Please leave all press releases to Jo and me. I have asked *The News* to publish that we are looking for CCTV images of the motorbike and side-car travelling between the college and the church. We are also requesting for anyone who heard a motorbike engine around midnight onwards on Saturday night to come forward.

However, we cannot rely on *The News* bringing someone forward, so Sergeant Oliver, could you please organise some Community Constables to check on all known CCTV and vehicle registration number plate recognition cameras (ANPR) to see if anything shows up. Please concentrate on the probable routes between the college playing fields and the castle and church. Do not forget the Cormorant Path that runs from Castle Street alongside the cemetery and the allotments. In fact, I am pretty sure that Cormorant House just up from the Castle street corner has a security camera. Please follow that up. The sooner we can locate the motorcycle registration number, the sooner we can find the registered keeper and confirm whether or not Simon was involved in Josh's murder,' continued Spencer.

'Simon could have had an accomplice,' interjected Jo.

'Yes, quite. Thank you, Jo. Bear that in mind please team. Don't forget the *English Heritage* owned camera along the Castle Path, Matt, as that may give us some idea as to which way the killer brought the victim to the church. However, the camera might be too far away from the seaside castle gate to record a clear image if the body was brought that way.'

Jo then turned to Sergeant Munden. 'Serg, in view of today's events, we know that Simon left the church at about the same time as Josh and before the vicar locked the church. This means that Simon would have somehow had to get back into the church with Josh's body, after the vicar had locked up. Could SOCO please address this, as we are bound to get a media question on it and this will be one more confirmation that we have solved this case.

'Yes, of course, Jo. I will let you know my findings as soon as!'

'Great and thanks,' said Jo.

She then turned to Spencer and asked, 'Sir, Simon told me when we were talking after Josh's death, that he would hopefully move up to the first choice for the number ten jersey, and one Raymond Salter would be the reserve. He could now be the number one choice for fly-half. Do you think that we need to interview him?'

'Well, we are only presuming that the common link between Josh's and Simon's death is jealousy and remorse, but a quiet word with the England coach might be helpful,' replied Spencer.

'Right,' said Jo 'I will get on to that today.'

Spencer then turned to the staff in the incident room, and said, 'Right, officers, those whom Sergeant Oliver has selected, off you go to locate any information about the killer's movements on Saturday afternoon at the college playing field, and Saturday night between the college and the church, and Monday morning at the college. We are particularly looking for camera shots of the motorcycle and side-car, especially the registration number. The rest of you can start looking for Simon's car. It must be around Portchester somewhere and probably near the college. If you find it, call it in and we will get a locksmith out to it.'

'Hang on sir,' interrupted Jo. 'I've got a spare set of keys for Simon's car from Mr. Cheyney, I will leave them with the duty officer.'

'Good work, Jo,' said Spence. 'When you do get the car, notify SOCO who can bring it in for forensic examination. Hopefully, it might reveal some information relating to Josh's killer being Simon. Jo, after you have spoken to the coach can you try and source the motorcycle with side-car? We will regroup here tomorrow afternoon at 2:00pm for updates.'

Jo returned to her desk, switched on her computer, and loaded the English rugby website, 'englishrugby' and scrolled down to the contacts link and found the direct phone number. She was soon speaking with the receptionist asking to speak to Glen Francis.

Initially she was fobbed off with the usual 'he's in a meeting' gambit, but as soon as she said who she was and that she was the lead investigator in the two deaths of Josh and Simon, she was immediately put through to the coach. After quick introductions, and expression of sympathies, she asked him whether he had spoken to Josh's and Simon's parents.

'Yes, I have spoken with both of them,' he said. 'I am finding it really hard to believe that Simon could do this, when he, of all people, knows how important having a stable squad is at this time. I really feel for his parents, as they will have to field a lot of flak. Also, I tried to speak to Josh on the Friday afternoon about scheduling an extra kicking practice session over the Easter weekend, but he was out training when I rang. Of course, that practice session never happened.'

'When will you appoint your replacement fly-half, please?' asked Jo.

'We have just had a pre-selection meeting and the contenders are the Number ten for Leicester Tigers, Raymond Salter, and the London Irish equivalent, Arthur O'Neill,' said the coach.

'Arthur O'Neill is, or should I say was a teammate of Josh's, so he has learnt quite a bit from him, especially regarding kicking. It is now down to the selection panel and they meet again tomorrow. There are preliminary enquiries to be made and pathways to follow, as his club coach also has a say and would have to agree to releasing him for England squad selection.

They usually do as it is a bit of kudos for the club to have players in the national team, so I will let you know, when there is a decision, detective. All this upheaval is not good for the squad's morale and internal integrity. Look Detective, if I can be of any help at all, please let me know, won't you,' implored Glenn.

'Well, thank you for your time, sir, and all the best for the forthcoming internationals. I will be watching the games with interest,' said Jo and she rang off.

Jo than wrote up the telephone call in her notes and went to find D.I. Bligh to give him a copy. Jo also thought that it could be worthwhile having a discussion with Chris Foley, the *Sportsman's Daily* rugby correspondent. He always seems to have his finger on the pulse and would know what was developing within the England Squad.

CHAPTER EIGHT

Detective Inspector Bligh was pouring himself a coffee when Jo caught up with him. 'Want a cup, Jo?' He asked on seeing her enter the tea-room.

'Yes please, sir,' she replied. She sat down at one of the small square tables in the staff tearoom and D.I. Bligh joined her with two coffees. 'It's milk, no sugar, isn't it?'

'Yes, thank you, sir. 'I have just spoken with the England coach, Glenn Francis, and he told me that a Leicester Tigers player, Raymond Salter and a London Irish fly-half called Arthur O'Neill are the likely contenders to replace Josh and Simon. There is a meeting tomorrow to make the decision.

'Also, sir, I would like to talk to Chris Foley, the *Sportsman's Daily* senior rugby correspondent as he always seems to have his finger on the pulse and will know what's developing within the England Squad.'

'Yes, that's fine, Jo, go ahead. Now go and find the motorcycle and side-car,' said Spencer.

'Sure, sir. See you tomorrow afternoon in the incident room.'

Jo returned to her desk and started searching for local motorbike dealers. A quick Google search showed five local dealers, and after contacting them she learned that none of them had sold a motorbike with side-car or a side-car on its own in the past three months. They all thought that ebay was her best bet, and so a quick search on ebay revealed that there were several motorbike and side-cars listed. What she needed, she realised, was information on recently sold motorbikes and side-cars.

She needed to contact ebay. She went on to the ebay website, and after clicking the contact link, filled out a query form and submitted her request along with her contact details. As is often the frustrating way websites are set up, she could not find a contact phone number, so she could now only wait for someone to get back to her.

She had only just returned to her desk with another coffee, when her phone rang, and it was ebay customer service. Jo explained what she wanted and she found ebay to be very cooperative. The fact that the customer services agent was a rugby fan, may have helped! She was promised a list of motorbike and side-car sellers who had made sales over the past two months, as a start. She would receive the seller's name and contact details and could take it from there. After she thanked the customer services agent, she hung up and on putting the phone down she suddenly realised that if Simon did not commit suicide, but was also murdered, then in the list could be the killer re-selling the motorcycle after the murders had been committed. All she needed to do would be match the ebay list with England team members and look for the same motorbike being sold and recently re-sold.

For the first time in a while, Jo was feeling a lot more positive. She would only inform Spencer of her theory that Simon was also murdered when she had hard evidence. She would have to convince Detective Chief Inspector Raylene Abbottsford as well. Now, she needed Sergeant Oliver and his team to come up with some identifying sightings of the motorcycle and side-car. A registration number would be good start, she thought.

Jo was about to ring Chris Foley when her phone rang. It was one of her girlfriends with whom she played rugby on

70

weekends, asking if she could play on Sunday. It was a friendly match between her team, Alton Ladies and Farnborough. As she had not played for a while, Jo thought that it would be a good distraction and a great way to spend Sunday afternoon. She said she would play and agreed to meet up with her teammates at the Alton clubhouse around midday on Sunday. She thought that they could have lunch together.

She then looked up the *Sportsman Daily* contact numbers and after a few minutes she was speaking with Chris Foley.

'Thank you for taking my call, Mr. Foley.'

'Chris, please!' he interjected.

'My name is Detective Constable Jo Fletcher, and I am investigating the deaths of Josh Christopher and Simon Cheyney, and I was hoping that I might be able to have a word with you,' Jo asked.

'What did you say?' Chris Foley almost screamed into the phone.

'Oh, I am sorry, I just presumed that you would have already been told that Josh Christopher was found dead on a cross in our local church on Saturday morning, and Simon Cheyney was found dead hanging from the cross bar of the local college rugby posts this morning.'

'No, nobody has told me anything. God that is terrible. It will really put the rugby world in a tizz, not to mention the England squad. Can you give me details, please Detective?'

'Call me Jo, please. For the press release I suggest that you contact Roland Marley, the sports reporter for the Portsmouth News, as we have released a press statement to him this afternoon and he will be publishing a news item in tomorrow's edition. Tell him that I requested that he email you his copy. He knows to keep on side with us, as we feed him anything useful.

71

It allows us to keep some control over what is released. He may insist that you do not print anything before *The News* goes on sale tomorrow.'

'That's standard practice with a scoop, but at least I will have time to do some background work. Does the coach, Glen Francis know?'

'Yes, he has been in contact with both families.'

'Oh, well, I can get to him tonight,' said Chris.

'Can I ring you, Jo, after I get his copy, as I may have some questions for you?'

'Well, Chris, if it is not too much of an imposition, I would prefer to meet up with you, rather than talk about sensitive matters over the phone. I have quite a bit to discuss with you, especially about who will be selected as fly-half and whether or not they could be in danger.'

'Meeting up is fine and the sooner the better, as this story is huge. Unfortunately I am tied up for the remainder of this week, and most of next week and of course on Saturday, watching and reporting on the main games, but I could do evenings, if that suits, as I sense time is of the essence for you right now.'

'Evenings are fine for me, Chris. How about tonight? You could get a train from Waterloo or Victoria to Portchester and I will meet you there. We could do dinner. I will cook. That will afford us some privacy.'

'Look, Jo, tonight would be fine. Give me your details, and I will text you the train I am on.'

Jo gave him her email address and mobile phone number and added, 'Come out of the station, down the steps, and turn right into Station Road, walk to the intersection and turn right. I will be there in a blue Vauxhall Astra. It is my own car so don't look for a police vehicle.'

72

'Right, Jo. See you later this evening. Shall I bring some wine?'

'That would be nice. It will be great seeing you and I can answer all your questions then.'

'Bye, Jo, and thanks. I will get on to *The News* straight away.'

Jo then put her handset on its cradle and suddenly thought, I have just made a date with Chris Foley! Whatever next.

She sat at her desk trying to remember when she last had a date. She had always kept to her rule of not dating police colleagues and although she still preferred that it did mean that with her long working hours, she was somewhat prevented in having much of a social life, especially when murderers had to be caught.

Jo decided that rather than remain in the office getting her notes together for tomorrow's Operation Golgotha meeting, she would do that at home once she had sorted out dinner. She knew that Chris would be a good two hours away, but she wanted time to get ready.

She quickly called in to Spencer's office and told him that she was meeting with Chris Foley this evening. Spencer nodded and said, 'Don't forget to put it down to expenses!'

Jo replied, 'I might just do that sir. See you tomorrow afternoon,' and left. She knew she had to get a move on to get home, shower, put some glad rags on and be prepared to entertain her guest!

Jo had plenty of time to organise her notes and write up her interviews with ebay, Coach Francis, and Chris, but she had only just arrived outside the station when she saw Chris, having recognised him from his mugshot in the paper that accompanied the by-line before his sporting articles.

She was nervous and anxious, feeling a bit like a young

teenager on her first date, it had been so long.

She had tried to dress well for dinner and just before she had come out of her bedroom she had checked in the mirror to assure herself that she would make a good first impression. In the mirror she could see an attractive twenty-something, with a smallish face, between centrally parted, long black hair. She had a small mouth, with pretty red lips, and she wore black rimmed glasses, which all gave her an air of having some authority. She was dressed in a smart jacket over open-necked sparkly blouse and black dress trousers. It was times like this, she thought, that she inwardly thanked her parents for her good looks.

Chris opened the front passenger door, popped a bag between his legs and shook hands with Jo.

'Nice to meet you,' he said. 'I nearly didn't make it as my editor wanted to know all about the deaths, so I pleaded lack of knowledge until tomorrow, which is in a way true. Thanks for picking me up. It doesn't look like there is a taxi stand at this station.'

'It's at the far end of the precinct over there,' said Jo, pointing across Chris in the direction of the Red Lion pub. She glanced at Chris and was quite pleased at seeing a smartly dressed, suited man, including a waistcoat. He was, she guessed, in his mid-twenties with a copy of the *Sportsman's Daily* in his hand. He had short black hair and a roundish face. Jo estimated that he would be about the same height as herself, which she appreciated as she did not fancy being with anybody that was either taller or shorter than herself.

Jo expertly drove along The Crossway, meandering the car around all the parked cars towards the petrol station. It was at earlier times than this, that she could have just crossed over into Rockingham Way and on to The Thicket but now that it had been pedestrianised, she had to go around the long way along the A27. She drove onto her drive and said: 'Right, this is my house, bring your bag and we will go in.' Once inside, Jo turned to Chris and said: 'I take it you are staying the night and going back to London tomorrow, Chris?'

'Yes, I thought that after our talk, I could get a room at the Marriott or the Village hotels, which I believe are quite close to here.'

'You don't need to do that. There are three spare bedrooms here, upstairs, just take your pick. The bathroom is on the left at the top of the stairs, or the bedroom on the right has an ensuite. Make yourself at home, while I get a couple of drinks. Wine or beer?'

'I'll have a beer, if I may, and here is a bottle I've brought that we can have later.'

Jo looked at it and said, 'Very nice, thank you. What is it? A Marlborough Sauvignon Blanc?'

'Exactly, the only white worth drinking!'

'I agree.'

'Right a pint of beer for you, it will be here for you when you come downstairs.

'Yes, I prefer lager now if you have it and I usually only have wine with food.'

'Have you tried the New Zealand Steinlager, Chris?' Jo asked.

'Yes, I have actually. I tried it when I was covering the America's Cup, and the New Zealand team were serving it as their main complimentary drink. Very enjoyable.'

At that, Chris picked up his bag and made his way upstairs. As he went up the stairs, Jo thought that he looked younger than his picture in the paper, but that he was still probably a couple of years older than her. She liked his charcoal suit and really liked his waistcoat. 'Yep, I could go out with this guy she thought. Jo knew that any person she started dating would get the once-over from all her colleagues, including Spencer, not to mention her rugby team mates. Perhaps she could invite him to the next work do, she mused.

Jo then went and put her bag away, took off her coat and made her way to the kitchen and the fridge. She poured herself a glass of wine from the already opened bottle in the fridge and took out a bottle of Steinlager that she had sourced on the internet and purchased direct from the SANZA shop in London. While she filled the glasses, she remembered the blurb about SANZA that she had seen when she first bought alcohol from the Southern Hemisphere. Established in 1999 for the antipodean ex-pat, SANZA combines the largest range of products from South Africa, Australia and New Zealand, which countries make up the company name.

Chris was pleasantly surprised when he came downstairs and saw Jo pouring his beer from the distinctive Steinlager bottle.

'You are very resourceful,' he said, 'but then that would be the hallmark of a good copper, wouldn't it?'

'Just like a journo, I presume,' retorted Jo.

'Snap,' said Chris.

They both took their drinks, walked into the main lounge, and sat opposite each other in the two large chairs. They talked small talk at first, about the train trip from London, and how each had spent their day.

Then, as if Chris was keen to get on to more serious topics, he stated, 'I received Roland's news story on the deaths, Jo. Thanks for the tip off there.'

'No problem. Have you got it with you, as I have not seen it yet and I am always interested in how the press re-interpret what is said in our media releases and interviews?'

Chris reached inside his jacket and brought out a small sheaf of papers. 'Here it is.'

Jo quickly scanned through it. 'Yes,' she said, 'that seems to be a fairly accurate summary of what we said to him.'

'Tell, me Jo, if you can,' said Chris. 'How did you come to the conclusion so quickly and affirmatively that Simon's death was suicide and that proved that he killed Josh? I understand that Simon could have murdered Josh, to take over his position in the England team and then had a huge attack of remorse, but I would like to know how you eliminated the possibility that both deaths are murders and the killer has been clever in disguising Simon's murder as a suicide?'

There was a pause, while neither spoke. It was obvious to Chris that Jo was pondering something. 'Have I said something to disturb you, Jo?' he asked.

'No, Chris. To be honest, I am just trying to decide how far I can trust you with sensitive information. I know that you are a great sportswriter and I do read your analysis of the rugby scenario and I really do like you, but you are a journo.

In my experience, journalists always seem to operate on the principle that the police are not revealing everything and they seem to think it is their prerogative and a mark of their expertise to fathom out what the police are concealing and in some extreme cases they will even enhance their stories to make their news reports more engaging to the reading public.'

'Yes, I do take your point, Jo, and some of my so-called colleagues are guilty of that, but I can assure you, that yes, I am a journalist, but my interest, my passion really, is sport, especially rugby, as I think it is treated badly by the media in favour of football. Even my own paper, only gives rugby a couple of pages at most, whereas football gets a whole section. I would never knowingly state mistruths just to get a story. There is enough interest and excitement in the rugby reality without making anything up. Also, I have always had a hankering to try investigative journalism and I admire those journalists who delve into the criminal word, set up stings and show some people up to be the low-lifes that they are. Especially when the lowlifes are celebrities or politicians. I think a bit of the underworld excites me!'

'Fair, enough, Chris. It is just that we often withhold some crucial evidence from the media, to be able to weed out the nutters and saddos who want to confess to the crimes, in order to get some notoriety, albeit fleetingly. There was one occasion when we had one persistent person who wanted to confess to a series of paedophile crimes and he wouldn't give up, even though we knew that he could not be the perpetrator as there was crucial evidence that we had withheld and that he could not tell us what it was. In the end my D.I told him that before he signed his confession, he needed to know that parliament had recently enacted legislation to make all paedophile crimes a capital offence, with no right of appeal and if he signed a confession, the DI said he could guarantee that he would be executed before the end of the month.

The nutter immediately stood up and said, 'Sorry sir, I believe I am not thinking straight and have it all wrong. May I go now?' The DI and I had a good laugh after he left!'

'I take it then that you have some crucial evidence in this case that you are currently withholding?' asked Chris.

'Yes,' said, Jo, 'I think that I can help you satisfy your desire to get a good rugby story straight and also do a bit of investigative journalism as well. I will tell you everything, but you must keep it secret, Chris for reasons that you will appreciate as you hear me out.'

78

'Yes, Jo, I swear that I will not report anything until you give me clearance.' returned Chris.

'Well,' said Jo, 'I will take you at your word, Chris, and I think that you will be able to help me investigate these crimes. We can do it together if that is okay?'

'Sure Jo.'

'Although, my boss, Detective Inspector Spencer Bligh believes this to be now an open and shut case of murder and suicide, I am not so sure. We know that Josh was murdered, by initially being strangled, and then dragged into the undergrowth by a rope around his neck and then stabbed in the right hand side, which we presume was to give the effect of replicating Jesus's death so that when the body was placed on the cross, it would look like a crucifixion. Therefore giving rise to their being a religious motive behind the killer's intentions and that regarding Simon's death that also has a religious motive in that it replicated Judith Iscariot's remorse at having betrayed Jesus to the Romans in the garden of Gethsemane as Simon's body was hanging from the cross-bar and it contained a coin bag full of thirty, fifty cent pieces.'

'Ah, the thirty pieces of silver,' interrupted Chris.

'Exactly,' said Jo.

'All a bit too pat, really. Meant, no doubt, to get us looking for some deep religious significance and a killer with a religious axe to grind, who then suddenly becomes totally remorseful and commits suicide. I do not buy it, but my boss seems to. I think he is more motivated by quick crime clear-up rates, and keeping in the good books of his Detective Chief Inspector, by limiting use of resources and keeping down costs, rather than actual justice. The bit of evidence that we have not released, in regard to Josh's death is that his body received severe bruising to his stomach, consistent with being heavily hit with an item like a dumbbell which our pathologist believes was severe enough to stun him and enable the killer to then tie a ligature around his neck and to drag him into undergrowth where he was then stabbed and left until the body was later retrieved and taken to the church.

In Simon's case there was no evidence of any bruising to the stomach. My boss interprets that to mean that he was not killed and then hung out to die but hung himself.

I am not so sure. I think that he was stunned in some way, either tripped or tackled, and then he was dragged by the neck or carried to the goal posts and hoisted up to hang from the cross bar being made to look like suicide. If I am right, this means that in both cases, the victims knew their killer and trusted him or her enough to train with them without expecting any harm to come to them.

In Josh's case, we believe that he was probably running in the opposite direction to his killer, and as they came together, the killer lunged forward with a dumbbell and slammed it into Josh's stomach, brought him down, then tied a rope around his neck and dragged him into the dense undergrowth behind the goal post at the end of the playing field.

It was different for Simon. He was probably brought down a different way, stunned and then dragged by the neck or carried to the goal posts. I understand Chris, that Glen Francis insists that his players train by jogging holding and swinging dumbbells to strengthen their arms,'

'Yes,' agreed Chris, 'it is a coaching trademark of his, and other coaches are now doing it as well'.

'Well, that would mean that Josh would not be surprised to see someone he recognised running towards him swinging a dumbbell. However, to prove that Simon was murdered, I need to find evidence that he was brought down, stunned, dragged and hoisted up onto the cross bar.'

'My God,' said Chris, 'this means that the killer is one of the England squad! As he would have to have been someone Simon recognised and trusted.'

'Exactly!' said Jo. 'This is why this evidence can't be shared, at least not yet, until I have more proof.'

'Jo?' asked Chris. 'Surely if someone had to haul Simon's body up to the crossbar and suspend it there, there would be some evidence of rope burn on the cross-bar?'

'Yes, Chris. I have thought that too. Although rugby posts today are made of metal, the school's posts are the old original wooden ones and so rope burns are a possibility. It was never examined by either the pathologist or the SOCO team and I intend to check it out. There should be a significant difference between throwing over a rope and tying it to the cross-bar with a slip knot and noose and hauling a body over it.'

'I would like to be there, when you check that out, Jo,' said Chris.

'You can come with me if you like. We could go at first light tomorrow morning, before you go back to London. I am sure that I could get the caretaker to open the gates early. He could probably supply us with a ladder to have a good look.'

I would like that Jo,' said Chris.

'See, I told you that this story would bring out the investigative spirit in you,' remarked Jo.

'I am very interested now, Jo.'

'What, at checking out evidence, or being with me!'

'Both!'

'Just kidding, Chris.'

'Well, I am not! For the record, I am not with anybody at the

81

moment, so I only have to account for myself.'

'Same here,' said Jo.

'Well,' said Chris. 'Presuming that both Josh and Simon were murdered and by the same killer. I am inclined to agree with your interpretation, Jo, not your boss, as although I have not had much to do with either Simon or Josh, I have never heard of any animosity or jealousy between them, but only the opposite. They come across to everyone as being a couple of *besties*.'

'I think the same, Chris. I interviewed Simon, virtually straight after we found Josh's body, and there was no evidence of jealousy or remorse, but only one of genuine shock and sorrow. Also, as you can imagine, it is dire for Simon's parents as they will be vilified by everyone, especially Josh's family who are or were their best friends too. I feel that we must do everything we can to show them that their son is not a murderer, by producing the real culprit. But, as you can imagine, I will have to do this on the QT as it were, because as far as the police are concerned, this crime has been solved!

'Is there any other possible scenario, perhaps one that is not rugby related, that might be worth investigating?' asked Chris.

'Well, there is another possibility,' said Jo, 'both Josh and Simon have dated the same girl in the past, but not lately, and this girl had another suitor who Simon told me was so keen on her at college that he tried to buy Josh off, so that he could date her. He could possibly have killed both Josh and Simon to clear the way for his romancing of this girl, but I'm not sure about this line of investigating as she is currently a student in Southampton and no doubt will have her own social network, which I am sure would not include a former school acquaintance from around here. It is worth just keeping in mind though, as a possible lead.

I think the rugby connection is more relevant and worth

82

pursuing.'

'Right,' said Chris, 'not something you should have to do on your own. I would love to help. Let us start with the England squad. Who stands to gain most by the absence of Josh and Simon?'

'Well, I asked Glenn Francis who will be the next fly-half, and he said that in his view it would be between Raymond Salter of Leicester Tigers or Arthur O'Neill of London Irish. Glenn said that the selection board will be making their decision tomorrow. My problem, Chris, is that if we are right and the murderer is still out there, then whoever is selected could be in danger, but in view of the situation, I cannot openly declare that.'

'Yes, I see your predicament. I could always have a quiet word with whoever is selected as it is part of my remit to interview players who become part of the England squad.'

'Well, I will leave that up to you, then. You can now start pondering over fly-half selections while I put dinner in the oven and set the table,' said Jo as she wandered off towards the kitchen.

'Well, Jo, that lasagne was absolutely divine. I also live on my own, and your lasagne obviously did not come from a supermarket, not even Waitrose!'

'No, I cook from scratch, when I have the time. I cannot stand all those preservatives that they put into food. If I were to follow the health advice that your paper writes, I would be too scared to eat anything?'

'Yes, it does seem to be a case of flavour of the month and I criticise them for so often saying one thing, one week, and the opposite the next. Anyway, as you probably realise, it is all about circulation figures and income, not about a healthy society. That would be pointless, as if we lived in a healthy society, we would not waste time and money reading inane articles in newspapers, but we would read quality literary works and proper research papers.'

'Talk about biting off the hand that feeds, you!' said Jo and they both laughed.

'Well, Jo, if we are going to work together as private investigators on these grisly murders, please tell me a bit about yourself.'

'Only if you will tell me about yourself later.'

'Deal!'

'Well, my full name is Josephine Agnes Fletcher, I am twenty-eight years old, birthday on 25th September. My Mum said that I was conceived on a Christmas Day when she was already full of turkey and plum pudding! Mum was a nurse, but after I was born, she gave up work. She died from dementia. My bra size is a 36D and I can barely just fit into size12 Marks and Spencer lingerie.'

'Too much information!'

'Not if you are going to buy me presents!!'

'True.'

'I am an only child and I have lived in this house since I was born. My Dad worked in the local Fareham Council Planning Department and he was murdered by his boss. This was because my Dad discovered that his boss was taking considerable bribes from large building firms in exchange for getting planning consents and was about to expose him.

At first everyone said that my Dad had had a massive heart attack but I did not accept that. I proved that he had been murdered. The police did not really want to know. That is what motivated me to become a detective. I went to local schools, and Portsmouth University where I took a criminology degree, and then I entered the local Police Specialist Entry Detective Programme. Initially joining as a student Police Officer, I completed a structured development programme which enabled me to progress to the role of Detective Constable and that is my current role.'

'Tell me about your Dad's murder, if that is okay, Jo.'

'As I said, at first it was thought that Dad had died naturally from a massive heart attack. The pathologist had argued that it was due to stress and high blood pressure. I had not accepted that as I knew that Dad had been no more stressed than usual and he had been meticulous about checking his blood pressure and taking his Valsartan tablets, morning and evening.

Dad had his own blood pressure monitor, an Omron M5-1 which was the same type as his doctor had and I had checked his last fifteen readings which were all in the normal range.

As Dad had talked to me about possible corruption over a planning permission, I believed that my father had been murdered as he was advising the council not to approve the application.

The applicant was a large multi-million pound house building company and they wanted to build in the green belt, which Dad argued went against the Borough Local Plan.

I knew that Dad's boss, the Director of Planning was in favour of approving the application and Dad thought that his boss was in the pocket of the applicant.

The police would not involve themselves due to the pathologist's report. I had been researching the internet as to causes of cardiac arrests and one possible cause that caught my eye was an air embolism, where an amount of air injected into a vein could cause an obstruction of the right ventricular outflow tract, leading to a cardiac arrest. I then decided to take the matter into my own hands and see if I could find any evidence on Dad's body of needle tracks.

At that time, Dad was in his coffin at home and the funeral was not for a couple of days. He would then have been cremated and all possible trace of murder would be erased. So I set about minutely examining his body. After a couple of hours I found some needle marks under both his armpits. I knew that I would have to get that confirmed.'

'That took some courage, love and commitment to examine your Dad like that.'

'Yes, it was not as gruesome as I thought it would be and I welcomed the challenge.'

Inwardly, Jo was quite pleased at Chris's remark, as she thought it showed him to be caring and perceptive.

'Carry on Jo, if you can, I am fascinated. You are opening up a totally different world to me.'

'Well, I knew that I would need to get another forensic pathologist's opinion and the only one I knew of was a man that I first met at university. His name is Peter Good and he is now our full time pathologist. Although we were both doing different degrees, we had a series of criminology lectures in common. We hit it off straight away and so I turned to him to confirm my findings regarding Dad.

Peter was hesitant at first as he had only recently been appointed as an assistant pathologist to the Portsmouth NHS and he did not want to step on the toes of the most revered Doctor Michael Thompson who had carried out the original post mortem on my father.

He did however examine him and was convinced that I was right. Peter considered that a twenty millimetre needle had been used, which was similar to that used by diabetics to inject

86

Insulin. I then remembered that my father's boss was a diabetic, as he had had a hypo attack during a staff social function and had to be given sugar to bring him around. I then knew that I had to find evidence of a needle.

The next day, I went to the site of the planning dispute and looked around the area where Dad was said to have collapsed and after some time in a nearby bush I found a syringe. Eventually, that syringe was traced to a pack that the Director of Planning had had prescribed, he was arrested and confessed.

That episode, emotional as it was for me, was the reason I decided to join the police and become a detective and is the reason that I am not prepared to let my boss seek the easy murder/suicide option in this case. I believe that there is still a murderer out there and we need to find him or her before the next fly-half gets hung out to die!'

'I think that you are one hell of a woman, Jo, and if I was a criminal, I would not want you on my case! Well, I suppose it is my turn, but not before we refresh our wine glasses.'

'Fine, I will get another bottle. Fancy a red?

'Yes, red would be great. Aussie is it?'

'Cab Sauv.'

'I'll drink to that! Well, as I am still alive.'

Chris started talking when Jo had returned with two glasses of red wine, 'I must have been born and as my Mum was present, I believe her when she says that I was born on April Fool's day, 1986. I am sure that many people think that I have been a joke ever since. Like you, I am an only child, and my Mum was a paediatric nurse until she retired two years ago. Dad was also in newsprint and edited a suburban paper until he retired last year when the paper was absorbed into a conglomerate.

I suppose I got the journalism bug from Dad, who had earned

a formidable reputation as an investigative journalist before he was promoted to the desk. I attended Newbury High School and then Newbury College where I did Politics and Sport and then I went on to Northumbria University where I got a B.A. in media and journalism. I played rugby both at school and college, but not very well, although I did enjoy playing.'

'So, Jo, as you can see, my current position as senior sporting correspondent combines all my education. Impressed?'

'Yeah, not bad,' said Jo with a large grin on her face, 'would you like a night-cap, Chris? It is not often I get to host a guest in my house. In fact, I cannot remember the last time. I have got some twelve-year-old Chivas Regal whisky, or a Napoléon Brandy, if you prefer.'

'I could definitely get used to this,' replied Chris,' I'll have the whisky please. My Dad would be impressed! He always had a bottle of single malt around, for reducing stress at the end of the working day.'

'Right, let us drink these and then I think we can have an early night as I don't want to be seen climbing over rugby posts tomorrow morning, so we will need an early start. I have already rung the caretaker and he will open the Sunningdale Road gate at 7.00am and leave a ladder near the goal posts. We can just drive in, collect the evidence, and leave. I will then take you to the station if that's what you want.'

'I'm impressed with your organisation, Jo, that is something I am not well known for.'

'Please remind me to take a camera tomorrow. You can now start your career as an investigative journalist. Under my supervision of course!' she added.

'Very happy to be supervised by you,' Chris replied.

'That's enough grovelling for one day, thanks!'

They finished their nightcaps and Jo then said: 'I'll get you some clean towels. No problem if you want a bath or shower as there is plenty of hot water.'

As Chris watched her go upstairs to get a towel, He thought that he and Jo could get along very well, but he was not going to start anything. Let her make the first overture, was his motto, or at least was now! Plenty of life left in them both without rushing things now. Now was bedtime, on their own!

'Wakey Wakey, sleepyhead', said Jo approaching Chris's bed with a cup of tea in her hand.

'What time is it?'

'6.15am. Time to get up and dressed. We need to leave about 6.45. Breakfast on the table at 6.30. OK?'

'Absolutely fine, Jo, Thanks for the tea. Just how I like it.'

By the time Chris had come downstairs, all suited and booted, Jo had breakfast on the table.

'Bloody hell, Jo. Bacon and eggs, orange juice, toast, jam, and coffee. This is better than most hotels I stay over in. Only for work, mind! I could really get used to this.'

The question, Jo pondered was, could I get used to you getting used to this? Ah well, time will tell.

They finished breakfast, and as Chris went out to put his bags by the car, Jo picked up a black pilot case and she followed Chris out, shut the door and unlocked the car.

As she drove along Sunningdale Road, to the playing field, she looked out for Simon's car, but it did not appear to be there. Hopefully, it had been picked up by now, she thought.

The gates were open, and the caretaker was standing just inside the entrance. Jo wound down her window and the caretaker looked in and said, 'I've left the ladder up against the

89

crossbar over there. Just leave it there when you are finished. I will come over in a minute.'

'Right, you are and many thanks for this. I hope I did not get you out especially.'

'No, I always get here about this time, so I am here before the kids arrive!'

Okay, we will see you later.'

Jo drove across to the posts and got out, collected her bag, and went over to the post. She opened her bag, took out a camera, tape measure and a short spirit level.

She then turned to Chris and said, 'Could you hold the ladder please but please put these on first, will you?' handing him a pair of latex gloves. I don't want to contaminate the scene.'

Jo then put gloves on herself as Chris went to the base of the ladder. Jo climbed up so that she was above the crossbar.

'It's as I thought Chris. There is quite a groove in the wood, where the rope was and the base of it is brownish in colour.'

She photographed the groove in the crossbar and then placing the spirit level along the bar, over the groove, she measured the depth of the groove.

'The groove is a good ten millimetres deep, so that depth could not be made by just throwing over a rope. There is also rope burn as the groove is brownish in colour.

I am now convinced that this is a case of murder made to look like suicide. I am theorising that the killer somehow stunned Simon, which brought him down, and then placed the noose around his neck and half carried and dragged him to the posts. Threw the rope over, then pulled his body up to the hanging position so that his feet were off the ground and then secured the rope.'

'You said to *The News* reporter, that there was a pair of steps lying alongside the upright here when you first arrived yesterday. Surely, they would not be high enough to be able to secure the rope to the cross-bar.'

'Good thinking, I'll make a copper out of you yet! That is why I have brought this with me. At that, Jo came down the ladder, and as she went to open her bag, Chris called out: 'Jo, is it okay if I go up and have a look, please?'

'Sure Chris.' Jo then removed a complete finger-printing kit from her bag and got it ready to take some prints.

'Chris, could you bring the ladder over here, please?'

'Sure.'

Jo then set about taking prints off the ladder. Just then the caretaker came over and Jo turned to him and said,

'Right on cue, sir. Could you tell me please where you store this ladder?'

'Oh, I just keep it over there, leaning up against the fence.'

'So, anybody could really take it and use it?'

'Yes, often tennis and footballs end up on those roofs and teachers use the ladder to get them down.'

'I'm dusting for prints in case the ladder was used by our killer.'

'But the paper said that Simon committed suicide.'

'I know, and that is the obvious conclusion from the evidence that we gleaned yesterday, but I just want to make sure that we have got it right.'

'Oh, I'm glad about that, as I know both those boys and they were like blood brothers. I cannot imagine Simon hurting Josh, or himself. It is just not in his character. He was tough and rugged while playing rugby, but otherwise, he could not hurt a fly. I remember teachers telling me that during biology class, he could not bring himself to even dissect a frog; and it had been

91

dead for some time. He was not a violent man.' Jo could not let him know that she agreed with him, so she just said: 'We will leave no stone unturned to get the truth, and I will keep you posted. Just one more thing, Sir,'

'Please call me Dave. Dave Edwards. I have been caretaker here longer than any other staff member has been here, so I like to think it is my college. I hate it when anything occurs that brings it into disrepute.'

'Okay, Dave. Do you ever wash this ladder?'

'Yes, occasionally, so teachers using it don't get themselves dirty, as they are usually in suits like your colleague here.'

'When would you have last washed it, do you remember?'

'Only last week, as it happens.'

'So probably not enough time for anyone else to use it other than yourself?'

'I imagine that is the case.'

'Right, then may I take your fingerprints, so I can eliminate them from my findings, please?'

'Sure.' Jo then took Dave's prints and said: Dave, I have just had an idea. In order to get conclusive proof, would you be prepared to help me in reconstructing this death scene?'

'Sure, I would like to.'

'Well, Simon was about fifteen and half stone in weight, so could you get weights to that amount from the college gym and I will get the pathologist present and we will drag the weights across the field and haul them up to the crossbar and see what type of groove they make.'

'Yes, Jo, that's fine. Happy to do that.'

'I'll just make a call.' After she had spoken on the phone, she said: 'That's all sorted. Could we do this after school today, say 4:00pm? Peter, the pathologist will attend as well. With this

92

evidence, I am sure I can convince my boss that Simon's death is murder, not suicide.'

'4:00pm would be fine. There won't be any kids around by then.'

'Great, I will see you later. And thank you.'

'Come on Chris. I will get you to the station.'

Jo then picked up her bag, put it into the car and they drove off. 'I'll drop you just around the corner from the station in The Crossways and you can walk from there to the station.'

They both got out of the car and stood together beside it. Chris turned to Jo and said, 'Jo, this has been fantastic. You have been fantastic. I would really like to see you again, may I?'

'Of course, Chris. I think you will be seeing a lot of me! You will let me know the outcome of the selection committee decision, today, won't you?'

'Yes, I have a good source on the committee, so I will let you know immediately. I have your mobile number. If you are still playing rugby on Sunday could I join you please. I have not really taken much interest in ladies rugby, apart from the English Squad, but I sense that is about to change.'

'Sure, Chris, come up on Saturday after the rugby, and you can stay over, and we can go to north Hampshire together and make an afternoon of it.'

'Sure, it's a date.'

Chris picked up his bag and made for the station. He turned and waved, and Jo waved back. What, two dates in the same week and staying over!!

CHAPTER NINE

D.I. Bligh was already in the incident room standing at his podium when Jo entered. They acknowledged each other and then Jo took her seat with the coffee that she had brought in with her.

It was another five minutes before everyone was assembled and Inspector Bligh called the meeting to order.

'Thank you all for coming. This is the second meeting of Operation Golgotha. You may have already read the headline in this morning's *News*, but if you have not then there are copies over on that table by the door.

Alex has reported quite faithfully the facts that we gave him yesterday and you can see from the photos that their illustration department has been a bit imaginative in portraying the bodies of Josh and Simon in their *Hung Out to Die* mode, as the article is headlined. I don't think these illustrations denigrate from the facts but now that these crimes are in the public forum we can expect some serious community reaction. I have got a police liaison officer working with the Cheyney and Christopher families, although I think the Cheyneys have engaged a lawyer to speak for them. The telephone staff downstairs have been prepared to take any messages from the public which will come to me in the first instance and I will farm them out to you all to follow up.

I would like now to hear from Sergeant Oliver as to how his team has progressed in locating relevant CCTV footage. Then from Jo, who has spoken to the England Coach, SOCO regarding Simon's car, and Peter, if he has the toxicology results, and anybody else who has something useful to offer. Sergeant Oliver, please.'

Matthew Oliver made his way to the front. He stood by a large map of Portchester that had been attached to one of the white boards. Picking up a pointer, he said, 'Good morning. My team started here at the college playing fields, and half of us went towards White Hart Lane along this path down the side of the school, then along White Hart Lane to the Castle Street intersection. They then went down Castle Street to the church.

There were no cameras visible along this route, except for the camera owned by *English Heritage* opposite the entrance to the castle. We collected their footage covering the Friday afternoon procession that Josh and Simon starred in and their Saturday afternoon and evening footage. The only really significant thing we found was a rather blurred image of what we believe to be the motorcycle and side-car coming in the seaside gate and turning in through the Lych Gate of the church. The image is not clear enough to pick out the bike registration number and despite Graham trying to enhance the image we still could not read it.

Unfortunately the camera arc stops at the Lych Gate, but we know from the photographic evidence we saw yesterday that the cycle tracks go right around the south side of the church. The Friday afternoon footage shows the procession clearly and the congregation leaving the church at the end.

There is clear evidence of both Josh and Simon leaving the church and going up the Castle path and out the large grey doors. This means that Simon did not stay back in the church, and so somehow, he must have had means of getting back into the church when he brought Josh's body in on the motorcycle. We still need to investigate that. My other group went from the playing fields straight down to the coast and along the coastal path, past the allotments and cemetery on the Cormorant Path and on to the church where we met up.

We could only find one camera, and that was attached to Cormorant House, along the Cormorant Path and Castle Street. The owners were extremely helpful and their son who is good with IT, has a very clear cataloguing system for the footage.

We struck gold here. There is a noticeably, clear image of the motorcycle and side-car travelling past the house at 2.30 on the Saturday morning. The registration is visible and it is BYH 693. We called it in and the DVLA gave the registered keeper as Simon Cheyney.'

With this revelation there was an audible gasp from the group in the incident room.

'The vehicle was registered three weeks ago and so Simon has been planning this for some time. It was not been a spur of the moment stuff,' Sergeant Oliver continued.

'The DVLA also confirmed that the bike has not been re-registered and so it has not been sold. It will be around somewhere, or it has been scrapped. We contacted Silverlake the local vehicle scrappers around here and they have not scrapped a bike within the last six months. It took a bit of persuading, but they checked out the main websites for scrapyards and confirmed that no other scrapyard was offering relevant bike parts for sale. We also saw on the video footage, both Josh and Simon walking along Cormorant Path, either to their cars parked nearby or straight to the playing fields.'

Sergeant Oliver finished and went back to his seat.

'Thank you Matt,' said Spence, 'This seems to further confirm our view that we have a murder/suicide crime situation.'

Jo was about to interject, but then thought better of it,

thinking it could keep.

'Now Jo, please.' said Spence.

'My first task was to try and track down the motorcycle side-car through dealers and I have drawn a blank locally, but ebay have been helpful and I am expecting anytime soon to receive a list of all buying and selling of motorcycles and side-cars over the past two months. As Spencer said, I have also been in contact with the England rugby squad coach, Glen Francis, regarding the likely player or players who will be selected to replace Josh and Simon.

The selection board is meeting as we speak and so later today I will know the outcome. Apparently, it seems to be between two players, Raymond Salter from Leicester Tigers and Arthur O'Neill from London Irish, which was the club that Josh played for. It does not seem relevant now to consider whether the selected player needs any special protection.'

Jo had already decided that she was not going to mention Chris Foley at this stage, as she did not think that that would offer any further relevant information.

'Thank you, Jo. If your enquiries with ebay work out, then we should find out whether Simon bought the motor-cycle or someone else did on his behalf. If so, we may have someone to prosecute after all, for aiding and abetting. Now, Sergeant Munden. Can we have an update on Simon's car. Please.'

'Yes, Inspector. We located the car in Sunningdale Road as Jo suggested and took it away for forensic examination. There were only Simon's fingerprints that were legible on it but we did find some incriminating evidence in the boot, in the spare wheel footwell.

The spare wheel had been removed, probably to make room. We found a roll of white rope which Peter has confirmed is identical to the rope both used to tie Josh to the cross, and to

97

suspend Simon from the rugby posts cross-bar. We also found the two clamps that Peter presumed were fastened to the cross bar of the cross to haul Josh's body up so that it could be tied on around the wrists. Further we found the new pair of Adidas boots that Simon told Jo, Josh was wearing during their rugby practice. We intend to return the car to Simon's parents tomorrow.'

'Arthur, did you manage to work out how Simon got back into the castle grounds and church with Josh's body at half past two in the morning?'

'Our best guess is that at some point during the service on the Friday afternoon, after the procession, he must have gone into the tearoom and unlocked the fire exit door and secured it in such a way that the vicar missed it when locking up. It would be easy for him to slip into the tearoom as the only toilet is just outside it and people are nipping in there all the time during services.

After he had completed hoisting Josh's body onto the cross, he could have locked the fire door and slipped out of the main exit from the tearoom which can easily be opened from the inside, as it only has a turn key. Getting into the castle grounds at that time, after they have been locked requires a bit more ingenuity. The gates have a strong padlock and you would need heavy bolt cutters if you didn't have a key. Sometimes you can be lucky by bumping the lock with a heavy hammer, but that method would leave traces.

We think that Simon, at some stage in the evening, must have cut off the lock and replaced it with a similar one which he could open later. We did check with *English Heritage* who are custodians of those gates and they reported that they did have difficulty opening the lock on the Saturday morning and had to call out the locksmith.

We think that that is proof enough that Simon got in that way, rather than involving the locksmith.'

'Thank you, Arthur. Peter, do you have anything to add?' asked Spencer.

'Only to say that from our toxicology results, we found no traces of poison in either victims' bodies. My examination of Simon's neck confirmed what I thought at the scene, that he died as a result of the classical hangman's fracture, where the head is virtually dislocated from the rest of the body.'

'Thank you, Peter. Is there anything else?' asked Spence.

No one commented, so Spencer continued, 'Well, that looks like we can close Operation Golgotha.'

Not for long, Jo said to herself.

'Thank you all for your participation, especially involving your bank holidays, and hopefully the England team have time enough to prepare themselves for the Autumn Rugby Internationals.

There was a bit of a flurry as they all tried to leave the incident room at the same time. Jo caught up with Peter.

'Peter, have you got a minute, please? I would just like to ask you a question.'

'Yeah, sure Jo.'

'Are you still available to come to the Cheyney murder scene at 4:30pm today?'

'Yes, I can, Jo, what is this about?'

'Between you and me, I think that Simon Cheyney was murdered, and I would like to show you my evidence for thinking this. I have arranged a reconstruction at the scene and I would like you to be there to witness it.'

'Does Spence know about this reconstruction?'

'No, not yet. He is so certain that he has solved this case with his murder/suicide theory that I do not want to challenge him until I have proof.'

'Well, I am intrigued,' said Peter.

'I will definitely be there this afternoon.'

'Peter, before you go, I have another question.'

'Okay.'

'Theoretically speaking, if someone is hanged, and there is clear evidence of the hangman's fracture, could you also ascertain if the victim had been strangled first, or would the hangman's fracture obscure that evidence?'

'Are you referring to Simon's injuries?'

'In part, yes. It just occurred to me how could you tell whether a victim was strangled and hung, or not.'

'Death results from strangulation from the shutting off of air or blood. This of course can be done by hands around the neck, but this could be detected by forensic study. If, however a ligature was used, such as garrotting, which would effectively cut off blood and air, and then the body was hung, as long as the distance of the hanging was equivalent to the body length then the hanging would result in the hangman's fracture and I would venture to suggest that the hanging fracture would disguise the previous act of garrotting.'

'Thank you, Peter. I am always trying to expand my learning, and that distinction just came to me, so I thought I would ask you. That's all.'

'Fine, Jo, Anytime. See you later.'

Jo returned to her desk, switched on her computer, hoping to find some response from ebay. She was also hoping to hear from Chris, regarding the selection committee's decision and she could not help feeling excited that she would soon hear his voice. Inwardly, she wished it would be him not just his voice, but for that she would have to wait until Saturday evening. There was an email from ebay, with an attachment, and so with some excitement she opened the email and the attachment. It was a short list of recent motorcycle and side-car sales. There were five in all, complete with name and email contact address. Jo sent a thank you email to ebay. She then composed an email stating that she was investigating a murder where a motorbike and side-car were involved, and could the seller please send her any details they had about the purchaser. She sent the same email to each of the five sellers and could now only await their replies.

Jo reckoned that Simon would not have had time to dispose of the motorcycle and side-car between Josh's murder and his suicide, which meant it should still be around somewhere.

However, if her theory of two related murders was correct then the real killer would now be in the process of disposing of the motorcycle and side-car. She wondered whether she could involve other police forces to try and locate it. Perhaps some officer had issued a speeding ticket. She knew however, that would declare her hand and she was not prepared to do that yet. She would wait and see what the ebay sellers would turn up.

At 4.00pm Jo drove onto the college playing field and made her way over to the goal posts. The caretaker was already there with weights tied to a piece of rope and a ladder up against the cross bar.

Five minutes later, Peter drove up and all three then set about the reconstruction.

Jo threw the rope over the cross bar and then Peter started pulling the weights along and up to a level equivalent to the neck height of a hanging body. They then lowered the weights, pulled off the rope and climbed up to see the groove. Just as Jo expected, the groove that they had made was exactly the same as the groove that they had photographed in the morning.

Jo showed both grooves to Peter, who then said, a bit ashamedly, 'Jo, I am mortified that I omitted to check this groove out when we were first called out here. That was an error. I think that you are right and I will have to change my opinion. I agree with you, Simon was murdered. This is not suicide. I will have to tell Spence and he will have to re-open the case. Operation Golgotha is not closed.'

'Hang on Peter, please,' said Jo. 'I just want to try one more experiment. Throw the rope with the weights over the cross bar, and tie it to the bar, so the weights are a body length off the ground.' Peter did this.

Then Jo said, 'Now drop the weights please.'

Peter did that, and as the weights fell, they pulled the rope over the bar, until the weights stopped. Jo then inspected the bar and there was only a slight groove in the wood.

Jo got down and called out to Peter, 'Come and see the groove. You will see that it is a lot shallower than the other grooves.'

Peter climbed up and took a look. Jo gave him her camera, and he photographed the groove, so that they could make a comparison. 'You are absolutely, right, Jo. This confirms murder.'

'Don't say anything to Spence, yet Peter, until I clear this with the chief. I want to avoid getting us all into trouble for setting up this reconstruction without prior approval. Spence, as you know, can get quite prickly about people going behind his back.'

'Okay, Jo. But I cannot sit on it for too long.'

'Just give me until after this coming weekend, please?

'Okay. Well done on this piece of excellent detective work. You have taught us all a thing or two.'

'Well, this is what comes from watching too many crime dramas on TV. See you later, Peter, and thanks for coming along this afternoon.'

'No problem and thank you Jo. Well done.'

Jo then turned to the caretaker and thanked him for bringing out the weights, rope and ladder. They said farewell to each other and Jo set off for home to prepare dinner.

As she was driving, she thought about what she had in the kitchen and settled on creating a Beef Bourguignon. She would usually prepare enough for at least two meals, so she could freeze one for later, which often saved her from having to buy take-aways when she had no time to cook. She had put her mobile next to her chopping board, waiting for Chris's call. She looked at her watch and thought he should have rung by now as surely the selection board meeting had finished. She knew in her heart that she was more interested in talking to Chris than finding out who was the next fly-half in the England squad.

She had just put the casserole in the oven along with a jacket potato and was preparing the broccoli for the regulation green vegetable when the doorbell rang. She was not expecting anyone, so being the cautious policewoman that she was, she made sure the chain lock was on and opened the door slowly. Her heart skipped a beat when she saw Chris standing there with a bunch of flowers. She frantically slipped off the chain and threw open the door.

She could not control herself and she screamed, 'Chris, I wasn't expecting you,' and she flung her arms around his neck, and gave him a kiss, full on his lips.

'Well, I definitely wasn't expecting that,' replied Chris.

'Come on in,' said Jo, 'oh, it's so great to see you. I have been waiting for you to ring all day and now to see you, it's great.'

'Well, I did not just want to ring you, but I wanted to see you too.'

'Obviously, you will stay over, won't you, and have dinner

with me. It is all prepared, I just need to put another spud in the oven.'

'If that's OK, I would like to stay over but I could get a train back.'

'God, no,' said Jo, 'You can get the train in the morning. Come in and put your bag upstairs. I'll get you a drink. A Steinlager?'

'Yes, Jo, that would be very welcome. I'll take my bag upstairs and then tell you about the selection meeting.'

With another jacket potato in the oven, some more broccoli in the pot ready for cooking later, a glass of red in her hand and a bottle of Steinlager for Chris, Jo sat in the lounge and felt like a young girl waiting to meet her first date. She knew that Chris's spontaneous arrival in person rather than a phone call, meant that he had feelings for her too. She had surprised herself with her response to his arrival, especially the full on kiss, but she knew that it was right. She did like him enough to kiss him, but she knew that she needed to progress slowly, because it could be so easy for her to throw caution to the wind and take him to her room for the night. I suppose that what happens when rain comes after a drought, you cannot just get enough of it. She then became all serious and said to herself she needed to slow down. She was not ready or prepared for a full on relationship just yet. It had been some time since she had been in this dilemma.

Chris came back into the lounge, took the drink offered by Jo and sat in the chair that he had sat in the previous evening.

'Sorry Jo to barge in on you like this but I enjoyed yesterday evening and the excitement of being an investigator this morning, and I just wanted to see you again. Tell, me. How did the reconstruction go this afternoon?'

'Chris, really it's fine. I am really happy to see you. The reconstruction went well. We did get the same type and depth of groove with the weights that we photographed this morning, and the pathologist was there. We also experimented with simulating how the suicide would affect the cross-bar, and the groove was nowhere as deep as the one made by pulling a body by a rope over the bar. We are agreed that Simon's death was murder. We are going to keep it under wraps until I have cleared it with my Chief Inspector. I have some news from today's crime meeting, and I hope that you have news for me, then we can forget about crime and talk about other things. Dinner will be about an hour.'

'That's fine. Well, shall I start. The selection meeting lasted quite a while and finally Raymond Salter was selected as the main fly-half with Arthur O'Neill being first reserve, just as we suspected. Apparently, according to my source, London Irish wanted O'Neill to be selected since Josh, was London Irish he should be replaced by a London Irish player.

This argument could not swing the selection away from Salter although the whole panel thought that there was very little difference between them. What is interesting, according to my source, is apparently one of the selectors, he would not say which one, argued quite vehemently for O'Neill to be selected. At one point, my source thought that he was going to make it a condition of his continuing on as an RFU official but he surrendered to the majority decision when Francis told him that as he had full power to make his own team selection for each game, he would make sure that if at the time of selection O'Neill was the better choice than Salter, then ability and skill would overrule priority.

This means in effect, that if O'Neill is the better player, then he will get selected. It gives him some reason to make a good impression on Francis. If he does, then I would not be surprised

105

if we see a lot more of O'Neill playing with Francis bringing him on earlier in the game than only in the last twenty minutes when substitutes are normally played.'

'That is interesting,' said Jo, 'it would seem that perhaps that selector has some vested interest in O'Neill playing.'

'Or he was given an inducement to promote O'Neill over Salter,' said Chris, 'I will keep my ear to the ground. Now what's your news?'

'Well, we concluded our meetings on this case, and it is now officially closed with the murder/suicide as the conclusion. My sergeant and his team have located the registered owner of the motorcycle and side-car that was used to transport Josh's body from the playing field to the Church. Guess who it is.'

'Simon?'

'Yes.'

'Well, does that put paid to your theory that Simon's death was murder?'

'No, not at all. In fact, I think it supports my theory. I have examined the V5C form section 6, issued by the DVLA. All that is required when a vehicle changes hands is for the registered keeper to notify the DVLA of the new keeper's name and address and send it to the DVLA. Section 10 also needs to be completed and handed to the new keeper. The murderer purchasing the bike just needed to destroy that section. No signature of the new keeper is required. All that our murderer needs to do is pretend to be Simon, pay for the vehicle in cash so that there is no trace of payment, like credit card details, and give Simon Cheyney's details to the seller to pass on to the DVLA.

In time, they will issue the new V5C form to Simon's address. I have checked with Simon's father and he has no knowledge of his son purchasing the bike. He also has access to Simon's bank account as he made deposits into it and kept an eye on it. He confirms that there were no unusual withdrawals which would have been necessary to provide the cash for the bike.

The bike is obviously around somewhere but no doubt it will be sold again. I am waiting for information from some recent sellers on ebay who have sold bikes and that may provide some leads, or perhaps a description of the person who purchased it.

Also, today we were told, that Simon's car has been located. They found in the spare wheel compartment Josh's new Adidas rugby boots, and some rope and clamps, all of which are items relating to Josh's murder. They could not find the car keys, neither on Simon's body, nor on the ground near the rugby posts or in the car.

Again, I think that Simon's murderer could have planted them in the car, after he killed Simon. The key for me, however that Simon was killed is the groove in the cross-bar that we found this morning. I cannot discuss that with anybody, as they all believe the murder/suicide theory, and If I raise it with my D.I. the SOCO team and the pathologist will look incompetent.

I will have to wait until I have more concrete evidence and know who the actual killer is. I still think that we are looking for someone currently involved with the English squad, and so this new selection, Raymond Salter is possibly at risk, unless he is our killer. I think that the fact that both Josh and Simon were fly-halves is relevant, but I do not know yet what that relevance is.'

'Bloody hell, Jo. That was really a speech. Can I refill your glass?'

'Yes, please. Do you think that I am making sense, Chris?'

'Absolutely Jo. I am sure we will get a break soon.'

Jo liked the way Chris said 'we'. She knew that she needed help and support with this as she was going out on a limb,

107

against more experienced detectives and forensic experts. She knew that she would have to be very sure of her ground before she told them all that they were wrong.

'Is there anything that you would like me to do Jo?' asked Chris.

'Anything you can find out about these new selections, Salter and O'Neil would be helpful.'

'Have you written anything yet for your paper?' Jo asked.

'I have written an article based on Alex's article in *The News*, but nothing about your theory or what we did this morning. When I decided to come down here to see you, I thought that tomorrow morning I could interview both the Christophers and the Cheyneys.'

'So, you just didn't come to see me, then?'

'No, but I decided to see you first before I thought of interviewing the victims' families. I am really doing that to give my boss a reason for this trip to be on expenses! I was going to take you out to dinner tonight, until I realised that you were already cooking something which smells marvellous.'

'God, the dinner,' blurted out Jo, 'the spuds will be cinders.'

'Don't worry, we can still go out if dinner is spoilt, but it smells fine from here.'

'No it's alright. I will serve it up. We can take a rain check on the going out. Perhaps next weekend.'

The dinner turned out to be fine, and Chris was very complimentary. He had brought with him an Australian Merlot and between them they finished the bottle. They spent the evening talking about their past lives and rugby. Chris seemed quite serious when he said he was looking forward to going to north Hampshire on Sunday and he was considering doing an article on woman's club rugby.

When it came to bedtime, Chris was quite the gentleman, and made the first move by saying that he would go on up to bed and he went over to Jo, gave her a peck on the cheek, and went upstairs.

Jo resisted the temptation to fling her arms around his neck, so she lightly kissed him back and went out to the kitchen to do the final clearing up. While putting away the cutlery, Jo thought about how and where their relationship was going, and she decided that it was getting serious and that she might in fact be falling in love with Chris. This was both an exciting and terrifying thought for her. As usual, when she has been in these situations, she regretted that she had no immediate family to discuss Chris with and so she would have to make do with her rugby girl friends whom they would meet on Sunday.

As previously, Jo woke Chris up with a cup of tea and her cry of breakfast on the table in half an hour. She had slept well, but twice she had woken up half-hoping that Chris would sneak into her room uttering the basic concept of foreplay, 'Hey, you awake!'

She was really quite relieved that he hadn't, as she was not ready for that yet, but she soon intended to be. Chris came downstairs, again all suited and booted and he sat down to omelettes, toast, and coffee.

'Very nice Jo, and very welcome,' he said.

'Well, just don't think that you will get a cooked breakfast every morning after you stay over,' she said.

'I can cook, too you know. I'll do breakfast next time.'

'I'll hold you to that,' she said.

As they went out of the door, Jo locked it and said, 'Do you want me to drop you somewhere?'

'Do you know any rental car places around here, as I could do with one, to visit our victims' families?'

'I can do better than that, Chris. I'll go to the police station and then you can have my car. I just need to make a phone call. I will need some information from you for this.'

It only took Jo five minutes to ring her insurance company and give them Chris's driving history to get him fully insured to drive her car.

She was aware as she was doing that, she was allowing him to get closer and closer to her. Next minute, she thought, she would be giving him front door keys. Good point, she thought and decided she would get a set cut today. She drove to work, stopped and got out.

She turned to Chris and asked, 'What time do you think you will want to go to the station?'

'Well, I have been thinking about that, I don't really need to go into work until tomorrow. I will do my interviews and I have my laptop and phone, so I will find a nice comfy cafe with Wi-Fi and work from there. I can also do some research into Raymond Salter.'

'Well, could we meet up for lunch after your interviews?'

'That would be great. Say 1.00pm. How about that *Ask* restaurant I noticed on the corner as we drove here?'

'*Ask* will be fine, 1.00pm. You're paying!'

'Agreed!' Jo saw Chris drive off and then she went into the police station and up to her office and desk. She felt in a funny mood. She was excited at once more being in a romantic relationship, which she thought, and inwardly hoped, could develop into something special. But on the work front, she was torn between knowing that for her the case of the murders of Josh and Simon were definitely not closed, but she had to pretend that they were, and make out that she was ready to move on to the next file.

She knew that it would be difficult to juggle her work but she had the feeling that Chris would be a great help in doing some of the enquiries for her. She turned to her computer, opened her emails, and was grateful to see some replies to her requests of the ebay bike sellers.

There were five, and so they had all replied. She took them in order and the first one revealed that she had sold the motor bike and side-car to a Walter Armstrong, who paid the full price through his PayPal account. There was no vehicle registration number given. Jo disregarded that sale, as in keeping with her theory, the purchaser would not identify themselves, or if they did would impersonate Simon and would pay by cash so it was untraceable.

It was the fourth email that gave Jo the information she was looking for. The purchaser had bought the motorcycle and side-car by couriering cash direct to the seller. He had given the seller buyer details over the telephone to enable the seller to complete the V5C form, which he said was one Simon Cheyney. Jo then rang the seller, and asked him,

'Did you speak to the buyer over the phone, please?'

'No, detective, all our contact was done by email.'

'Are you able to tell me the buyer's ebay username please?'

'Yes, it was a Hotmail account, *rugbyposts*,' he replied.

'Thank you, sir, you have been a great help,' replied Jo

She knew that the Hotmail account was probably just set up for the transaction and would now be deleted. She then took out her mobile and rang Chris.

When he answered, Jo asked, 'Are you still with the Cheyney's, Chris.?'

'Yes, I am.'

'Can you ask them whether or not Simon had an ebay account, and what was his username?'

'Sure, Jo. I have already established that they have no knowledge of Simon buying a motorbike and he does not even have a license to drive one. In fact, they say he detested bikes as being too dangerous as one of his school mates had been killed in a bike accident five years ago.'

'Yes, Chris, I think I remember that. It was before I joined the cops, but it was in the papers. He was a pillion passenger, only about thirteen, I think, and the bike was hit by a drunk driver and both rider and pillion were killed. The drunk got eight years. Chris, tell the Cheyneys, that I have managed to trace the seller of the bike and side-car, and the buyer paid by cash, and gave Simon's details. We don't know any more about him, except that he used the ebay username of *rugbyposts*. Please reassure them that between us, we are doing everything possible to find the killer and restore Simon's good name but impress on them to keep stum until we can name the killer.

We do not want him or her to get wind of us being on to him and flee. The killer is probably quite happily thinking that they have got away with it and so hopefully they will slip-up soon enough.'

'Right-ho Jo. See you around 1.00. Bye for now.'

'Bye, Chris.'

Jo then replied to all the five emails, thanking them for contacting her. She then went to her in-tray and picked out a file on a youth suspected of shoplifting in *Freshcos*. This should be an easy one, she thought, I'll pop over the road to *Freshcos*, interview the manager, and track down the shoplifter after lunch.

The manager at *Freshcos* was more interested in asking Jo questions about the deaths of Simon and Josh, than worrying about a case of shoplifting. Jo fielded them as best she could, without letting on that she thought her boss's solution was false and the case was far from being solved.

The manager was also a rugby fan and a member of the local rugby club. He seemed really pleased that Jo was able to tell him that Raymond Salter had been selected as part of the England squad.

'Oh, thanks for that titbit, detective. I should be able to barter a few pints out of the boys at the club tonight to pass that on.'

'Glad to be of help,' said Jo. 'Now, back to this shoplifting. What did the rascal take?'

'Well, he did not get away with anything, as it happened. My staff apprehended him just outside the main door and took the items off him. They brought him up to my office, and I spoke to him. He is just a kid, around fourteen I would say, and very scared. I would not be surprised if he had done it as a dare, in order, perhaps, to get accepted into some sort of group or gang.'

'Did he take alcohol?' asked Jo.

'No, it was meat. A joint of beef. The security guard had picked him up on the cameras and kept an eye on him. He was obviously inexperienced as he kept looking furtively around all the time. He was carrying a small knapsack and stuffed the beef into it. He was seen just walking straight out of the shop from the meat aisle. He made no attempt to stop and even pretend to pay for it.

One of the big problems we have since the installation of the self-pay terminals, is shoplifters pretend to use them and just bag their goods and leave. I don't like them, and I tried to argue against them as they take up just as much staff time as the normal checkout does, as they are always going wrong and requiring an assistant to attend, but there is no customer contact.

I was overruled by my area manager. It was not worth putting my job on the line for it. Now, detective, I don't really want to see this young guy get a criminal record just for a joint of beef. I work with similar lads in the rugby club and when you get them fit and playing in a team, their attitude changes and they mature. What he needs is to be sentenced to one season's attendance at a rugby club. Without any conviction. He would not be interested in theft, after I've finished with him!'

'Are you saying that you do not want to press charges?'

'Yes, I suppose so, but I don't want him to get away scot free, without some effort to help him.'

'If I brought him in would you be prepared to talk to him, especially about rugby?'

'Yes, I would be happy to.'

'Okay, I will try and see him this afternoon and bring him in and we can be a bit canny and say that if he attends the rugby club for a couple of training sessions, then *Freshcos* will not prosecute him for shoplifting. How does that sound?'

'Yes, I can go along with that. This could become quite a trend and definitely a new way to attract players!'

'Right,' said Jo, 'I will be in touch.'

Jo crossed the road back to her office and wrote up her interview with the manager and added it to her case file. She thought that she should just check it out with Spence, so she went along to his office.

'Hi, Jo, how are you and what are you working on, now that we have wrapped up Golgotha?'

'I'm fine, thank you sir. I am working on the *Freshcos'* shoplifter case. I have spoken with the manager and he said he does not really want to prosecute and so I have suggested we deal with it by way of a Youth Conditional Caution. I intend to see the young lad this afternoon and put it to him.'

'And what does the manager want as a condition? Compensation and a week's cleaning the store?'

'No, Sir, he is into youth rugby in the local rugby club, and he is prepared to mentor the youth if he is made to attend so many training sessions. You never know, he might like it and join one of the youth teams.'

'Well,' said Spence, 'that's a bit different. Yes, by all means, give it a go. Let me know how you get on. I am sure DCI Abbotsford will give us both brownie points if we can pull this off and save a prosecution with all that attendant use of time and resources. I have the statute here somewhere; in case you need it.'

'Oh, it is The Legal Aid Sentencing and Punishment of Offenders Act 2012 and it introduced Youth Conditional Cautions for ten to seventeen year olds on 8th April 2013.' said Jo.

'I should have known that you would have that at your fingertips, Jo. How old is this youth?'

'I have to confess, sir, I have just looked it up to refresh my memory, but we did cover it in training, so I knew it existed. The offender is about fourteen, according to the manager of *Freshcos*.'

'Right, go ahead, and see what he says to your proposal. It sounds quite good to me and I am sure the rugby club would love to get another player. You can put a bit of pressure on him, and say that if he does not accept the condition, we can still prosecute him and he could go to youth prison. Well, you know the drill.'

'Yes, sir. I will let you know the outcome.'

'Oh, Jo, before you leave, are you happy with the outcome of

Golgotha, as yesterday I noted that you did not seem overjoyed that the case had been solved?'

'Well, I just like to think I am a good judge of character and when I interviewed Simon and his family, I did not get any inkling that he could be capable of murder. So, sir, I can see that that was the only verdict presently available and so I am happy with that until or unless something else rears its ugly head and makes us think again.'

'Fair enough. Your investigations were very thorough as usual and immensely helpful in solving it.' said Spence.

'Thank you, sir, I will keep you posted on this Youth Caution.'

'Yes, do. If it is a runner, I will speak with the CPS to clear the way for a caution. Often the big firms like *Freshcos* like to see public prosecutions to give a clear message that thieves will be prosecuted, but at the same time, display their goods in such a way that it is very tempting and easy to just take them. The self-pay tills don't help either. It is heartening to see a manager prepared to buck the *Freshcos'* policy. We will see whether we have a CPS decision that's not swayed by corporate pressure.'

Jo just nodded and left her office. She went downstairs and booked out a police car for 2:30pm. It was best to show a public police presence when interviewing suspects, as they usually co-operated better in order to get it over with so that the car would leave the area and not draw attention to the fact that the family were being interviewed.

It was nearly one o'clock, so she grabbed her coat and left for the Ask restaurant. Chris was already there, with a beer and Jo could see a small glass of red wine. She went to Chris, gave him a kiss on the cheek and sat down opposite him.

'I'm interviewing a shoplifter this afternoon and so I can only drink about half that,' she said, 'how has your morning been?'

'Quite fraught, really. Understandably the Christophers are angry with the Cheyneys, as both families have been friends long before their children were born. I couldn't really help them much, but it really reinforced for me how important and urgent it is for us get to the bottom of this case, so that the families can be reunited again and support each other in their mutual grief.'

'I had to see my boss today and he reinforced how we had come to the only possible verdict and so I know that I cannot raise any objections until I have unassailable evidence that Simon was murdered.

What we gleaned yesterday from the cross-bar is not enough, especially in face of the registration of the bike in Simon's name and the evidence found in his car. We definitely need a breakthrough. As much as I hate to say it, it might take a third related murder before we can get much further. Have you managed to find anything out about Raymond Salter yet?'

'No, but I will do this afternoon. Your phone call to me at the Cheyneys was helpful as it showed that we were still working on the case. We checked Simon's computer and he does not have an ebay login or account. From what I could see, for a twenty something, he did not seem to be into much on-line activity or social media.

The Cheyneys like you Jo, and they really believe you when you say that you will be able to prove that Simon is not a murderer and they do understand that they cannot say anything yet, but they are finding it hard to deal with the backlash that they are getting and so I would suggest you keep updating them, as that will help them to cope, as long as they know steps are being taken.'

'Yes, I intend to. Shall we order, as I have only got an hour?'

They then talked about each one's rugby playing career as they ate their lasagnes and garlic bread and Chris repeated that he was looking forward to being with Jo at rugby on Sunday.

As they got up to leave the restaurant, Jo said to Chris,

'You keep the car, go home and work from home. Help yourself to anything that you need. The switch behind the TV turns on the Wi-Fi if you need the internet. The password is on the router. I have booked out a police car for the afternoon, so I should be able to bring it home. If I need you to pick me up, I will ring you. OK? Here are my house keys. Thanks for lunch. See you later.' Again, she reached up and planted a kiss on his cheek and left the restaurant.

Michael Potter aged 14 lived in the council houses opposite the Red Barn Primary School and Nursery which is situated near the Portchester Crematorium. Jo had not rung ahead, so she was lucky to find Michael at home. His mother let her in and Jo asked that her mother be present while she interviewed Michael about the shoplifting, as Michael was a minor and a responsible adult needed to be present, although how responsible his mother was would be was a matter of conjecture.

Jo started with the heavy act of saying that shoplifting was an offence of theft and although it was only a piece of meat, the courts saw it as theft and the government had insisted that the courts impose heavy penalties against shoplifting as it threatened the whole economy of Britain.

After some questioning and cajoling, Michael admitted what Jo suspected, that he had done it as a dare in order to get accepted into the local *Barnies*, a gang set up by some of the older council house lads. Michael's mother said that she was at her wit's end with Michael. It was obvious that there were no evident social outlets for young teenagers and so it was inevitable that gangs would emerge to provide some relief from the boredom of school and homework.

After about an hour, Jo decided to work towards a result. She turned to Michael and said, 'Michael, do you want to be prosecuted, found guilty and sent to youth detention? There is no question of a defence, as you are on CCTV as taking the meat and leaving *Freshcos*. Also, the security officer was watching you all the time.'

'No, Miss. I only did it as a dare and because Mum cannot afford roast beef.' At that, Michael started to cry.

Jo just wanted to go over and give him a hug, instead she said, 'Michael, I have an alternative for you to consider. Instead of having you taken to court and prosecuted, I am able to offer you a caution, but there is a condition. Do you want to hear what that is, or do you want to go to court?'

Michael stopped crying and brightened a little. His mother turned on him and said, 'Answer the policewoman, Michael!'

'Yes, Miss, what is the condition?'

'You would have to attend Portchester Rugby Club each week for a minimum of two months, training and playing rugby.'

'And what would happen if he couldn't do it. detective?

'He would then still be prosecuted.'

'But doesn't joining those type of clubs cost a lot of money?'

'Normally, yes, but in Michael's case we would find the money for him, as part of the condition.'

'What do you say, Michael?' asked Jo.

'Yes, that would be better than going to prison.'

'Right, to do this we need to get agreement from *Freshcos*, but I have spoken to the manager and I know that he will agree. He likes rugby too. Okay, Michael?'

'Yes, Miss.'

'Right, Michael, get your coat and we will go and see him.' Turning to Mrs. Potter, Jo said: 'I will bring him back here, Mrs. Potter, we will only be a couple of hours.'

'Thank you, detective. He is a good boy, really. This hopefully will be the making of him.'

'Well, it will at least give him a different group of boys to mix with rather than the *Barnies*.'

Michael followed Jo out to the police car, and they drove off. The meeting with the *Freshcos'* manager went very positively.

Michael apologised for stealing the meat, and the manager outlined what he could expect once Michael joined the rugby club.

Without prompting from Jo, the manager said: 'You probably realise, Michael that there are some costs involved. But I know that your family probably cannot afford them. I run a fund to help with these costs, so you will not have to pay anything. I will pay your club fees and when you first come to the club, I will supply you with jersey, shorts, socks and boots, all in the rugby club colours. Can you come tomorrow at 5.30pm? Do you have a cycle?'

'Yes, I can come tomorrow, but I do not have a cycle.'

'Wait a minute,' said Jo, 'I'll just make a call.'

She was on the phone for about five minutes and said, 'I have got a bike for you, Michael. It's from our lost property and has not been collected. It is yours to keep. We will collect it after this. You will need to secure it and not loan it to anybody, OK?'

'Yes, thank you Miss.'

Jo thanked the manager and ushered Michael out of his office. As they were leaving, the manager picked up a *Freshcos'* bag and handed it to Michael.

'Give this to your mother, he said, and next time pay for your purchases.'

'Yes, sir and thank you,' said Michael.

Once back in the police station, Jo took Michael up to D.I. Bligh's office, and after he had read him the riot act, issued him with a caution with the condition of attending Portchester Rugby Club each week for a minimum of two months. Jo got him the bicycle, a helmet and security chain, and watched him head off home. Back in her office, she updated the shoplifting complaint file, and stamped it 'Case Closed'.

She wished she could do that with Golgotha file but that would not be so easy.

As Jo reached for the next case file in her tray, she wondered how Chris was getting on. She had a gut feeling that he was how he seemed to be and she could usually trust her gut feelings. Thinking about the lunch that they had just had, she realised that they both liked the same food and wine. She felt like a break and so said to her colleague on reception, 'Just off to the Precinct, so see you in about fifteen minutes.'

When she got back to her desk, she realised that she should check on Michael to make sure he had got home alright and that his mother knew that he had not stolen the bag of stuff that the *Freshcos'* manager had given him. She presumed that it was meat.

She briefly looked at the case file she had taken from her tray and decided that it could wait until tomorrow. Once again, she pulled up outside the council houses. Michael was fine, and his mother grateful for her intervention and the bag of meat. The cycle was securely fastened and locked in a shed, so they all agreed that there was nothing stopping Michael from playing rugby. As she left, she turned to Michael and said: Michael you will enjoy rugby. It is a great game, and I play it.'

'Who for Miss? Portchester?'

'No, for north Hampshire, but we often play against Portchester, so I may see you at the club. Goodbye and good luck Michael.'

Jo then drove home and parked the police car out of view behind the garage. Chris had heard her drive up, and so he was at the door, when she reached it. Another quick peck on the cheek and they were inside the house.

'Great to see you Jo. I have started dinner. I just rummaged around the fridge and vegetable drawer and we are having a chicken casserole. Is that okay?'

'Fine, Chris. I can take over now if you like. you get some drinks poured.'

'Fine, how was your afternoon?'

'Quite eventful, really. An attempt at prosecution diversion.' Jo related the shoplifting case and the result. Chris was quite impressed.

'I wish that I had you around as the copper when I got nicked for shoplifting,' he said. When he saw Jo's face he quickly added, 'Hell, I was only eleven and my Mum would not get me a chocolate bar when we were shopping. I just took one and she noticed me eating it later and I admitted that I had taken it.

She dragged me back to the shop and made me confess and pay for it. It so happened that there was a copper doing his shopping and he overhead my admission of guilt and he really laid into me berating for what I had done, saying I could go to prison for six months, and then he said that instead of prison he would clip me over the ears.

He then gave me quite a belt round my head, and it really hurt. I was petrified of coppers for years afterwards, so I suppose it did some good. But I assure you Jo, I have been totally clean since then, as you probably know because you have probably

122

pulled my rap sheet.'

'I believe you Chris and no, I have not pulled your rap sheet, because it is illegal for a copper to get that information unless it is relevant to a crime that is being investigated. Incidentally, the copper who hit you would today have been expelled from the police and prosecuted. It is the way things are now, although there are many old hands who reckon a kick up the backside behind the bike shed was much more effective than a prosecution. Anyway, how did you get on this afternoon. Did you find anything out about Raymond Salter?'

'A little. His family comes from Alton, His father owns a garden centre just out of the town and apparently the family is fairly wealthy. Raymond attended Alton School and then went on to Churcher's College in Petersfield. He started playing rugby at North Hampshire, and did quite well, which apparently helped him get into Churcher's as they are a sporting college. I don't know how he did academically, but he must have done okay as later on he went to De Montfort University in Leicester, after working for three years for his father after he left college. He did excel at rugby, getting into the college first fifteen, and after leaving college he played for the North Hampshire Senior First Fifteen. You may have come across him there, Jo.'

'When was he there?'

'About eight years ago.'

'No, way before me. I only started playing two years ago after leaving university. I had met a couple of girls at uni who played there and they persuaded me to play with them. I still play with them and you will no doubt meet them on Sunday.'

'Well, anyway, Raymond's father thought he had his son's life planned out for him, so after he finished college, he employed his son to work at all aspects of the garden centre business, from growing plants, to wholesale, retail and finally into the accounts section. Although his father did not have a degree, he thought that his son should get a business studies degree. He was accepted at De Montfort and once again excelled on the rugby field. He was spotted by Leicester Tigers, and was encouraged to join with them when he graduated from De Montfort.

That has somewhat delayed his return to his father's business and so Raymond got a management position with a garden centre on the outskirts of Leicester. The plan was for him to get as much experience as possible so he can take over the family business when his Dad retires. I think that Raymond Salter would be a good catch for somebody, if they can put up with the rugby lifestyle. The fact that he has now been chosen to play for England, probably will keep him down this end of the country and disrupt his father's plans for him, regarding taking over the family business for a while, although Alton is not far from London.

The only other thing that I found out is that Raymond turns twenty-eight next month, and he has decided to celebrate it in style as it is the average age of most World Cup Rugby players, including the All Blacks. He is having a party at the Whiteley Hotel and I hope to get an invitation!'

'You can take me as your guest, then.'

'Yes, then you can meet the real rugby players!'

At that, Jo hurled a cushion at him, saying, 'You can sleep on your own tonight, for that. Now I am going to get dinner.'

'I did not know that there was any other option, Jo.'

'Neither did I so I don't know why I said that. Just forget it.'

'We'll see! More wine vicar?

'What did you put into this casserole, Chris. It is really tasty.'

'Just some of your herbs and spices that I found in the cupboard.'

'Well, I am impressed.' After dinner, they turned on the TV, and watched a film on the Film 4 channel. Jo joined Chris who was sitting on the sofa opposite the TV and so they watched the film together. At the end of the film, Jo turned to Chris and said, 'Oh, well, tomorrow is another day. What time is your train to London?'

'Oh, I'll get the 9:18 from Fareham, as I can use my railcard on that one, to keep expenses down. Can you drop me off at the station, please, on your way to work?'

'As long as you don't mind travelling in a police car?'

'Police car will be fine Jo.' Chris then turned to Jo, and said, 'Look Jo, I know we have only really just met but I really like you, I like you a lot. I think that you are an intelligent and incredibly attractive ...'

Jo cut him off and said, 'Don't talk soppy and just kiss me!' The kiss became a lingering one and then another, and soon Jo could feel Chris's hand creeping up her thigh. She reached across him, and thought to herself, the moment of decision. Brush his hand away from her thigh or respond in kind. Decision made, she started to undo his belt, then she squeezed him, stood up and took his hand and led him to the stairs. She turned off the downstairs lights and they went upstairs by the light of the top landing and into her bedroom.

Chapter Ten

Anyone who saw Jo give her customary peck on the cheek to Chris as they left the *Ask* restaurant after lunch yesterday, would have had to think that there had been a major development in their relationship if they also saw Jo and Chris saying farewell to each other at Fareham railway station. Such a passionate farewell kiss was not that of just work colleagues, but definitely of new lovers. With a 'See you Friday', Jo finally disentangled herself from him, waved, and returned to the police car.

'Thank God, she was not still in uniform', she thought as she drove back to the police station. Once back in her office, she opened her crime bag and took out the fingerprint evidence that she had taken from the caretaker's ladder. She located one of the fingerprinting team, took her aside, and said, 'Can you check these for me please, but please keep it secret for now. They are off an aluminium ladder. Suffice it to say that I am just wanting to confirm some of the evidence in the Golgotha case but I don't want the hassle of Bligh knowing as you know what he's like, he'll think I am undermining him and go berserk.'

'No problem, Jo. Mum's the word. I can do it when the rest of the team are out at lunch.'

'These prints are the school caretaker's, so you can disregard them when you find them on the ladder. There may be smudges as I used rubber gloves. Any other prints you find could be useful.'

'Fine, Jo. Come and see me about 2.00pm today. I should have the results by then.'

'Thanks, Anita. I really appreciate this.'

Back in her office Jo tried to busy herself with the pile of paper in her in-tray, but her mind was elsewhere. She had really enjoyed last night and she felt that it was right. She could not wait for the weekend. At one point she thought of taking the train to London and surprising Chris, like he had done to her, but she dismissed that as being seen to be just too keen. The weekend would come soon enough.

Her thoughts then drifted to Sunday's rugby game. It would be good to see her girlfriends again and introduce Chris to them. They would soon let her know what they thought. Especially Sarah and Anne, her girlfriends who were also an item, and were generally good judges of men, as men did not present any sexual threat to them.

She could also ask if any of them remembered Raymond Salter when he played for the club. She thought it co-incidental that she was investigating the murders of fly-halves, as that was the position that she played in her team. Perhaps one day she could play for England, especially if by then they fielded mixed teams. 'Scrums and rucks would be interesting!' she thought mischievously.

At 2.00pm precisely, there was a knock on her door and Anita came in. 'It's all done, Jo. There is one set of prints indicating a person carrying the ladder, and climbing up it, but I have run them through the database and there is no match. I will store them, however, in case you need to check them later.'

'Thanks, Anita. I am really grateful. I owe you one.'

'I'll remember that if my boy gets into any more scrapes, just joking!' and she was gone.

The weekend came soon enough and Jo and Chris spent the

Saturday morning as young lovers do, walking, talking, drinking, eating and making love.

Chris spent the afternoon watching rugby and making notes for his analysis of the match for Monday's edition of the *Sportsman's Daily*. On the Sunday, after a full breakfast, they set off for the rugby club. Once they were travelling up the A32. Chris said: 'My boss has authorised me to do a series on women's rugby, so this trip is business, but with a lot of pleasure thrown in, he added. It does mean that I can claim expenses, so drinks are on me.'

'Good, but I warn you that these girls can really put it away. They would give your testosterone fuelled mates a good run for their money. But at least they will talk to you, but don't go all funny asking about painful boobs, and groping in rucks, as often that is all the blokes think about, and these girls are much more professional than that.'

'Both good points, Jo. I will steer clear of any sexual references.'

'I am going to ask them about Raymond Salter, to see what they remember, I am mindful that there is still a killer out there, and he may need some protection.'

'So might you, Jo, If someone has got it in for fly-halves.' replied Chris.

'I doubt that I will ever play for England, Chris. No, the motive for these murders is specific. We just have to find out what it is!'

Jo pulled into Anstey Park, and parked in front of the club house. She went in with her kit, and most of her team were already in the lounge. Jo greeted them all in the usual girlie way of 'mwah', 'mwah', 'mwah', and then introduced Chris as her friend. As she did so, she caught Sarah giving what she hoped was an appreciative look to her partner Anne. Anne was a bit more forthcoming, and went to Chris, gave him a peck on the cheek, and said: 'Cor, if Jo ever drops you, give me a ring!'

'I thought that I had heard that you didn't really go for men?'

'Well, no harm in just making sure, is there?' replied Anne.

'Anyway, thank you Anne.' Jo had already suggested to Chris that he tell the girls that he was doing a story on women's rugby, and so she said, 'I'll leave you with them, Chris.' Turning to the girls she said, 'Now, be nice to my friend.'

It was while they were eating lunch together that Jo raised the appointment of Raymond Salter. She turned to Sarah, and said, 'Did you see that Raymond Salter has been selected as the replacement fly-half for the England squad? He used to play here, didn't he? Did any of you know him?'

Jo did not expect the vehemence in Sarah's reply. 'Know, him. Sure, I know him. He might be a good rugby player, but he is an arsehole as a person.'

'Sarah, I am surprised. What makes you think that?'

'Well, his family are wealthy and he thinks that he is God's gift to women, but he has no respect for them. He takes what he wants and makes it very difficult for a woman to refuse him. His reputation is that he can get quite rough with a date who does not cooperate with him.'

'And some say that he virtually raped a couple of his dates.' cut in another of the group.

'But to change the subject, Jo continued, 'I understand that he is giving a birthday party next month.'

'Yes, there is an open invitation on the club notice board,' said Anne.

'Are any of you going to go?' asked Jo.

'A couple of them said they were thinking of it and Sarah said, 'Anne and I will go, just for the free drink and food, and to see all our friends. If you are going, can we stay over with you Jo?'

'Normally, as you know I would say 'yes of course', but I am detective on duty that weekend and so I will not be able to look after guests. I have to be prepared to be at the cop shop the whole weekend. It's a bore, but it only comes around every six weeks, and I get overtime.' As they got up from lunch, Jo turned to Chris and said in a low voice: 'I didn't expect that response when I mentioned Salter. There is more to this than they are letting on.'

'Yes, I picked that up too, Jo. The birthday party could be quite interesting with drink flowing and if feelings are running high, or Salter is true to form and starts on the girls, there could be fireworks. I will definitely go. You never know what I might pick up. It is a pity that you are on duty but will it be alright for me to stay at your place, anyway?'

'Of course, but you will not be driving. I can drop you there, and you can get a taxi back. Anyway, Chris, I must go and get my boots on. See you later, darling.'

Chris was very impressed with the standard of the girls' rugby. He knew that they were only in the third division, but there were definitely skills and flair on show. They beat Farnborough 15 to nil and Chris was a bit surprised at how proud and elated he felt when Jo scored a try and converted it herself. His surprise made him realise that he really did care for her. In fact, he knew that he was falling in love with her. It suddenly occurred to him that it was time that he introduced her to his parents. Perhaps in a week or two. He would discuss it with Jo later.

Jo knew that their relationship was developing fast, and that was confirmed for her when Chris suggested she meet his parents. She could take the train to Waterloo, meet him at the station and then get the tube to Twickenham where his family lived. It would be another milestone passed in their relationship. In her heart of hearts, she knew that he was the one and the thought of looking at engagements rings suddenly occurred to her.

Despite being on call, Jo managed to leave work in time to meet Chris's train from London. She didn't mind the fact that he would mostly be on his own for the weekend, that was the reality of her job, and he just had to accept it.

She knew that he would spend Saturday watching rugby and writing his press release, Saturday night at the party and on Sunday they should have some time together, unless something blew up during the weekend. There had been nothing since Easter and so Jo thought the omens were good. She dropped Chris off at the Whiteley Hotel and then returned to the office to clear up a couple of outstanding matters.

By 9.00pm she was able to leave, pick up a Chinese takeaway and go home, hoping that the drunks of Fareham could be handled by uniform without the need for her to return. She was in bed, when Chris came in and she was too tired to grill him about the party so just kissed him and said they would talk in the morning.

Jo was awoken at 9.00am by her mobile. She jumped out of bed, so as not to wake Chris, and went downstairs to take the call. It was the Duty Officer who had been on during the night and her professional training kicked in as soon as he said,

'Jo we have got a suspicious death at the Whiteley Hotel. Apparently, the maid entered a guest's room, because he wasn't responding to a wake-up call and she found him to be lifeless, and get this, he was just lying on top of the bed, dressed in a bra and panties!'

'Do you have a name, Sergeant?'

'Yes, detective, the victim is Raymond Salter. Apparently, it was his birthday party.'

'Thank you, Sergeant. I happen to know the victim, so I can confirm that when I get there. Please can you alert D.I. Bligh, and Sergeant Munden of SOCO. and the photographer. I guess we will need them. Please get Peter Good to attend also. Can you give me the hotel number please?

I will come in straight away, draw a car and go to the hotel.' Jo then rang the hotel. 'Good morning, it is Detective Constable Fletcher, here, may I speak with the duty manager please?

Ah, good morning, sir, its DC Fletcher here. I am on my way. Please do not let the staff touch anything and have the glasses been washed yet that were used last night? No. that's great, please do not touch them as I may need to get them fingerprinted. I will be there in about thirty minutes.'

Jo then went upstairs, and woke Chris, and started dressing and said, 'Salter has been found dead in a hotel bed this morning and so I am going there now. I will keep you posted, but I will probably be away all morning. Please do not leave yet, as I may have to talk with you, since you were there. This may be the break that we have been waiting for. Bye for now.'

She gave him a kiss and left the room.

The hotel was quiet when she got there, with only a few cars parked out front. Good, she thought, not too many rubbernecks. She entered and asked for the duty manager. Being a Sunday, she did not expect to see the hotel manager there, but he had been called in by the duty manager. He came over to her and introduced himself as Lionel Rafferty.

Jo introduced herself, and said, 'Not a very good birthday present for him, is it?'

'Oh, so you knew it was his birthday.'

'Yes, some friends of mine were invited and so I am intrigued to find out what has happened.'

'I should warn you, detective constable, that we have not disturbed the bedroom, in case it is a crime scene, but the victim was found dressed in female undergarments and just lying on top of the bed.'

'Yes, the duty sergeant told me that this morning. I am a bit puzzled as he was more famous for trying to undress women, rather than dress up as one. But I am sure we will uncover what has been going on.'

I do hope so, and quickly, as it is not good publicity for a hotel that is meant to offer a relaxing sleep to be found to be offering death instead!'

'We will be as quick and efficient as we can, Mr. Rafferty, I assure you. Now, may I please have a list of all your staff who were on duty last night and this morning and their contact details, and their next shift here. It will probably be easier to interview them here so we can check out places if we need to. Also, my boss, DI Bligh will be joining me along with Scenes of Crime officers, a pathologist and a photographer. Could you show me the room please?'

'Definitely, follow me.'

It was a typical hotel room, basic furniture of built-in wardrobe and drawers, fridge, mini bar, ensuite bathroom, desk, heavy blue curtains, and the double bed taking up most of the centre space. The victim was lying on his back on the bed, and only dressed in a frilly brassiere with the cups obviously stuffed with something, Jo guessed, socks, as the victim had bare feet, and matching sexy type panties. Jo thought that they looked as though they were from the Marks and Spencer Valentine range. It was obvious looking at the panties, that the girls had been right in saying that Salter was well-endowed. They were definitely not designed for men!

Jo looked around for his clothes and found them under the end of the bed. She noticed that something was missing, and it took a bit of time before she realised that there was no suitcase, or overnight bag and so Salter had not intended to stay the night.

Something obviously happened during the party for him to be brought to this room and she hoped that Chris could probably enlighten her. There was about a third of a bottle of whisky on the desk and one glass beside it. She bent down to smell the glass without touching it and there was the whiff of whisky, so it had been used. The room key card was also beside the whisky bottle. Her first thought was that he could have drunk himself to death. From her training she knew that the victim would have needed to absorb about fifteen shots of spirit to become unconscious and die. Jo also knew that the amount of alcohol in his blood would continue to rise even after he had stopped drinking as the alcohol in the digestive system carries on being absorbed into the bloodstream, and that causes the body to stop working properly and death then occurs. The question then was did Salter just have too much drink at his party and pass out or was he deliberately poisoned with alcohol. Peter would have to answer that for Jo.

At that point in her deliberations, the door opened, and the hotel manager ushered Spence in. Jo nodded to Spence, and then turned to the manager and said, 'Mr. Rafferty, are any of last night's bar staff or reception staff on the premises at the moment, please?'

'Yes, the duty manager downstairs was working last night. His shift finishes in thirty minutes.'

'I would like to see him before he goes, if I may, please?'

'Certainly, detective. I will make him available to you.'

'Thank you.'

'Morning Spence.'

'Morning Jo. It seems when you are on weekend duty, you get all the fun!'

'Well sir, just don't roster me on duty on weekends, then.'

'Humph! What have we got here then?'

'Well sir, the victim's name is Raymond Salter and it was his birthday party here yesterday. He is twenty-eight years old and was also celebrating being selected to join the England Rugby squad as a replacement for Simon and Josh.'

'Not another rugby squad death. Do you think it is related to Golgotha, Jo?'

'I am not sure yet, sir. Obviously, we need to find out the cause of death and whether it is self-inflicted or murder. I imagine that it is alcoholic poisoning but until we can find out how much is or was in his system and how it got there we don't know. I have called Peter in so hopefully, he can shed light on that. If it is murder, then the modus operandi is quite different to before. There is no religious significance that I am aware of that combines alcoholic poisoning and cross-dressing if that is what this is. The bra and panties set up seems to be mocking Salter, as he was known as a bit of sexual predator and is more used to undressing girls rather than dressing up as one, there could be some revenge connection, so just because there is a rugby connection I am not going to make the jump to say that all three murders are connected until I get more evidence.'

'Yes, Jo, I think that you are right. We will have to wait for Peter to get the toxicology results. You take the lead on this and we can meet tomorrow in the incident room at 2.30pm. I will get the station sergeant to alert the crime team.'

'Fine, sir. I have noticed that there is no suitcase or overnight bag, or any pyjamas or toiletries in the bathroom, which suggests

135

that the victim did not originally intend to stay overnight here and so I want to go downstairs and talk to the duty manager on how this room came to be booked. He goes off duty shortly and I would like to talk to him before he goes, if I may?'

'Absolutely, Jo, please do. I will wait here for Peter and SOCO. Is Graham coming in?'

'I am not sure, sir, I asked the station sergeant to contact him.'

'I'll check and if not, I will ring him. After SOCO has arrived, I will go. See you tomorrow, Jo.'

'Bye sir.'

Jo left the room and went to find the duty manager. She noted his name badge telling her that his name was Michael Armstrong. After getting his permission to record their conversation, Jo pulled out her Dictaphone, turned it on and asked him,

'How did it come about that the victim was in a room, as there doesn't appear to be any overnight bag there?'

'It was the victim's birthday party and he was drinking quite heavily throughout the evening. He became more and more intoxicated and when he started to come on to some of the female party goers, one of the party members came up to me and said that he needed to lie down for a while, so could he get a room for him.

Fortunately, there was a room vacant and the party goer paid the £60 in cash and as he had bought it, I gave him the key card. He organised some of his friends to virtually carry the victim up to the room. I went up about half an hour later, to check on him, using my pass key and he was lying on the top of the bed asleep. I could hear him snoring, so I turned him over into the recovery position, in case he vomited.'

'How was he dressed on the bed, please?'

'Not like he is now. He was fully clothed, lying on his back.'

'Did you notice a bottle of whisky on the desk?'

'No, there was no whisky. If there had been, I would have confiscated it, as we have a rule that you cannot bring alcohol onto the premises. Obviously, we want you to buy from the hotel. Many guests do smuggle it in, but if we find it, we confiscate it.'

'Can you describe the person who paid for the room, please?'

'Well, I don't think that he was a teammate, as he was older than the others. He was possibly around thirty-five or a bit older. He had a bit of a belly on him, black hair, wore glasses and was well dressed in a suit and tie.'

'Could it have been his father?'

'No, Salter told me when he booked, that his parents were away on a cruise and would be gone for two weeks. I think that they are due back next Friday.'

Jo wondered whether the police could wait until then before they told them, since Peter would probably not release the body for burial until after then.

'Mr. Armstrong, did the person who paid for the room sign the hotel register?'

'Yes, he did. I handed him my pen and he signed.'

'Could you show me please where he signed the register?'

They both went off to the reception desk and the duty manager opened the register, and pointing to an entry and signature, said 'There's his signature.'

Jo looked at it and saw the name 'Raymond Salter' scrawled in the signature box.

'He signed the victim's name!' she said.

'Oh,' I did not read what he signed and we are not like European countries that demand to see passports or any ID. I don't know why we bother with registers, as a lot of people do not like to leave any evidence of their being here in case their spouse should find out!'

'In that case, could I take this page please as I can get a handwriting expert to look at it. It might throw up some valuable information?'

'Okay, detective, I will just photocopy it for our records.' He tore out the page and took it into the office behind the reception desk. He soon came back and gave Jo the page. 'Could you sign this copy please to say that you have taken the original?'

'Sure,' said Jo as she took out her own pen and signed the copy. When she looked up, she could see the duty manager holding his pen out to her.

'Is that the pen that he used?' asked Jo.

'Yes, it is actually,' he said showing it to Jo.

'Could I borrow it for a moment to get our guys to dust it for prints? It will help us to locate him.'

'Okay, as I am going off shift soon, could you return it to my colleague who will be here on reception?' he said, dropping the pen into the evidence bag that Jo was holding out to him.

'Just a bit more information please, if you don't mind, How many guests were there in total last night?'

'We catered for one hundred and thirty.'

'That must have cost a pretty penny,'

'Yes, the invoice was for £5,230 in total counting room hire, catering and open bar.'

'Open bar with a group of rugby players. He must have been mental or wealthy.'

'Wealthy, paid with his Dad's credit card.'

'Were there any really big drinkers, please?'

'Not really, but most of the women drank spirits, so we got

through a lot of vodka.'

'How many bar staff did you have on last night please?'

'I had one waiter in the house bar for the resident guests and the few patrons we get on a Saturday night and Manual and I ran the bar for the party.'

'What about our birthday boy? Did he drink much and what was his tipple?' Jo realised that she just stopped herself in time from saying 'poison'!

'He got his first drink himself which was a pint of Guinness and thereafter others got him the drinks. He was the only person drinking Guinness, so I remember pouring about seven or eight pints. A couple of the girls were keeping him topped up and I know that they were lacing his drinks, as they would come to the bar together and order a pint of Guinness and a vodka. I noticed that as they left the bar they would pour the vodka into the Guinness.'

'You mean that Salter could have drunk at least seven or eight pints of Guinness and seven or eight shots of vodka?'

'No wonder he got drunk so quickly. I will check, but that would be enough to put him to sleep, but probably not enough to actually kill him. Can you tell me any more about the girls that did this?'

'Only that I remember one of them calling the other 'Sarah'. They were about twenty-ish, and 'Sarah' seemed quite keen on our Manual as she started dancing with him in a sort of *Dirty Dancing* sort of way, if you know what I mean.'

'Ah, that is interesting and very helpful, thank you.'

'When is Manual back on shift please?'

'Tomorrow at lunch time. Oh, here is the staff list that you asked my boss for.'

'One last question, please? What CCTV coverage do you

have around the hotel?'

'Well, we have security cameras outside around the front so we can see who had driven here and one in reception but we do not have any in the bar area as that would be too invasive on guest's privacy.'

'Could I get my team to view the footage please, especially the outside ones?'

'Certainly, I can get them for you.'

'Thank you, Mr. Armstrong. You have been immensely helpful. Enjoy the rest of your Sunday, and when you come in next, everything will be shipshape again.'

While Jo had been talking to the duty manager, she had noticed Peter and the SOCO team come in and go upstairs, so she decided to go and join them.

She entered the room and said hello to them all. Sergeant Munden said, 'I should have known with you on duty, Jo, we would get called out, and on a Sunday too.'

'Yes, Spence said the same, so I told him to stop rostering me for weekend duty!'

'Look, Arthur, I have spoken to the duty manager and I have a lot of information. Could you fingerprint this pen, first, please, so I can give it back to the duty manager? It should have the prints on it of the person who signed the register and organised for the victim to have this room. As you can see, there is no overnight bag or toiletries, so the room was not booked in advance. I don't think Salter planned to stay here last night.'

'Sure Jo,' replied Detective Munden as he took the evidence bag from Jo, 'and I agree with you that this was probably not a planned stay-over.'

'Also, I have asked the hotel not to wash the glasses from last night, in case we can find further fingerprints.'

'I don't think that is necessary as I know that Salter was drinking Guinness, spiked with vodka, and I think I know who was spiking them. Is it okay for me to advise the staff that they can wash the glasses, Arthur?'

'Yes, I have no interest in them, then.'

Jo went to the room phone and dialled reception and told them that she had released the glasses for washing.

Jo then turned to Peter and asked, 'Peter, from what I know I estimate that the victim had drunk seven or eight pints of Guinness and at least seven of them were spiked with a shot of vodka each, so he was brought semi-conscious to this room. That would not be enough to kill him though, would it?'

'One pint of Guinness is about 2.3 units times seven, plus the seven vodka units, that is about 24 units of alcohol in all. That's a week's allocation for a male. A bloody lot, Jo, enough to put him out, but probably not enough to kill him. He would need about another seven or eight units to finish him off and so I am guessing he got that from the whisky over there,' said Peter.

'The duty manager checked up on the victim about half an hour after he was placed on the bed, he was in his own clothes and there was no whisky in the room. He was virtually unconscious.

Somebody or bodies came here and planted the whisky and put him in this underwear. I doubt that he was in any state to drink whisky. Peter, please can you check how that may have been administered? We are talking about giving him around two hundred millilitres of whisky equivalent to eight shots. About a full glass of whisky. No doubt an autopsy of his mouth can show whether he was forced to drink it, or it may have been injected. Remember Dad, Peter?'

'Yes, of course, Jo. When I get him back to the mortuary I will find out and I will look for needle tracks.'

141

'To avoid needle tracks, Peter, the killer might have injected through the nipples or the penis. Please check,' said Jo.

'Ouch!' came a reply from Arthur.

'Peter can you tell the time of death. Please?'

'I would say nine hours ago, which would make it about midnight to one o'clock last night.'

'Thank you. Peter. Are you finished here now?'

'Yes, I cannot do any more at the moment. Nick is on the way so we will get the body to the mortuary and I will see you tomorrow.'

'Thank you Peter. Arthur are you and your team finished?'

'Yeah, there is not much for us here. There are no useable fingerprints on the pen, or the bottle of whisky and it is not easy to get fingerprints from fabrics, but Peter may get some DNA off the underwear. I think that you will find out easily enough who dressed him up like that once it gets out that he is dead. I think that possibly the dressing up and the alcohol poisoning are two separate activities.'

'Yes, Arthur, I am inclined to agree with you and I think I know who will be able to shed some light on this. Graham, have you got all your photos that you need?'

'Yes, fine thanks, Jo. I will get off now.'

'Well, team, if we are all finished, I will hand back the room to the hotel once the body has been removed. See you in the crime room tomorrow. Thank you all for coming out.' When it was just Jo and Peter in the room. Peter asked,

'How did Spence react to the results of the re-enactment regarding Simon's death?'

'I have not told him yet. I am going to speak to the DCI first, and then if she agrees, I will approach Spencer on his own. I have been waiting for a suitable moment and I think that this death

142

has given it. I think it is related to the other two deaths, and the same killer is responsible for them all. That is why it is important to know how Raymond died, and whether the alcohol was self-administered or not. I am guessing not!'

'I agree with you.'

The door then opened, and Nick came in with the gurney. Jo left them to it, saying as she left, 'I am just going to retrieve some CCTV footage, and then I will go. See you tomorrow Peter.'

'Bye Jo.' Jo left the room and went and found the duty manager, 'Your colleague Michael said he would have some CCTV footage for me from last night.'

'Yes, here it is, on this data stick. Have you all finished yet?' he asked as he handed over the data stick.

'They are just bringing the body down now. You can make up the room and thank you for all your help. Please give this pen back to the manager.'

Jo left and decided she would not go back to the office, but set off home to question her lover about a murder.

Chapter Eleven

Chris opened the front door for her as she got out of the car, and they kissed. After settling down in the lounge, Chris turned to Jo and asked, 'It was Salter then?'

'Yes,' said Jo.

'Murder, suicide, or death by misadventure?'

'I think murder, made to look like self-inflicted alcohol poisoning. The strange thing is he was lying on top of the bed, dressed only in a frilly bra and panties.' replied Jo.

'Not the image of a tough, efficient, hard playing rugby player, Jo!'

'Not at all. That's what troubles me. Well, you were there, Chris. Please tell me what happened.'

' The drinking was....'

'No don't tell me yet, Chris,' Jo interrupted 'because what you tell me is evidence, and so I have to do this properly.'

'What I am a suspect?'

'No, silly, a witness. I usually record my interviews, so do you mind if I turn on my Dictaphone?'

'No, Jo, that's fine. Now that we are ready, I was going to say, the drinking was manic. I suppose that it was because it was a free bar. Drinks and food must have cost somebody a small fortune. There were over a hundred people there, mostly rugby players, both girls and boys, in their twenties, and about six older men, whom I believe to be Rugby Football Union wallers.'

Ray paid £5,230 according to the duty manager.'

'Probably put it on his Dad's credit card,' said Chris.

'Anyway, Chris, go on please,' said Jo.

'Well, I think that Ray had had a few before any of us arrived, because when I arrived, he was already finishing a pint of Guinness. All through the evening, guests were handing him pints of Guinness. Especially one of those girl friends of yours, the blond one, Sarah, I think you said her name was, well she was really plying him with them. He would hardly finish one, and she or her partner, Anne, would be handing him another. Ray slowly got drunker and drunker and then his bad behaviour started. He would approach the female guests and ask them for a birthday kiss and, if they let, him, he was immediately groping them either trying to get under their tops or under their dresses.

Obviously, the girls were reacting, but Ray just got drunker and kept slurring his speech. It was embarrassing. One of the older guests came over and told Ray that enough was enough and that the girls didn't want him groping them. He then said to Ray that he had had enough to drink for the night, and he went off to arrange a room. He came back and got two or three of the boys to help take Ray upstairs to his room. I never saw him again after that.'

'Thanks Chris, for that. It is how I have understood the evening played out from speaking with the hotel staff. Was there anything else a bit out of the ordinary that you noticed, please?' Jo asked.

She was hoping that he might throw some light on Sarah and Anne's involvement, but she did not want to prompt him.

'Only that Sarah was acting a bit weird, especially since she is already in a relationship.'

'How do you mean?' asked Jo.

'Well, after Ray had left the party, she started dancing with the waiter. I think he was Spanish or Mexican. He must have thought that he had pulled, as Sarah was really doing the *Dirty Dancing* routine, with grinding and swaying to the music. At one point, she put her hand in his back pocket and pulled him right into her, and then she left him but returned about five minutes later and did it again', said Chris.

'You mean like this', said Jo as she pulled Chris up from the couch and drew him into her and started grinding against him, and then she plunged her hand into his back pocket and found something. She pulled it out and it was his railcard. 'Of course!' she yelled, 'that's what Sarah was doing, she wanted the waiter's pass key so she could get into Ray's room. She and Anne must have gone up to the room, opened the door, retrieved the pass key that would have been left for Ray, and then come down and Sarah would have started dancing with the waiter again to replace the pass key. I bet she never danced with the waiter again', she said to Chris.

'Not that I saw' replied Chris.

'Now we need to find out what Sarah and Anne were up to in Ray's room, although I can guess. I don't think they poisoned Ray, but I think that they might have dressed him up in female undergarments. I am fairly sure that seven pints of Guinness, even if some of them were spiked, would not be enough alcohol to kill him. Somebody had to administer something else. We will have to wait for Peter to tell us the toxicology results to know more about that.' said Jo.

As if on cue, there was a knock on the front door. Jo went and opened it, and Sarah and Anne were standing there.

'We thought that you would want to talk to us', said Sarah, 'we heard about Ray and thought that we could throw some light on the matter.'

'I am sure that you can,' said Jo. 'Come in and take a seat. You remember, Chris. Well, as he was there last night, he has been helping me with this. Is it alright for him to stay, please?'

'Yes, sure Jo.' said Anne.

'Well, this is official as you both are witnesses, at least to what went on last night and, as you can see, the Dictaphone is recording this. Although this is official, and as it is a Sunday, a glass of wine may help jog your memory. Okay?'

'I'll get them,' said Chris.

'Tell, me Sarah, was there a bottle of whisky in the room when you and Anne went to Ray's room?'

'How did you know we went to his room?'

'I'm a detective, that's what I do!'

'Well, to answer your question, no, there was no alcohol or whisky in the room when we went in,' replied Sarah.

'If you think that we killed Ray then you are wrong. The amount of alcohol that we supplied him with was enough to make him drunk and pass out but not enough to kill him,' said Anne.

'How do you know it wasn't enough, especially since you were spiking the drinks with vodka?'

'We are nurses. That's what we do!'

'Touché!' said Jo. 'Let me tell you what I think this is all about. Let me know if I'm correct and then you can fill in any gaps. Okay?'

'Fine Jo.' said Sarah.

Jo leaned forward, put her two index fingers together and said, 'Well, it is obvious that you do not like Ray as a person. You told me that during lunch at Alton on Sunday. I imagine that something occurred for you to feel this way about him, which no doubt you will tell me about. You were obviously waiting for an

147

opportunity to avenge his wrongdoing, whatever that was.

The birthday party invitation was heaven sent. You could go to the party, spike his drinks, and watch while he made a public fool of himself, which he did, to the point that he was carted off to bed.

You saw this as an opportunity to further avenge his wrongdoing, and so you, Sarah, started dancing with the waiter, to distract him so you could get his room pass key from his back pocket and then you and Anne went to Ray's room, took the pass key left for him, and returned downstairs and returned the waiter's pass key to him. You both then returned to the room, stripped Ray's clothing off him and dressed him in the Valentine's bra and pants. I can only imagine you took photos. How am I doing?' said Jo as she paused in her explanation.

'Absolutely right, Jo. We still have the photos. Do you want to see them?'

'Okay,' said Jo. She took the phone from Sarah and looked at the image of Ray. 'That would have made a stir on social media.' said Jo.

'We didn't bring the underwear with us as we did not think we would get the opportunity that we did. The underwear belonged to Anne, and so she had to continue the evening commando!' said Sarah.

'I was wearing top and black satin finish trousers, which were a tight fitting, and one of my friends came up to me and asked where do I buy my lingerie as she said she could not see any panty lines beneath my trousers. I did not have the guts to tell her that I was commando!' said Anne.

'We intended to post the photos on social media, Facebook, Linked-in and Instagram, but when we heard that he had died, we didn't of course.'

'How did you hear so quickly that he had died. That information has not been released yet,' asked Jo.

'One of my friends who knew what we were up to, left an earring at the party, and when she went back for it, she asked the hotel staff, how Ray was this morning and they told her that he had died.

They also said that the police had been and thought that he had been murdered, so she rang us and told us. This is why we have come to see you because we knew that you would suss out that we were somehow involved with Ray being dressed up,' said Anne.

'Okay, so you did not kill Ray, but why did you want to embarrass him so much?' asked Jo.

'Because he raped me!' said Sarah.

'Can you tell me about it, Sarah?' asked Jo in a quiet voice.

'It was about three years ago, when Ray was still playing for Alton Seniors,' began Sarah, 'I'd watched a few games and I was impressed with his ball kicking skills, so in the bar after the game, I went up to him and told him I thought his kicking was great and what wouldn't I give to be able to kick like him – that sort of thing, you know?

Well, I was over the moon when he offered to give me some coaching. We agreed to meet up at the club the following day – Sunday – after all the matches had finished. So around 3pm, we went out onto the number three pitch.' Sarah paused, gathering her thoughts before continuing.

'I have to say that Ray was an excellent coach. We did some warm-ups, running up and down the field, some stretching which he said was really important before you do any kicking, to make sure you don't get a strain injury. So already he was giving me good advice. Then he taught me how to place the ball correctly for place kicks and I managed to kick a goal from thirty yards out and on an angle, which was a first. We moved on to doing drop kicks, and he coached me not only in dropped goals, but especially in the drop kick to start or restart the game after a try.

You play, don't you, so you probably know the idea is to kick the ball so that it's high enough and long enough for your side to chase and catch it ahead of the opposition. That way, you don't lose possession, so this was a skill I definitely wanted to learn. After about an hour, I started to get the hang of it and I became pretty good at getting the distance and height right.'

After another reflective moment, Sarah went on, 'And then he said we ought to call it a day because the light was starting to go. Now I don't know whether it was me saying I'd do anything to be able to kick like him, or he just felt that he deserved something for sharing his rugby skills, but during our warm-down run up and down the field, he suddenly dropped behind, then tackled me and brought me down. Before I knew what was going on, he had me on my back and was pinning me down on the grass. As you can imagine, I was shocked as well as furious and I asked him what he thought he was doing and he said something like, What do you think? It's how you're going to pay for my coaching you, and I said, not like this I'm not, but not only did he ignore what I said, he already had his great big hands mauling my breasts.

At this point, he was lying half on top of me and to my dismay, I realised he was both too strong and too heavy for me to fight him off. And what was even worse, I could feel him getting hard! When he started trying to drag my shorts down, I yelled at him to stop and reminded him that I don't go with men, as he bloody well knew. Telling men that usually puts them off, but not this one. 'Effing lesbian,' he scoffed, 'what you need is a real man like

150

me. Once you've experienced a real man, you won't want any of that lesbian crap!'

'In under five minutes, he'd gone from being Mr Nice Guy to being a total shit. I tried telling him that I was still a virgin and that he wouldn't be able to penetrate me, but all he said was that he'd had virgins before, and he was sure that I would be no problem. I then tried to explain to him that actually it would be a problem as I had a medical condition called imperforate hymen that makes penetration impossible but he just snorted and tore my pants off before he began pulling his thing out of his shorts.

As soon as I saw it, I really panicked and started screaming for help, but he smothered my mouth, then shoved himself between my legs. Once he was there, he kept trying again and again to get it in me, but it wasn't happening.

Maybe playing rugby had taught him never to give up, though I think it's more likely that he'd got himself so aroused that he couldn't stop. Whatever the reason, when it still wouldn't go in, he must have either tried to tear me open with his hand or else he cut me with something. I have no idea which because the pain was so intense, I must have blacked out. When I came to, he'd gone and Anne was standing over me, talking into her phone.'

'I was ringing for an air ambulance,' continued Anne, 'I went looking for Sarah when she hadn't returned from her practicing, then I found her half-naked, unconscious and covered in blood. There also appeared to be a lot of semen on her so it seemed likely Ray had got what he wanted. I wasn't going to move her, mainly because I couldn't carry her to my car, plus I had no way of knowing what other damage might have been done to her. So, she got airlifted to hospital and underwent immediate surgery. When I found her, she was in a dreadful state, and I reckon it's only by sheer luck that she didn't bleed to death.'

151

'That must have been absolutely horrific for you, Sarah,' said Jo, 'and of course my question is why did you not report him to the police?'

'Jo, surely that is obvious.' replied Sarah. 'Rugby is my world, and Ray was the best thing in rugby to happen to the club. Because of him, the club was in the running to move up to the premier league and if I were the cause of his being removed and imprisoned, my rugby life would have been ruined and I would have been ostracised. It would all have been my fault. Being raped by Ray would be considered a tolerable experience for the skills that he taught me. You heard the girls when you recently came along to play on Sunday, they all would like a piece of him. Anne and I just decided that we would get back at him in our own way. That was what we were trying to do yesterday,' said Sarah.

'I think it is customary for the air ambulance to report their call-outs to the police?' said Jo.

'Yes, I was contacted, but I refused to report it and offer testimony.'

'How bad were your injuries?' asked Jo.

Anne replied, 'Well the surgeon who performed the surgery was the chief gynaecological consultant at the hospital and she said that it was the worst case of internal damage that she had seen in her career. I managed to snaffle a copy of her report from Sarah's file, and I have it here. Would you like to read it, Jo?'

'Yes, please,' said Jo taking it, 'I'll look at it later if I may. I do have a question, Sarah. Why did you not get your medical problem treated after you reached puberty?'

'Well, I did have some surgery but at that time my parents would not consent to a complete resolution of the problem as they thought it would help me safeguard my virginity. No one could have foreseen the consequences of being raped. When I decided that I was not going to go with men, I did not see the need to have any further medical intervention.'

'What happens now Jo?' asked Anne.

'Well, you have not committed any offence, as far as I can see and so nothing really,' said Jo.

'The fact that somebody else has killed Ray, if it is murder, and I think that it is, means that it could be connected to Josh's and Simon's death. I think that it will re-open the original case and that hopefully will mean that Simon is exonerated from being Josh's killer.

I will obviously have to discuss this with my boss tomorrow, but please keep this confidential. I presume that you don't want your situation made public either, Sarah?' asked Jo.

'Oh God, no,' said Sarah, 'it would be totally misinterpreted. I don't want to keep going over it. It has been bad enough reliving it with you, and I know you, so I definitely do not want it out in the public domain, and that goes for your paper also, please Chris.'

'Of course, Sarah,' replied Chris, 'despite what you might read, we don't speak ill of the dead!'

'Sarah, you do know that you can still get counselling from *Rape Crisis*, without first having to report your rape to the police. They can be extremely helpful and totally non-judgmental,' said Jo.

'Yes, I am aware of that Jo, and I may yet do that,' replied Sarah.

'Well, it really is time for some lunch. Do you both want to stay. It's only pizza and salad, but Chris has brought some good wines to wash it down,' said Jo.

Sarah looked across at Anne and as she nodded, Sarah replied, 'Thank you Jo, that would be very welcome.'

After lunch Anne and Sarah left and, just as Jo and Chris were settling down together on the sofa, there was a knock on the door. Jo opened it to find Peter on the doorstep.

'Oh, hello Peter, I did not think we would meet up until tomorrow,' said Jo.

'Well, I am unable to attend tomorrow's meeting as I have an urgent autopsy to do on a young mother who died in childbirth this morning. The hospital want to make sure that there are no suspicious circumstances. I just wanted to give you the results of my autopsy on Ray, so that you have them for the meeting tomorrow.'

'That is very good of you, Peter, do come in,' replied Jo.

Peter entered the lounge and took a seat beside Chris after Jo introduced them.

'You were right, Jo,' he started. I could find no trace of whisky in his mouth, gullet or stomach and so he did not drink any once he got to his room and he wasn't force fed either. I looked for needle tracks and found that he had been injected in the nipples and the penis as you presumed. There were traces of whisky in his breast tissue and in the corpora cavernosa and the corpus spongiosum in his penis. I would estimate that a 20ml needle was used to inject the whisky, which would mean that he was probably injected about ten times. That would be enough to kill him, particularly as injecting alcohol directly into the blood stream is a lot worse than it being absorbed more slowly through the digestive system and more fatal.

The alcohol affects the nerves and the breathing, which causes disruption to the heartbeat and can stop the heart. In my judgment, the alcohol could not have been self-injected and there was no sign of any needles.

Jo, Ray was murdered. He did not die by his own hand.'

'Thank you, Peter. That confirms my thinking as well. I will convey your autopsy results to the team tomorrow and we can go back into hunt the murderer mode,' said Jo.

'I will also talk to my chief inspector tomorrow about our experiment with the rope and the rugby post cross-bar. It is about time that this investigation got back on track.'

Peter got up and made his way to the front door. 'I will take my leave now, Jo, as I have got an early start tomorrow. I am not looking forward to it either. Maternal deaths are so upsetting for everyone, with the husband looking for someone to blame and the hospital staff hoping that they have not messed up. The husband in this case is a lawyer and so he will no doubt be right on top of us to ensure that there has been no slip-up. Please, Jo, let me know if I can be of any more help. Cheerio Chris.'

Jo returned to the couch and sat beside Chris. 'Well, Chris, I would like to plan where do we go from here? We have three murders, all rugby players selected to play for England and all fly-halves. Despite the change of *modus operandi*, from religious symbolism to alcohol poisoning, I still think that we are looking for one killer, and in light of the physical requirement to crucify a body and haul one up onto the rugby post's cross-bar, I think we are looking for a male killer.'

'Yes, Jo, I would agree we are looking for a male killer and someone who has had some close connection with English rugby,' replied Chris.

'I am going to try and see Detective Chief Inspector Abbottsford tomorrow,' said Jo, 'hopefully before the team meeting and tell her about our investigative work in respect of Simon's death. I want to get this investigation back on track. I think it would be good if you could come with me, as I need to let her know. Also to tell D.I. Bligh that you are assisting us.

155

He knew that I was going to contact you, but I have not told him of your complete involvement. I will introduce you as my specialist rugby contact and important to the case to get more information on Arthur O'Neill who no doubt will be the next fly-half. Somehow, I think he is very important to unlocking this case. What do you think, Chris?'

'That's fine, Jo. I am happy to make some enquiries into O'Neill. I can shroud it by saying that I am doing a background article on him as the incoming English fly-half.'

'Right, I will go and see Abbottsford first thing and ring you when we can go and see her together. Are you able to stay around here and go up to London later?'

'Yes, Jo, that's fine. I will write up the birthday party and death of birthday boy here and email it to my editor. He is getting used to my 'working from home' as it were,' Chris sniggered.

'Chris, I need to get clearance for what you write about Salter's murder, before you publish. Is that okay?'

'Of course, Jo, but as I was at the party quite legitimately, so surely, I can write up what I know as a party guest, rather than what I know as part of the crime team?'

'Of course, you can do that, but I am sure that I can get consent to allow you to write about the murder. Well, Chris, I think I will turn in now, as tomorrow will be a big day. See you upstairs.'

'Yes, I will come upstairs with you.'

Jo arrived at the police station at 8.00am and was pleased to find that Chief Inspector Abbottsford had already signed in. She went up to her office and tentatively knocked on her door.

'Come in.' Jo entered and the DCI immediately looked up and said, 'Oh hello Jo? A busy weekend, I hear!'

'Yes, ma'am, you could say that. Look, there is something that I need to tell you about this case, so when would be a good time for me to see you please? The sooner the better.'

'Shouldn't you be talking with Spencer. Rather than me, Jo, as he is after all leading this investigation?'

'Well, it is about him that I want to talk to you about, in a way,' replied Jo.

'Oh, I see,' said the DCI. 'In that case, how about in thirty minutes, as I have an urgent call to make to the Chief Constable.'

'In half an hour is simply fine, thanks. I will see you then.'

Jo left the DCI's office and went to her own office to organise her notes relating to the investigation of Simon's murder and to ring Chris to get him to come to the station in time for the meeting. Twenty minutes later, the duty constable rang Jo and said that Chris was downstairs. Jo left her office, went downstairs and signed Chris in. They went back to her office talked briefly over what Jo was going to say and then arrived outside Abbottsford's office exactly on time.

'Come in again,' was the reply as Jo knocked on the door.

Jo and Chris entered and the DCI showed a bit of surprise, that Jo was not on her own. Jo immediately took the initiative and pointing to Chris, she said, 'Ma'am, may I introduce a friend who has been helping me in this case. This is Chris Foley, who is the senior rugby correspondent for the *Sportsman's Daily* and he has been gathering background information on the England Rugby scene which is really involved in these murders. Chris, this is Chief Inspector Raylene Abbottsford who is in charge of this police station, so my big boss,' said Jo.

'Sometimes, I don't think that I get treated as the 'boss' but thanks Jo. Welcome, Chris. Jo, I trust that you have not let a journo run amok through this case?' said the DCI.

'Oh no, he is very well trained and has been extremely helpful. For instance, he was able to attend the birthday party of the latest murder victim, Raymond Salter and so I have got first-hand knowledge of what went on. I will pass that on at the meeting this morning. He is also going to get invaluable background information on Salter's replacement, which we believe to be one Arthur O'Neill who is either going to end up dead like his predecessors, or, as I think, going to be a major player in helping to solve this case,' replied Jo.

'Very well, Jo,' said the DCI, and turning to Chris, she said, 'It is a bit unusual to allow civilians to work with us in murder investigations, but I can see your expertise will be helpful, so please feel welcome. At the same time, please do not abuse the privilege by publishing any information that has not been sanctioned. I can trust Jo to be your censor. Is that understood, Mr. Foley?'

'Of course, ma'am,' said Chris, 'I am grateful for the privilege of being able to assist. I truly respect Detective Constable Fletcher, and I will not publish anything without her approval.'

'Fine, well, Jo what is it that you wanted to see me about and do you want Mr. Foley to remain while we discuss it?'

'I want to see you about some evidence that I gathered regarding Simon Cheyney's death and as Chris was with me, when I found this evidence, I would like him to be present now.'

'Okay, Jo. What is this evidence, and have you spoken to D.I. Bligh about it?'

'No, I haven't as yet but he needs to know and basically I would like your support in telling him.'

'Why is that?'

'Well, Inspector Bligh was quite forthright in deciding that

158

Simon's death was suicide brought on as a result of his remorse after killing Josh Christopher and he did not want any further investigation into those two deaths.

Well, you know what the inspector is like and he does not take kindly to being gainsaid. I did not accept his analysis, and I decided to carry out my own further investigations as I thought that there was evidence to suggest that Simon had also been murdered. The evidence found at the time by the team, including the pathologist, could be interpreted as either suicide or murder. The inspector chose suicide, but because I know the victim, I thought murder.

In order to back up my suspicions, I returned to the scene of Simon's death to examine the crossbar of the rugby posts. Fortunately, the school has retained their original posts and because they are over fifty years old, they are made of wood. We would not have been able to do any reconstruction with modern posts which are metal.

Chris came with me to the posts and I took out a camera, tape measure and a short spirit level. I had arranged for the caretaker to place a ladder nearby and so Chris held the ladder, wearing protective gloves to prevent any contamination and wearing gloves myself I climbed up so that I was above the cross-bar. As I expected, there was quite a groove in the wood, where the rope supporting Simon's body had been and the base of the groove was brownish in colour. I photographed the groove in the cross-bar, and then placing the spirit level along the bar, over the groove, I measured the depth of the groove.

Here is the photograph that I took. You can see the groove clearly. My measurement showed the groove to be a good ten millimetres deep, and that depth could not be made by just throwing over a rope. There was also rope burn as the groove was brownish in colour.

As a result of my findings, I am now convinced that this is a case of murder made to look like suicide. I am theorising that the killer somehow stunned Simon, which brought him down, and then placed the noose around his neck and half carried and dragged him to the posts. The killer then threw the rope over, and then pulled Simon's body up to the hanging position so that his feet were off the ground, and then secured the rope.'

Jo paused, and then the DCI said, 'But the pair of steps lying alongside the posts would not be high enough to be able to secure the rope to the cross-bar.'

'I know that the steps were too small and so I reasoned that there had to be another ladder involved. The ladder that the caretaker had supplied to us was usually left in the vicinity to enable balls to be retrieved from trees and roofs and so we took prints from the ladder. I also took prints from the caretaker to eliminate him.

The caretaker also confirmed that the ladder was just leaning up against the fence nearby over the Easter weekend and so it would have been easy for the killer to use it and put it back. The caretaker also offered an observation that he could not believe that Simon could kill Josh or himself as he said that he knows both the boys and they were like blood brothers. He said that Simon was tough and rugged while playing rugby but otherwise, he would not hurt a fly.

He also related an occasion when a teacher told him that during a biology class Simon could not bring himself to even dissect a frog, and it had been dead for some time.

I also asked the caretaker whether or not he ever washed the ladder. He replied that he did occasionally, so teachers using it would not get themselves dirty, as they were usually in suits.

He told me that he last washed it a week before Easter and so it is a fair assumption that no-one had used it prior to the Easter weekend.

Then, acting on a whim, we decided to reconstruct the death scene. The pathologist had told us that Simon was about fifteen and half stone in weight, so we got weights to that amount from the school gym and I organised for the pathologist to be present.We then hauled them up to the cross-bar to see what type of groove they made. The groove was identical to the one in the photograph. This just confirmed my view that Simon was murdered. Also, I sent the prints that I took off the aluminium ladder to the lab and the result is that there is one set of prints indicating a person carrying the ladder and climbing up it.

They have since been run through the database and there is no match. They have been stored so we can check them later. I have told the pathologist this and he now also agrees with me. He wanted to tell the D.I but I asked him to hold fire until I saw you. I recognise, ma'am that I was probably going outside my remit, especially with the reconstruction, and so I am hoping that you will accept that it was all in good faith to get to the truth, not to undermine the DI.

Now that we have a third murder, again the same rugby player position, then I think that Operation Golgotha should now be expanded to include the murders of Cheyney and Salter.'

'Bloody hell, Jo. You have been busy! What made you think of measuring the groove?'

'Well, I remembered it from an episode of 'Foyles War' on TV. They were investigating the death of an RAF serviceman who was found hanging from a branch of a tree. The sergeant got the groove checked and the depth of it was consistent with a body being pulled up, not just a rope being thrown over. I have

161

always remembered that. The RAF airman was murdered by the local priest who was a German Patriot or spy, and the airman had sussed him out.'

'Well, Jo, we now have to move this forward. I can understand your reluctance to confront D.I. Bligh with this new information and so I will go and see him before this afternoon's meeting. He may want to see you, but don't worry, you are not going to get into trouble for your investigations. You may even get rewarded. Come back and see me just before the meeting, please.'

'Certainly ma'am, and thank you.'

'Bye Jo, and you too Mr. Foley.'

'Bye ma'am,' answered Chris.

Jo and Chris went downstairs and said their goodbyes. Chris set off for the station to get a train back London and Jo returned to her office to prepare her notes for the meeting.

At 2.00pm, half an hour before the start of the meeting, Jo knocked on Chief Abbottsford's door.

'Come in, aah, it's you, Jo. Is it that time already?'

'Well, we have half an hour, ma'am,' replied Jo.

'Right. Well, I have spoken to D. I Bligh and he agrees to re-open Operation Golgotha to cover all three murders. Although he was very impressed with your investigative prowess, he was a bit concerned that you did not feel that you could approach him yourself but had to go through me. I pointed out however, from my own observations of his responses to people that he does come across with a bit of the 'I am right, and so don't argue with me' attitude. He made all the right noises of saying that he would make himself more approachable and so we will just have to wait and see.

It was a conversation that I needed to have with him, and so thanks, Jo for the opportunity. He did ask, however, that he would be able to tell the team why he is re-opening the Cheyney murder in such a way that he does not come across as a complete fool.

So I agreed with that. He will give you, your due, although Jo, it will be clothed in such a way that it appears that he initiated it. Can you live with that, Jo?'

'Of course, ma'am. I am not about scoring points but getting at the truth.'

'I also told him about Mr. Foley's involvement and he is okay with that. On that subject, can you assure me that he will not publish anything that could compromise our case?'

'Yes, I can. ma'am. Just let us say that it is not in his interests for him to cross me, or the department.'

'Do I read into that what I think that you are saying, Jo?'

'Yes, we are an item, but it's early days. We get on very well, and I know that Chris would not do anything to jeopardise that. We both enjoy the benefits!' laughed Jo.

'Well, good for you, Jo. Thanks for letting me know, as you know any personal liaisons between staff or in this case staff and co-opted persons, if I can call Mr. Foley that, should be disclosed. Once this gets out, however, there will be a few blokes in the department that will have their ardour somewhat dampened.'

'Well, I have always made it clear that I will never date a copper. It is bad enough spending all day discussing policing, crime and punishment without spending the evenings doing that too!'

'But for these red-blooded males, that just heightens the challenge.'

'Well, if I did, it would be our luck that the serg. would put us on opposite shifts and we would never see each other.'

'You are probably right, and talking of sergeants, I have been discussing you with Spence, and we would both like to put you

163

forward for promotion to sergeant.'

'What, is there a vacancy?'

'Well, it is not common knowledge yet, but Sergeant Oliver has handed in his notice. He intends to set up his own security company. He hopes to leave by Christmas and so that would give you three months to complete the Objective Structured Performance Related Examination. You will have completed the required initial training and probationary period by then. What do you think, Jo?'

'I am truly flattered, ma'am. I would very much like to have a crack at it.'

'Well, that's great. I know that Spence likes having you in his team and so he can get the ball rolling for you to get back studying!'

DCI Abbottsford glanced at her watch and said: 'You better get off to the meeting, now, Jo. We will obviously keep in touch, but not a word about Sergeant Oliver, okay?'

'Of course. Thank you, ma'am. Goodbye.'

CHAPTER TWELVE

Jo was last but one to get to the meeting. As she walked in, D.I. Bligh was on the telephone but he looked up and nodded at her. He then completed his call, came up to her and said,

'Oh good to see you. I have just been speaking to Peter and he told me that he cannot join us this afternoon. However, he said that you have his report and can present his findings to the meeting. Is that right, Jo?'

'Yes, sir. He came around to my place on Sunday evening and gave me his findings.'

'Fine, Jo. I will start the meeting and if you could then take over. I am sorry that you felt me to be unapproachable but I do understand. We will have to talk later. Did Abbottsford mention OSPRE to you?'

'Yes, sir, she did.'

'And...?'

'Yes, thank you. I am flattered and really pleased.'

'Well, we think that you are ready for it. I will get all the information for you. I better get started now that Graham has arrived and we are all here.'

'Good afternoon ladies and gentlemen. Unfortunately, we meet again as we now have a third rugby related murder. I am going to stop rostering Jo on at weekends as she keeps getting us all called out!'

As nobody seemed to make a comment, he then quickly added, 'Only kidding and we will hear from Jo shortly.

As a result of this third murder and the similarity to the

other two in terms of the rugby connections, we have reviewed the evidence of the first two murders, and consider that that all three are related. We also believe that Simon Cheyney's death may well be a murder as opposed to my original view of it being a suicide.

This change in thinking has come about as a result of my speaking with our pathologist, Peter, who has re-visited the crime scene of the hanging. This was due to some further evidence that Jo has ascertained.

The confusion is best explained by the fact that the neck injuries that Simon sustained by the hanging of his body from the rugby posts cross-bar, which are commonly known as the hangman's fracture, masked the fact that Simon could have been strangled prior to being suspended from the cross-bar. Also, there are marks on the cross-bar that were not seen during the original crime scene assessment. These are more consistent with dragging the body over the cross-bar rather than the marks that would be caused just by a suicide.

For this reason, Operation Golgotha is now re-opened and we have three murders to solve. Jo, I know that this will bring some relief to Simon's parents and so I wonder if you could go and tell them about this change in our thinking?'

'Yes, of course, sir. I know that they will be relieved because they did not accept that their son was a murderer. I will go after this meeting. Would you like to hear from me now, sir?'

'Yes thanks, Jo. Jo will also give an account of the Pathologist's findings, as Peter is occupied with a sensitive maternal death case.'

Jo walked up to the lectern. 'Sorry to have called you all out again yesterday but Spence will keep rostering me on duty because he thinks that I will die of boredom sitting at home on my own. But I don't mind really, as I do like your company!

Well, for me this all started with a phone call from the duty sergeant at 9.00am yesterday. When he told me that there was a suspicious death at the Whiteley Hotel I immediately thought that it would probably have something to do with rugby, as I knew that the victim, Raymond Salter was hosting his 28th birthday party there, together with a celebration of his being selected to play in the England squad.

The duty sergeant confirmed to me that the victim was the birthday boy and that he was found by a maid who entered his room after he had not responded to a wake-up call. He was found lying on top of the bed dressed only in a bra and panties!

I went straight to the hotel and spoke to the staff and viewed the body. Well, most of you turned up sometime after me and so you know the crime scene layout. There was a bottle of whisky beside the bed which was about a third to a quarter full. From speaking to the hotel manager, who was on bar duty on the Saturday evening, the victim had drunk a lot, and so the question was did he die of alcohol poisoning. This could have been self-administered or was he poisoned by someone?

From my enquiries, I know that as a result of the victim's drunken behaviour, he was taken up to a room. and lain on the bed to sleep it off. The room was paid for by an unknown adult who was one of the guests. He signed the hotel register as Raymond Salter, so we do not know who he was. We will need to try and locate him. As you are aware, the victim was found dressed in female underwear, namely a brassiere and panties. I now know that these belonged to one of the guests at the party who entered the bedroom after the victim had been taken up there. This guest and a female friend put Salter in her underwear in order to photograph him and embarrass him by posting the

167

photos on social media. They confirm that the victim was alive but unconscious when they dressed him. The photos were never posted on social media in view of his death. The reasoning behind this intention to embarrass Salter is unrelated to the murders we are investigating. It relates to a violation that the victim allegedly undertook against one of the women some time ago. These women know me, and they knew that they would be suspects and so they came forward and explained their actions to me yesterday.

The evidence I have gleaned so far shows that they did ply the victim with alcohol in the form of seven pints of Guinness spiked with vodka, but that level of alcohol although sufficient to bring on a complete state of inebriation, was not sufficient to cause death by alcohol poisoning.

Sometime later, some person or persons unknown entered the victim's room and administered a sufficient amount of whisky to bring the alcohol level in the victim's blood to a fatal dose. As well as hearing from these women, I also interviewed another guest who attended the party, and he confirmed the women's account of their actions, the state of the victim at the time he was transported to his room.

When Peter, our pathologist realised that he could not give his report directly to this meeting, he came to my house last evening, and gave me the results of his preliminary findings. He stated that he could find no trace of whisky in the victim's mouth, gullet or stomach and so in his view he did not drink any whisky once he got to his room, despite their being a glass beside his bed that obviously smelt of whisky. In his view, Salter would have been too comatose to drink any whisky, on his own, and according to Peter, he wasn't force fed either. Peter then looked for needle tracks and found that the victim had been injected in the nipples and the penis with whisky. There were traces of whisky in his breast tissue and in the corpora cavernosa and the corpus spongiosum in his penis. Peter estimated that a 20ml needle was used to inject the whisky, which would mean that he was probably injected about ten times. That would be enough to kill him, particularly as injecting alcohol directly into the blood stream is fatally worse than it being absorbed more slowly through the digestive system. The alcohol affects the nerves, and the breathing, which causes disruption to the heartbeat which can stop the heart.

In his judgment, Peter said that the alcohol could not have been self-injected, and there was no sign of any needles. In his view, Raymond Salter was murdered. He did not die by his own hand. As I left the hotel, I was able to retrieve CCTV footage that covers the twenty-four hour period up until the time I asked for them and hopefully will show all the guests arriving and leaving in their vehicles. This footage still has to be viewed. There are reports on my interviews on the evidence table for you to peruse.'

'Thank you Jo,' said D.I. Bligh, 'that is a very thorough account and it is obvious that you did not get much time to yourself yesterday. Sergeant Oliver, may I leave it to you and your team to examine the footage that Jo retrieved. I think we need to list the vehicle numbers and locate their registered owners from the DVLA. We especially need to find out who the man was who booked and paid for the room. I understand that there were about six older men at the party, and that it was one of them who booked the room. Jo, was the hotel manager able to approximate this man's age?'

'Yes, he placed him at around thirty-five or a bit older. He said that he had a bit of a belly on him, black hair, wore glasses and was well dressed in suit and tie.' replied Jo.

'Sergeant, if you locate a driver that fits that description then

169

hopefully the DVLA can get a photo from his photocard to us.'

'I can get the person identified, sir, once I have a photofit,' said Jo.

'Right sir, I will follow that up,' replied Sergeant Oliver.

'Graham, can you take us through your crime scene photos, please?' said D.I. Bligh.

Graham moved up to the lectern and turned to the table beside it where there was a laptop, clicked a few keys and suddenly on the screen appeared a man lying on a bed dressed in red lacy female attire. The inappropriateness of the attire on a male, caused a few sniggers throughout the room.

Graham reported, 'You can see how that picture on social media would have been an embarrassment.' Graham then clicked through the rest of the photos showing the hotel room, the bottle of whisky, key card, and more photos of the victim on the bed. When he had finished and sat down, D.I. Bligh turned to Sergeant Munden, and said, 'Can SOCO add anything else at this stage sergeant?'

'Not much sir, but we can confirm that there were no usable fingerprints in the room, on the bottle of whisky or the glass and so the perpetrator covered his or her tracks well. I think the real work now is to find out who the guests were and what else is on the CCTV footage.'

'Yes, sergeant, I would agree with you. Did you say that there were about one hundred and thirty guests, Jo?'

'Yes, sir, that is what the hotel manager told me.'

'Right, I think that we can adjourn this meeting now, Sergeant Oliver. Perhaps when you have some more relevant information you can let me know and we can continue with this meeting?'

'Yes sir.'

'Jo, could you find out more background information on

Salter's replacement at fly-half, and keep me posted?'

'Yes sir.'

'Has anybody got anything else to add?' asked D.I. Bligh.

'Sir?' Jo spoke up. 'The victim's parents are on a cruise, and they have not been told yet. I think that they are back next Friday.'

'Fine, Jo. I will get one of the liaison officers to handle that. Thanks for reminding me.' At that Spencer picked up his folder made a note and left the meeting room, which everybody took as the signal to leave.

Jo looked at her watch, and deciding that there was still time, she set out to visit the Cheyney's to tell them that the police no longer considered their son to be a murderer or suicide victim. The meeting was quite brief, and the parents were quite relieved. It occurred to Jo that it was a strange situation when parents felt happy about receiving news that their son was no longer considered a murderer but a murder victim. They did ask if Jo could also tell the Christophers.

As she still had time Jo did that after leaving the Cheyney's. She thought that their response was brilliant as they both said that they would go immediately to the Cheyneys to rebuild some bridges. 'We will probably all get horribly smashed, detective,' said Mrs. Christopher.

'Well, just be careful,' said Jo, 'as we don't want you all down the nick for being drunk and disorderly!'

'No chance!' she replied.

Jo said her goodbyes and made her way home. She decided that she would give Chris a ring to discuss with him how they were going to proceed with finding background material on Arthur O'Neill.

CHAPTER THIRTEEN

When Jo entered her home, she noticed that her answerphone was blinking. Her heart quickened as she hoped that it might be Chris. It wasn't. It was her rugby team captain asking her if she could play a game against Fareham Ladies on the forthcoming Saturday. She dialled three to return the call and told her captain that she was available. She knew that Chris would be busy with his rugby watching and game analysis ready for the Monday rugby special feature.

She then rang Chris, related the days events, and when she told him that her bosses wanted her to study for the sergeant exams, he was really thrilled for her. She felt very warm towards him when he said, 'It's only what you deserve, Jo.'

She told Chris that she was playing rugby on Saturday, which was a re-match following a cancellation, and as she suspected, he was too busy to come and watch her play. 'Now, if it was on the Sunday,' he said, 'I could come down for that.'

'Well come down for Sunday, anyway,' said Jo. 'I am sure we can occupy ourselves!' Chris laughed over the phone and agreed, and Jo then asked him, 'How are you getting on with background material on O'Neill?'

'My editor is happy for me to do a background article on him and so I am going to see his parents tomorrow. They are Agatha and Ryan O'Neill, and they live in a village called Terling in Essex. I am going to drive across there tomorrow. It should take about two hours. Obviously, I will let you know what I find out.'

'I wish I could come with you but I am going to have to spend the next few days going through the CCTV footage from the hotel with my sergeant. We hope to make up a list of the guests who were at the party. Actually, Chris, you could help by listing those that you remember were there,' said Jo.

'I have actually been thinking about that, Jo and there are very few that I recognised. I would guess that most of them were from his previous clubs of North Hampshire and Leicester. I have a file on Rugby Football Union Officials and could not recognise any of them who were at the party, and so the six or so adults that I saw, including the one who organised the room for Ray must have a different connection to him than through the England squad. I did not recognise any of the party goers as being English squad members. Probably too soon for him to have established any main contacts.'

'Oh, that's a bit of a bummer, Chris,' said Jo, 'we really need to locate and talk to that guy who paid for the room. Hopefully, we can pick him up from the CCTV.'

'Well, Jo, it is great to hear your voice again, and I will be in touch tomorrow, after I have spoken to the O'Neil's. 'Bye for now', and he rang off.

Jo went into her kitchen to start to prepare some dinner and while doing that she started to think about something different and interesting that they could do together on Sunday. She suddenly remembered getting her 'Stay Local' booklet through the letter box, so she thought she would check out what was on offer in that section of the magazine. As she was flicking through the pages, she suddenly saw something that caught her eye. She stopped, read it and exclaimed out loud: 'The D-Day revival!' She immediately knew that that would be a great outing, as she had attended it previously. It was now an annual event over the second

173

weekend in June, put on by Southwick Village. Southwick played a crucial part in the preparation for the D-Day landings on 6 June 1944, and the Revival turned the village back into a second world war scene with stalls, vehicles, and the memorial flypast. There was still the giant map of 'Operation Overlord' built by the Chad Valley toy company. This was housed in the old Southwick Manor that before, the military took it over, was the home of the Thistlethwaite family who still owned the Southwick Estate. It could only be visited during the revival weekend, so Jo stopped preparing her dinner and fired up her computer to order two tickets for the *Revival* and tour of the map room. Jo knew that this would be different but interesting type of date to have with Chris, and she was really pleased with herself. She decided that she would not tell Chris but keep it as a surprise.

Jo arrived at the police station at her usual time of 8.00am but she had mixed feelings about sitting down all day looking at videos, yet she was positive that something would turn-up that would be a good lead to follow.

After her last telephone conversation with Chris, she was not that hopeful as she was still sure that the murderer had connections with the English rugby squad, and so if Chris was right and all the guests came from North Hampshire or Leicester, then they were probably wasting their time.

She was optimistic, however, that they would be able to identify the man who paid for Ray's room. The team all loaded the images from the memory stick that Jo had got from the hotel and worked through them noting the registration, make, and model of each car that was recorded. They discovered to their dismay that the function room and bar where the party was held had its own entrance, which was not covered by any camera, and so they could not see images of the guests arriving. They would have to rely on the DVLA giving them driver details, that they would then have to manually follow up. It would take three days for the all the information to come from the DVLA.

The only intervention during that time was when Chris rang Jo following his visit to Arthur O'Neill's parents, in Essex. Chris had just said that he had the information regarding Arthur's schooling and university and rugby career, but there was nothing that really helped them any further. He told Jo that he would provide her with the details when they met on the weekend.

Jo took copies of the driver's licence photos of the six older guests so that she could show them to the hotel manager, to try and discover a a more detailed description of the man who paid for the room. She thought that she could also show them to Chris to see if he could identify any of them.

They were just preparing to call it a day, when suddenly an image emerged of a person walking to the hotel towards a door at the far end, away from the car park. Jo thought that it might be a staff member coming on shift and entering the hotel through a staff door but when she saw the time on the recording as 2.30am she thought that was an unusual time for a shift change.

She turned to Sergeant Oliver sitting beside her and said, 'I will discuss this with the hotel manager when I go to show him the pictures of the older guests. I better get off now, Matt, as I have agreed to see him tonight before he goes home.'

'Fine, Jo,' replied the sergeant, 'can you ring me when you find out who the room booker is please, as I will get in touch with him and hopefully see him tomorrow?'

'Of course, Matt.'

Jo was a bit disappointed that she could not attend that interview as she would like to be there to see how the man

175

justified not signing the hotel register in his own name. Just as she was about to leave, Matt called out to her, 'Jo, do you still have the page from the hotel register showing the signature of Raymond Salter that I can show to this chap, please?'

'Yes, I will get it for you now, and then I am off to the Whiteley Hotel,' she said picking up the laptop that she had been viewing the images on.

Lionel Rafferty was in reception when Jo arrived, and he took her into an adjacent office. Jo took out the file of photos and handing them to the manager she said, 'Thank you sir, for seeing me. I would be grateful if you could look at these and tell me which one paid for the victim's room last Saturday evening. I am sorry that they are not noticeably clear, but they are from the DVLA.'

The manager sifted through them and pulled out the third one in the pile. 'That's the man. I am certain of it, detective constable.'

Jo took the photo and turned it over to read the name. 'Thank you, sir. That is extremely helpful. Acting on information from the DVLA, we believe that his name is Keith Brown. My colleague will interview him tomorrow and hopefully that will throw more light on the identity of the murderer. There is just one other thing, if you do not mind sir, we also picked up this image.'

Jo opened her laptop, and soon the image of the person walking to the end of the building was revealed. Jo showed it to the manager. 'Would this be a staff member entering a staff entrance, sir?' she asked.

'No, that is more likely to be a guest returning to the hotel late. That door is an after hours guest entrance. There is no CCTV covering that entrance, and I cannot pick up who it was from this image.'

'Is there any other way that we could ascertain who that is?

Perhaps it is the murderer entering the hotel to go up to Ray's room?' Jo said hopefully.

'Yes, of course,' splurted out the manager. 'That is a room key-card entrance. I should be able to track back through the computer to see which room key card was used to open the door at that time. Can you give me five minutes? Pop into the bar and get a drink, on the house, of course. I will come and see you in the bar.'

True to his word, the manager came back into the bar swiftly and said the door lock was activated by a guest in room five, our deluxe suite. It is a man by the name of Frank O'Glynn. He was here for the Saturday night only, and to the best of my knowledge he was not associated with the birthday party. He must have been out all evening, as I do not remember him being around on the Saturday night. I have also checked the table reservations for the Saturday evening dinner, and he was not listed. He must have just checked in and left and then returned at 2:30am. Sorry, I cannot be more helpful.'

'On the contrary, sir, you have been extremely helpful. Tell me, may I presume that room five is adjacent to room six, Salter's room?'

'Well, yes, it is.'

'Is there a connecting door between those two rooms, please?'

'Yes, in fact all those rooms have them. It is great for wedding parties as all the guests can go into all the rooms.'

'Is it possible,' Jo continued, 'that the door on the room six side could have been left unlocked?'

'Well staff are meant to leave them locked when they make up a room, but it is possible, I suppose.'

'Thank you. We can now follow up both Mr. O'Glynn and the

mysterious Mr Brown, and I will check if any of our team tried the connecting door to see if it was unlocked?' said Jo. 'Thank you for the drink as well, sir. This hotel looks really nice, I might just come here with a friend, when this case is all over.'

'Yes, please do. I guarantee that you will both be well looked after. Well, detective, is there anything else?'

'No, sir. That's all. I will be in touch when we know a bit more. Goodbye and thank you.'

Once, back in her car, Jo rang Matthew Oliver and told him the identity of the man who booked the victim's room.

'I will be very interested in the results of your interview, Matt.' she said.

'Thanks Jo. Yes, I will let you know as soon as I am back tomorrow. Good night.'

'Night, Matt.'

Jo spent the Friday with Detective Inspector Bligh recapping over the case but mostly spending time on Jo's forthcoming training to pass her promotion exams to become a sergeant.

She was looking forward to the weekend, to playing rugby on the Saturday, and being with Chris on the Sunday.

Sergeant Oliver interrupted them to recount his interview with Keith Brown. 'I'm afraid he is not our murderer and is not attached to rugby in any way. It turns out that he is the accountant with the victim's father's Garden Centre, and he had come to the party at the request of Raymond's father to keep an eye on Raymond, as his Dad knows what he is capable of when he gets a serious amount of drink in him.

Apparently, Raymond hated how his father tried to keep tabs on him and that is why he signed the register with Raymond's name, as he thought when Raymond sobered up the next morning he would want to know who put him to bed, so to speak, and he did not want Raymond to realise that it was further his father's request, in effect. Matthew ended his account by saying, 'I could not find any evidence of any wrong-doing, but at least that is another lead closed.'

'Thank you Matt, another piece of the jigsaw in place,' said D.I. Bligh.

Matt then just happened to look down at Jo's notes and realised that she had put down information regarding promotion. He turned to her and said: 'Jo, are you going for promotion? Well, you deserve it. In fact, you can have my job, if you like! I'm going to go out on my own.'

He must have seen a funny look on Spencer's face, as he quickly added, 'Oh sorry, sir, have I said something out of order?'

'No, not really, Matt, but Jo has been told that you are resigning and we would like to put her forward for promotion.'

'Quite right too, sir, if I may say so, and Jo if I can be of any help in your studies, let me know. I still have my own notes from my OSPRE if you would like them.'

'I really appreciate that, Matt. Thank you, I may just take you up on that.'

'Yes, please do,' and he left the office.

'That was a bit of a surprise, sir,' said Jo. 'We have not really been bosom buddies, but we worked well together over the CCTV tapes this week.'

'Yes, Jo. Matt is a bit of a complicated fellow, and often I just do not know what he is thinking. Although I wish him well in his new venture. I keep thinking that when I walk into his office, he will be working on his business plan for his new venture, rather than clearing up his in-tray. Wouldn't blame him, really, as once you decide to leave a job, your enthusiasm and commitment goes out the window.

179

Well, we are not much further on, so let us hope that next week brings us the breakthrough we need as the All Black game is now only a month away, isn't it?

'Oh, a bit later, sir as the Autumn Internationals are in October and November. Saturday 10th November is the All Blacks match at Twickenham.'

'Well, I am sure we will have this all wrapped up by then. A good target to aim for.'

'Exactly, sir. Thank you for today and enjoy your weekend.'

It had been some time since Jo had visited the Fareham Rugby Club and as she drove past the Royal Mail postal centre to the ground, she remembered being called out with Spencer to a drunken brawl about a year ago. Two or three patrons just had had too much to drink, and one of them assaulted another whom he thought was flirting with his wife. It was really just a matter of too much alcohol being served to patrons who were already too drunk. Spence really laid into the bar manager, telling him it was his duty to ensure his staff did not serve alcohol to drunk patrons. The bar manager's excuse was that the patrons were the club executives. Spence made it clear that their status was irrelevant. He also made it plain that if the police were called out again, then he would personally refuse a continuation of the liquor license to the club. The bar manager knew that that would be very costly to the club in lost income, and to date there had been no more incidents. Jo thought that it would be good to observe how the bar was being managed today.

As usual, Jo enjoyed her game, again scoring a try. She wished that Chris had been there to see it, but she did not realise it then, but she did have an admirer.

Once, Jo had changed and was in the bar for the after match

function, she noticed Michael Potter standing somewhat aloof towards the end of the room. She went over to him and said: 'Hi Michael, have you been playing today?'

'No Miss. I actually came to see you. I saw on the club fixtures list that our women's division were playing North Hampshire, so I presumed that you would be here. I watched you, Miss, and you played very well. Yours was a great try. North Hampshire deserved to win.'

'Thank you, Michael. How is the rugby going for you? I presume your police caution condition is now terminated so are you still attending the club?'

'Oh, yes Miss. I really love it. I play for the under 15s and our games are a lot of fun. The coach tells me that I am quite good, too. I scored two tries last week, and our team is top of the competition.'

'What position do you play at, Michael?'

'I am fly-half. Number ten jersey. I have discovered that I am quite a good kicker too. That manager from *Freshcos* has been coaching me in kicking. He has been particularly good to me, Miss, and he always brings me something to take home to Mum. I have you to thank for all of this, and I am incredibly grateful.'

'Well, that's really good, but don't look upon shoplifting or theft as getting on in life, even if it has done you no harm! Are you still with the *Barnies*?'

'Oh, no, they think rugby is for toffs and puffs. They are into football, but that is not for me. I just hang around with my rugby mates now.'

'That is great, Michael it is good to see you and to know that things are going well for you.'

'Thank you, Miss, I really came down here today to see you, as I have something to tell you.'

'Okay, Michael. What do you want to tell me?'

'It's about those three fly-halves who were murdered.' Jo, suddenly became very interested, and said,

'What about them?'

'Well, I overheard some of the guys talking in the bar, last Sunday. Our firsts were playing a team from London Irish, and one of the London Irish supporters said that O'Neill, you know the guy who has just been selected to replace Salter, he said that O'Neill was meant to have been selected before Salter. That one of the selectors had been paid to ensure that O'Neill was selected, but he could not swing the vote. Apparently, the guy who paid him was really angry. According to this guy at the bar, O'Neill is adopted, and his real father wanted him to be selected over Salter. I just thought, Miss, that somebody from the police should know this, and I thought of you.'

'Michael, you have done well to tell me. Yes, I know the case very well, as I was the detective that was first on the scene when Josh Christopher was murdered. What you have told me is particularly important and very helpful. I do not want to alarm you, Michael, but do not tell anyone else this. It is very sensitive information, and when people have committed murder, they will do anything and everything to keep it hushed up.

If you talk to the wrong people, then you put yourself in danger, so it is best not to talk to anyone, except me of course. Here is my card, with my mobile number. You can ring me at any time. If anyone asks you what we are talking about now, just say that I was asking you how you were getting on since I introduced you to this club. I would like to see you play some time, so let me know when there is a suitable game.'

'Thank you, Miss. I understand what you are saying. I can keep secrets. I'll let you know when our team are playing North

Hampshire, and you can see Fareham beating them in return for you beating Fareham today,' Michael said with a wide grin across his face. 'Goodbye Miss.'

'Goodbye Michael and thank you,' she whispered.

My God thought Jo. It is now starting to make sense. We will now crack this case. All we have to do is find out who O'Neill's biological father is. What a heinous way to get your son selected for a rugby squad by killing all the opposition. Jo couldn't wait to tell Chris so they can work out a plan together. Jo always thought it a strange factor that resolving one criminal case can lead to the solving of another. This latest piece of information only came to her because of her handling of the *Freshcos* shoplifting case. This was true policing.

Probably, because she had been looking at CCTV footage all week, Jo went up to the bar manager whom she remembered from the call-out the previous year and asked him: 'Hi, I'm Detective Constable Jo Fletcher, do you happen to have CCTV that covers this area?'

'Yes, I remember you detective, your boss gave me a right bollocking, last year! Yes, we do have CCTV. What date are you looking for?'

'Last Saturday.'

'No, it will be re-recorded over now. It only lasts two days for staff to view it if there has been an incident. What were you after, as I was here last Saturday? I don't remember any incidents.'

'No, it wasn't an incident, apparently a group of your patrons from a visiting team were talking about the current murder investigation relating to the English fly-halves that we are investigating and I wondered who they were, as they may have some valuable information.'

'All I can say is that they were London Irish supporters.'

183

'Oh well, thank you anyway,' said Jo, 'I'll follow it up with them.'

Jo stayed at the club for another hour, talking with her teammates, especially Anne and Sarah, reassuring them that they were not in any trouble after their escapade at the birthday party.

Remembering that Spencer was on duty for the weekend she decided to call in at the police station to see if he was there and leave a message regarding O'Neil being adopted.

As it happened, D.I. Bligh was in his office. Jo knocked and went in. 'Hello, Jo, I didn't expect to see you until Monday. I am just getting some paperwork out of the way. My wife and the kids are at a relly's birthday party, and I cannot stand her relatives! Sometimes being a copper on call can be a blessing,' he said with a sly grin.

'I just heard some news that hopefully will put us on the right path. You remember that youth, Michael Potter for whom we organised a caution to attend the rugby club, well, he sought me out this afternoon as he had overheard in the club bar that not only was O'Neill adopted but one of the rugby selectors had been paid to try and get him selected for the English squad at the time they selected Salter. Chris had told us that there had been a selector holding out for O'Neill, but we did not know that he had been paid. We need to find out who his biological father is as he may be our murder suspect. I was wondering if I could have permission to interview the O'Neill parents on Monday and see what more information I can glean? As you know, Chris has spoken with them, but this adoption did not arise.'

'Yes, of course, Jo. Will you be wanting a car?'

'No, sir, I think I will go by train and taxi if I need to.'

'Yes, I am happy to approve both.' At that he rang down to the duty sergeant and said, 'Can you please prepare a travel warrant for Detective Constable Fletcher to travel by train to?'He looked up.

'Hatfield Peverell, sir, in Essex, is the closest station to Terling.

'Hatfield Peverell in Essex. She will pick it up in a few minutes. Thank you, Sergeant.'

'Thank you, sir,' said Jo, as she left the office.

As she drove home, she tried to remember what she had in the cupboards for tea and thought she had enough in stock to choose from. She had hardly got her key in the front door, when it suddenly opened, and Chris was standing in the doorway with a large grin on his face and a glass of red in his hand. 'Surprise!' he said, and he then handed Jo a glass of wine. 'I thought I may as well write my article on the train and email it to my editor rather than do it at my flat.'

'I am really glad you did,' said Jo as she flung her arms around him and gave him a big hug.

Well, I have got some news for you, but first I must see what we have got for dinner.'

'No need, I have already reserved a table for us at Antonio's in Port Milton. My treat.'

'That's great, Chris. What time?'

He looked at his watch: 'a couple of hours.'

'Right, I will tell you my news and then I must get ready. Let's get a taxi, so we can both drink. '

'Already booked.'

They sat down on the couch and Jo related the events of yesterday evening at the Whiteley hotel and the conversation at the Fareham Rugby Club. Chris listened appreciatively and when Jo mentioned the adoption, he exclaimed, 'Of course, that is why they were a bit reticent talking about their son's rugby

185

heritage. Their whole family are well into football. Big Arsenal fans. I had asked the Dad that if he were faced with watching his son playing in an English Rugby International or an Arsenal cup final, on television, which one would he watch and he said that without doubt it would be the football. So, Arthur is not their son, so perhaps the biological Dad is the rugby player. We need to find out who he is.'

'Exactly, and Spence has authorised me to go to Terling and visit the parents on Monday. I am taking the train.'

'I will be on tenterhooks waiting to find out who the real father is. The only bit that I really found out about O'Neill is that he attended Harlow College for his A levels, and he studied Sports Sciences gaining an Extended Diploma,' said Chris.

'He obviously had a career in sport in mind from an early age. I noted that one of his subjects was sports anatomy and physiology together with sports nutrition. It occurred to me that he may know a bit about alcohol poisoning, but I reasoned that if he was at the hotel, he would have joined the party as it was an open invitation. O'Neill then played rugby for the Harlow Rugby Club, in their first fifteen, until he was spotted and invited to join London Irish. I wonder if his Irish sounding surname helped?' sniggered Chris.

'I must admit,' said Jo, 'that I have not really considered him to be our murder suspect, mainly because he did not need to kill Salter as he would be playing for England anyway albeit as a substitute, but he had every incentive and opportunity to get the top job. I wonder, Chris, whether there is any mileage in trying to find out who the supporters are that were at Fareham Rugby Club last week from London Irish?' asked Jo.

'That may be a bit difficult, without disclosing our hand, which could send the killer into hiding. Perhaps we should wait until we find out who Arthur's real Dad is and take it from there.'

'Yes, I think that you are right.'

'Oh, Chris, I have got some photos for you to look at,' said Jo as she opened her bag and pulled out the six photos of the adult birthday party go-ers. Do you recognise any of them?'

'These are the guests at Ray's party, aren't they? Where did you get them?'

'From DVLA when we sent them the registration numbers of the vehicles that were captured on the CCTV.'

'I only recognise that one, Jo. He is the guy who booked and paid for the hotel room and took Ray up to bed.'

'Yes. We have found that out ourselves, and my sergeant has already interviewed him. It turns out that he is an employee of Ray's father who asked by him to keep an eye on his son.'

'Makes sense, I suppose. He'll be gutted that he let his boss down. Well, he is the only one I recognise. None of the others are RFU Officials or anything to do with the English squad.'

'Yes, that is what we thought. They are probably from either the North Hampshire or Leicester clubs wanting a free night out. We are not following any of them up unless further evidence points to us in their direction.

There is one other image that we saw. Jo opened her laptop, and soon the image of the person walking to the end of the building was revealed. She showed it to Chris. The hotel manager said that it would not be a staff member entering a staff entrance, but a guest returning to the hotel late. The door the person was walking towards was the after hours guest entrance. There is no CCTV covering that entrance, and we could not pick up who it was from the image. The manager then said that the door had a key-card entrance, so he was able to track back through the computer to see which room key card was used to open the door at that time. The door lock was activated by a guest in room five. It was a man by the name of Frank O'Glynn. He was there for the Saturday night only, and to the best of the manager's knowledge he was not associated with the birthday party and was out all evening. He did not dine at the hotel either. We are now concentrating on Arthur's biological parentage.'

'Well Jo you get off upstairs and get ready.'

'Antonio's, Eh? I feel a lasagne and a tiramisu coming on washed down with a good rich red. Peroni to start of course. Be down in a jiffy.'

'I will still be here when you come down. What are we doing on Sunday?'

'It's a surprise!

Chapter Fourteen

They both woke up at about the same time on the Sunday. For Jo, the whole evening had just reinforced for her that she and Chris were right for each other. Again, Chris asked her about meeting his parents, and this time Jo agreed and they decided that Jo would travel to London the following Friday and Chris would meet her at Waterloo and they would get the train to Twickenham.

After breakfast, Chris asked, 'What's this surprise?'

'You'll soon find out. Get your coat as we are going for a short drive.'

It was only as they were driving into the designated field for public parking that Chris saw the bunting and realised that they were going to some type of festival. It was, in fact, the annual Southwick D-Day re-enactment with a ride on a 1940's bus to the map room in Southwick House, a talk on the decision by General Eisenhower to launch the greatest invasion ever held with the simple phrase: 'OK Let's go!' and a walk up the closed off main street with second world war vehicles, music, persons in uniform and the hog roast accompanied with a pint of Liberation brewed in nearby Wickham and obtainable in the local pub and the brewery museum.

The day was a great success, topped off with the Spitfire memorial flypast. Chris just said, 'Jo, I had no idea that this village and its annual pageantry existed. Thank you very much. It has been a marvellous day.'

Jo was happy that he was pleased, because it was becoming obvious that they both liked the same things.

Monday saw them on the train together going to Waterloo, with Chris going to his newspaper offices and Jo changing trains to go to Hatfield Peverell and then on to Terling by taxi.

Agatha O'Neill was very quick to open her door, when Jo knocked, and she immediately asked if Arthur was in trouble as she did not know what Jo wanted to speak to her about, as Jo had thought it best not to say anything over the phone, so that she could not prepare a deceptive or obstructive response.

After Jo explained that they were investigating the murder of three fly-halves, the position that her son now occupied, Mrs. O'Neill seemed to be understanding and willing to help. When Jo asked, 'Why did you not tell Chris Foley when he visited you last week that Arthur was adopted?' She looked stunned, and stammered out, 'How did you know?'

'We were told by some London Irish club members.'

'Well, I do not know how anybody knows, as we have not even told Arthur yet.'

'Why not?' asked Jo.

'Well, we could never find the right time, and we knew that he would then start asking questions and we would not have been able to answer them.'

'How do you mean you could not answer his questions, please, Mrs. O'Neill?'

Jo's heart sank, when she replied, Well, we do not know anything about his biological parents. We were never told. It was all handled by the adoption agency, and everything was kept secret. We presumed that there was some problem, but we were not told. We were just thrilled to get a baby, as up until then we thought that that would never happen.'

190

'Can you tell me anything about the adoption agency please?' asked Jo.

'Yes, it was a Catholic Adoption Agency in London that specialised in adopting Irish babies, because as you know there is no possibility of abortion in Ireland, although that may change now that the referendum has been passed. I remember that the social worker's name was Arlene O'Hanlon, although she may have retired by now, but she was quite young back then. I think that the agency was called 'Caring for Catholics,' or some such name.'

'Thank you for that. That is extremely helpful information. Are you going to tell Arthur?'

'Well, yes. We know that we have to, but we do not know how to go about it.'

'I suggest that you ring your local social services, as they should provide you with a social worker who could help and support you as you tell him. Your local catholic priest may also be of assistance.'

'Thank you, I will talk it over with my husband. Is there anything else, detective?'

'No, that is all for now. Thank you for seeing me. Goodbye, Mrs. O'Neill.

'Goodbye Detective.'

Jo rang for a taxi, and while she was waiting, she rang Spencer and briefed him on her visit to Mrs. O'Neill.

'I'm on my way back to London, sir, should I try and locate this adoption agency or hopefully the social worker Arlene O'Hanlon and get some more usable information?'

'Yes, Jo, give it a go, but they may try and block you under Data Protection, and if they do use the Court Order, thirty coppers ruse.'

'Right, Sir. I will let you know how I get on.'

A quick google search showed Jo that the agency still existed, so she noted the address and realised that it was in walking distance from Waterloo station. She could be there by lunchtime.

Thinking that it would be better not to be on her own, Jo rang Chris and they agreed to meet outside the agency. It was an office over an Indian Restaurant which was fortunately closed at that time. Jo gained entry via the intercom and was pleased that Arlene O'Hanlon still worked there as the social worker. So as to not reveal Chris's true occupation, Jo started with, 'Thank you for seeing us. My name is Detective Constable Jo Fletcher, and this is my colleague, Chris Foley. We are investigating a series of three murders, and I believe that you have some information that could help us. This is especially important as the information that you have may prevent a fourth murder.'

'If you are wanting personal information about adoptions, then I am sorry, detective, but the information here is all highly confidential, and protected under Data Protection legislation.'

'Yes, I appreciate, that Mrs. O'Hanlon, but...'

'It's Miss, detective.'

'Oh, my apologies, Miss O'Hanlon. I must stress that we do not come here lightly. We have evidence to believe that the life of one of the babies that you took in, who is now 28 years old, is in danger. We have spoken to this person's mother and she gave us your name, but she could not tell us the information that we require.'

'What specifically do you want to know, detective?'

'We need to know the name of the biological parents of Arthur O'Neill, an Irish boy adopted by Agatha and Ryan O'Neill about 28 years ago.'

'Detective, as I said before, I cannot reveal that or any other personal information.'

'Miss O'Hanlon. We can do this either the easy way or the hard way.'

'What do you mean?'

'Well, my chief is at this moment at the Portsmouth Crown Court, together with the Crown Prosecutor, ready to request a search warrant of these premises in order to find out the information that we require. I just need to send him a text and within half an hour, about thirty coppers from the Met will park their police cars outside and their inspector will serve the warrant on you and his team will search every file until we find the O'Neill file and the relevant adoption papers.

Now, these coppers are only human, but they are well trained, and have brilliant memories. As they search for the information that we require, they will no doubt remember information that may be useful to them in the future, or they may even uncover evidence of criminal activity such as underage sex producing unwanted babies that you have adopted out, and they would have to act on that. As you will already know, they are incredibly good at prosecuting historical sex offences. That's the hard way.

Now, the easy way, is for you to get the file that we need, place it on your desk, and then go and have some lunch. When you return, in say about half an hour, we will be gone, and the file will be on your desk, untouched. Now, Miss O'Neill, do I send the text?'

Jo glanced across at Chris, and he was desperately trying to avoid her gaze, but she could see a certain amazement on his face. Miss O'Hanlon did not speak. She just got up, went to a filing cabinet, one of several that ran the whole length of the side wall of the office and took out a brown manilla file. She placed it on her desk and turned to Jo with an angry look and said, 'I am just going to lunch. I will be back in half an hour.'

She then got up, put on a coat, stood as tall as she could and walked out of the office, pulling the door hard behind her. Jo immediately picked up the file, opened it and turned to Chris and said, 'Can you see if that photocopier is on, please Chris?'

Jo took two pages out of the file and handed them to Chris who photocopied them, and gave them back to Jo to return to the file. Within minutes, they were out of the office and walking away towards the station.

'Let's have a coffee,' she said, 'and I will update Spence.'

'Jo, you were amazing in there. So confident. I did not think that you would get the information. Where did you come up with the 30 coppers ruse?'

'Oh, it's a bit of psychology. People who are hiding dirty secrets do not want a reputation of having police around and the chance that a reporter might be present and able to photograph all the police cars turning up outside and a load of coppers storming through the office would not be good for business, and I knew that she would not take that chance.

Adoption agencies always have dirty secrets, as a lot of the babies are the result of underage sex, or inappropriate relationships, and so the appearance at least of utter confidentiality is essential for their business to survive.'

'Jo, I'm impressed. The image of 30 coppers rifling through files and telling their colleagues what they were finding, nearly sent me into hysterics.'

'Yes, I saw that you were trying to suppress some sort of outburst.'

There was only the birth mother's details on the original

birth certificate in the file. The address of the mother was in Ennistymon County Clare, Ireland. There were no details about the birth father.

Jo turned to Chris and pointing to the papers, said, 'We will have to talk to the mother who is in Ireland. I presume that Spencer will want to do that, as he always likes the trips away. He prefers to go himself rather than rely on the local police to do his work for him. I will talk to him about it tomorrow and let you know. Now, I'd better get a train back to Fareham.'

They walked together to Waterloo, and Chris waited with Jo until her train was due to depart and then he took his train to Twickenham.

The following day, Spencer somewhat surprised Jo, after she recounted her day's work by saying that he thought that they should both go to Ireland to interview the birth mother. Jo was given the task of organising the flights and transport and Spencer said that he would clear it with Chief Abbottsford and notify the Garda, the Irish police as a courtesy.

After a bit of website searching, Jo found that Eleanor Pickford's home in Ireland in Ennistymon, County Clare was close to the Atlantic Ocean and not far from Galway Bay. It was around twenty-three miles from Shannon Airport, and so she booked two tickets from Southampton for the Friday.

On the Thursday before leaving for home, she called into Spencer's office to find that he was on the telephone. He motioned for her to sit while he finished the call. On putting the phone down, he turned to her and said: 'That was Chief Constable Emily James. She has scheduled a meeting of all senior detective staff for tomorrow in Winchester, about some suspected moped robbers coming into the area from London.

It is a three line whip and so I won't be coming with you

tomorrow. However, I do not want you going on your own, and I know that Sergeant Oliver is tied up with interviews tomorrow, and so can you suggest someone, Jo?'

'I could see if Chris is free, if that is suitable, Sir?'

'Of course. Yes, that would be fine. His rugby knowledge may come in useful. You would have to notify the airline of the change of name and don't forget your passports, as it is not the UK you are going to.'

'Thank you Sir. I will let you know about Chris.'

Jo could hardly wait to get home and ring Chris. Hopefully, he will come up tonight, she thought and she started to ponder on a good dinner for them both.

The flight to Shannon was uneventful, and it only took them about half an hour to drive to Ennistymon in an Opel Corsa rental car. They decided to go straight to Eleanor Pickford's house and hope that she was in. It would be an unannounced visit as Jo and Spencer decided that it would be better that way, rather than give her any warning.

They arrived at Ennistymon and found the satnav had taken them to St Andrew's Church, a stone Church of Ireland building.

Chris somewhat surprised Jo when he said, 'Jo, I really think that you should talk to this lady without my being present. I think that it will be less threatening and so more revealing to be just the two of you.'

'Yes, you are probably right. Ah, that's her house, there,' said Jo, pointing out a two storey cream bungalow with a large porch and set back from the road. There was parking right outside.

'You go and have a look round the church and I will meet you there.'

Jo knocked on the door, and after a short while, a lady in her mid-forties, with long auburn hair opened the door. 'She was probably very pretty in her youth,' thought Jo.

'Yes, How can I help you?'

'Is it Eleanor Pickford?' asked Jo.

'I'm Mrs. O'Malley now, but yes I was Pickford once. Seems a long time ago now.'

Jo introduced herself and said, 'I've come from Fareham in Hampshire and we believe that you can help us in a murder case that we are investigating.'

'Murder, Glory be to The Father. How can I help you?' Her Irish accent was strong but unaffected.

'I think that I better come in, as what we need to talk about is a sensitive matter.'

'Oh, come in then. Would you like a drink of something?'

'Oh, no thanks,' replied Jo, 'I will not trouble you for long.' When they were seated, Jo started, in her quiet pensive way.

'Mrs. O'Malley, we know that about thirty years ago, you gave birth to a son and had him adopted.'

Jo paused, to wait for her reaction. There was a delay and then she said, 'Yes, I cannot deny that and not a day goes by that I don't think of him. I have tried to trace him, you know, but the adoption agencies will not help you and my local priest thinks I should just let things be.'

Suddenly, her face lit up, 'Have you traced him? Oh, please say that you have.'

Jo replied, 'Yes, we do know who he is, but what we need to know is who his biological father is please?'

'Oh, my God. I cannot tell you that, as we promised that we would never reveal that. We were both minors at the time, and we could go to prison, even now.'

'Even though I am an English policewoman, I am not

interested in historic sex offences. We are more interested in finding your son's father, to ensure that your son's life is not in danger. There have been three murders since Easter, and we do not want your son to be the fourth. I know that this is a bit unorthodox, Mrs. O'Malley, but can we do a deal? If I tell you your son's adoptive name and where you can locate him would you tell us his father's name and I will ensure that there are no recriminations resulting from your illicit sex thirty years ago.'

At that, Eileen O'Malley began to cry.

'I suppose so,' she said between tears.

'Well we have traced your son. Mrs. O'Malley, I know that this is a shock for you. My coming out of the blue to rake up long buried memories of a bygone age.'

'Oh, but they were happy times, then,' she said, 'until I found out that I was pregnant. Then I was cast aside. I ended up in a convent, had the child and only had a glimpse of him when he was whisked away to a couple I never saw or knew. I do not even know his name as I never got the chance to name him.'

'Well, his name is now Arthur O'Neill. He was adopted by Agatha and Ryan O'Neill who are from Ireland originally but now live in a little picturesque village in Essex, near Chelmsford called Terling. Your son is a very keen sportsman, Mrs. O'Malley, and he has recently been selected to play for the English Rugby Squad. They will be playing the All Blacks in November, and no doubt soon, he will be playing for England against Ireland.'

Jo then drew out a photo. and showed it to Mrs. O'Malley and said, 'This is your son dressed in the English rugby team kit, a friend took this photo two weeks ago.'

'Oh my God,' she said, taking the photo from Jo. She looked at the photo, kissed it, and then held it to her heart, and burst into tears.

'This is an answer to all my prayers. Thank you so very much. His father was a good rugby player, you know. I knew him from when we were ten, and by fifteen, we were stepping out together. I used to watch him play rugby for his school first fifteen each Saturday, and afterwards we would go for walks and usually buy fish and chips to eat in a park or on the beach.'

Eileen O'Malley suddenly seemed to have drifted away into the past, and Jo decided to leave her be for the moment.

She soon returned and said, 'We were sitting on Lahinch beach one Saturday afternoon, and after a while we started cuddling. We were both virgins at that time and very naive. Being Catholics, nobody talked about sex and although I had started my periods, I did not know anything about men and babies.

Frank made out that he was just as ignorant as me, but I think he knew a lot more than he was letting on, because he was telling me what boys and girls who are going out together could do with each other and because he paid me a lot of attention and I enjoyed being with him, one thing led to another and suddenly I was pregnant.

The local priest became involved and we were forbidden to see each other again and we never did. I was heartbroken and then I was sent to a convent for unmarried mothers. The nuns were quite good to me, as I was only fifteen then, and as I said as soon as I had had my baby, he was taken away.'

'Jo asked, 'What was Frank's last name, Mrs. O'Malley?'

'O'Glynn. Frank O'Glynn. He would be about forty-three now, the same age as myself. I heard that he had gone to England, so as to avoid the Garda, here, but I do not know anything more.

I met Mr. O'Malley, we married and have four children. He knows about my having a son, but it did not seem to bother him.'

The name O'Glynn triggered something in Jo's memory, but she could not place it. Perhaps a photo might help, she thought.

'Would you have a photo of Frank, please?' asked Jo.

'Yes, I do tucked away somewhere but he was only fifteen in the photo. I'll get it.'

She left the room and Jo could hear her climbing up the stairs. Jo thought this is a typical but sad Irish story. Catholics kept in ignorance. Contraception a sin. Pregnant girls told that they are sinners and hidden away in convents. Babies taken away and adopted as retribution for the sin of lust.

Steady on, Jo, she thought we are talking nearly fifty years ago. Things are more enlightened now, and with the abortion referendum, there will be a lot more choices for couples.

Unfortunately the name Frank O'Glynn didn't ring any bells for her. There was no RFU official by that name. It seems that I may be on a wild goose chase, unless he changed his name when he came to England. The photo might help, but it will be thirty years old.

Mrs. O'Malley returned with a photo and handed it to Jo.

'My, he was a handsome man. I imagine that you were very pretty too. You would have made a striking couple. May I copy this photo onto my phone, please?'

'Yes, of course. I cannot give it to you as it is the only photo that I have of Frank.'

Jo copied the photo and handed it back. They talked on for a bit, and she undertook to contact Arthur's parents and give them Eileen's contact details so that he could write to her, if he wanted to, after his parents had disclosed his adopted status.

On impulse, Jo turned to Mrs. O'Malley and asked, 'Is there anything more that you can tell us about Frank, please, any hobbies apart from his rugby?'

'Hobbies, ah yes. There was one. He was extremely interested in sailing. He belonged to the local sailing club and often said to me, 'One day, I will have a yacht, and we can sail around the world.' My getting pregnant put paid to that, though didn't it?'

Jo thought that she was going to cry again, and so she put her arm around her.

Jo suddenly remembered that something had sparked in her head when she had first seen Josh tied to the cross. Yes! she thought, the knots used on the cross were sailing knots, specifically the ones used by sailors to secure the fenders to the side of the boat. This means that O'Glynn could very well be the murderer and possibly now does own a yacht. Worth investigating, she thought.

When she said their farewell, caught up with Chris at the church and then drove to the Falls Hotel where they were staying overnight before getting the flight back in the morning direct to Gatwick so that Chris could go to the rugby game he was reporting on. They would meet up later and both go and stay with Chris's parents.

Once in the hotel, Jo emailed the photo of Frank to Graham, the forensic photographer with a request that he age it by thirty years. Jo then remembered the nagging thought that she had had triggered in her memory when the name O'Glynn was mentioned.

She suddenly grabbed her bag, took out the 'Operation Golgotha' file and looked through her notes. She looked up and yelled, 'I've got it! Frank O'Glynn. That is the name the hotel manager gave me of the image in the CCTV footage of the man walking towards the guest entrance of the hotel at 2.30 on the Sunday morning. He must be the murderer. His room was adjacent to Salter's and there is a connecting door. Why would he

201

give his real name? That is a slip up on his part. Every murderer slips up somewhere along the line, and this is his first slip-up that I am aware of. As soon as we can work out who he is calling himself now, we have got him.'

Then Jo paused for a moment, and said, 'My God, I have just worked out who he is. She took a piece of paper from her file and wrote down a name. She turned to Chris and said, 'I bet it's him, but I am not going to show you until we see what Graham sends us.'

It was not long before the e-fit image came back. Jo recognised it, and knew that she had been right, but she did not say anything but showed it to Chris, who exclaimed, 'Oh my God. I know who that is. He is very much involved in the RFU. Yes, it all makes sense now. I would put money on his being our murderer. Jo, this is dynamite. Once this gets out, all hell will break loose. I strongly suggest that you reveal this to no-one until all the evidence is gathered to put him away. In the meantime, call him Mr. X or just suspect.'

'Is this who you mean?' said Jo, showing Chris the name that she had written on the piece of paper.

'Yes, how did you work it out?'

'I'll tell you after we arrest him,' Jo teased.

'Yes Chris, we cannot reveal this to anyone. I will talk to Spence when I get back. We now need to get all the evidence and link it to Mr. X and put this whole case together to present to the Crown Prosecution Service. If the name gets out, he will scarper. I will get Spence to keep it from all the team as well just to be sure.'

CHAPTER FIFTEEN

After Jo had updated D.I. Bligh with the information that they had found out in Ireland, he immediately agreed that the suspect's name be kept confidential right up until his arrest. Spence then turned to Jo and said: 'Jo, you have done exceedingly well in solving this series of murders. You now need to prepare a brief for the Crown Prosecution Solicitor that outlines all the evidence and links it to our suspect. I have found that it is better to link the evidence to each victim, and to each witness, and then to the suspect, rather than outline the evidence in chronological order. This will enable the prosecuting barrister to question witnesses about all their evidence and for the police who question the suspect to cover all the ground in a logical sequence. This piece of work is essential to get the prosecution service to authorise the arrest of the suspect. It will probably take you some time. I am happy for you to work from home, just let me know if you need any help, as the sooner we get this to the CPS, the sooner we can get this murdering bastard behind bars. I will deal with the team, and I will not disclose the suspect's identity. I am sure it will make headlines when that happens!'

'Oh yes, it will, sir. Well, I will get right on to this sir. I will keep you posted as to progress.' said Jo, as she got up and left the office.

Jo returned to her office and sat down to just collect her thoughts and decide how best to proceed. She then remembered the knot that had been niggling at her and started to search through her photos. She picked up the large one of Josh being roped to the cross and studied the knots holding his arms to the cross bar. She could see that it was a type of clove hitch but specifically used to tie fenders to boats, as the knot is designed to allow the weight of the fender to hold it in place. Just as the weight of Josh's body was holding the arms in place against the crossbar.

Jo recalled that in her teens when she was a Girl Guide, she had done her knots badge. She mused that when she was studying for her knots badge, little did she know that she would later use that knowledge to help solve a murder case!

This knot was tied by a sailor, Jo said to herself under her breath. So, if the suspect was a sailor, did he have a yacht and if so, did he moor it near Portchester. Jo then remembered that there was CCTV at the entrance to the Castle Sailing Club off the large Castle Street car park. She could not remember Sergeant Oliver talking about this camera at any team meeting for Operation Golgotha, but she thought that she better check.

Fortunately, he was in his office, poring over some pages of A4 as she entered, and so she quipped, 'Giving your business plan, the once over, eh Serg?'

'Got me in one!'

'Tell me. Matt, when you and your team canvassed the area for CCTV, did you contact the Castle Sailing Club as I believe they have a camera at their vehicle entrance?'

'No, Jo, I must confess I did not know about that one and we didn't. That is remiss of me. Do you think that might be significant?'

'Well, it may be. I found out in Ireland that our suspect was keen on yachts and sailing, and it may be that he kept a yacht moored nearby. I think that I will go and check out their cameras, or at least speak to the commodore.'

'Sorry Jo. If you find something significant, I'll feel really bad.'

'I'll let you know, Matt. If you want me to, that is? Bye Matt.'

'Bye Jo.'

Jo had to make an appointment to see the commodore, as he was only available at the club in the evenings. Probably only when the bar is open, she thought, unkindly.

The earliest she could get to speak with him was the following Friday evening. That was fine with her as she would not see Chris until the Saturday evening anyway. She decided to use her own car, so as not to draw attention to her visit and as she walked from the car park to the club entrance she looked up and noticed the camera. That is quite obvious, she thought, how could Matt have missed that. She could see that it could cover all traffic down the road to the castle and so would pick up any vehicle going past to drive down the northern wall side of the castle and along the gravel coastal path towards the gate into the castle grounds and so to the church. She realised that any footage from Easter would now be recorded over, and so they had missed a vital evidence gathering opportunity.

Spence will not be happy when he finds out, mused Jo. Matt might get an earlier departure date then he intended!

Jo announced herself through the speaker phone, as the entry was keypad secured and there was a click and the gate started opening. As she walked through, she noticed the cars parked around and the boats and their tenders all over the yard. The clubhouse was towards the back end of the hard standing and so she made her way there. As she opened the entrance door, she was met by a very fit looking man of average height with black hair.

'Commodore Nick Massey?' she asked.

'Yes, detective constable is it?'

'Yes, sir, Jo Fletcher.'

'How can I help you, detective constable?'

'Well, commodore, this is rather sensitive, can we go somewhere private, please?'

'We can go into the bar. There is quiet nook by the window, where we will not be disturbed. There is no one in there at the moment and the members will not be coming in for an hour or so yet.'

'Fine, sir, I am part of a team investigating a murder committed around here last Easter. It has come to our attention that a person whom we believe to be involved is a keen sailor, and so we wondered if he was known to the club or to you?'

'Do you have a name for this person, detective?'

'Well, I have an e-fit photo. Do you recognise this person? sir?' she said handing the photo to the commodore.

'Ah yes, we do have a member who resembles this photo, if fact, if I am right, he has a yacht moored out in the channel over there.' He replied pointing to the east.

Jo took the photo back from the Commodore and turned it over. 'Would that be the name of this member, sir?' she asked.

'Yes, detective. That's him.'

'And you say that his yacht is moored out there now?'

'Yes, it is just over to the left, in the channel. It is called 'Eileen.''

Well, that sort of clinches it, thought Jo. Calling the yacht after the mother of his illegitimate son.

'Commodore we would like to search that yacht please, but we do not want to alert this suspect, by serving a warrant on him. Any suggestions?' Jo was hoping that he might just say go and search it anyway but instead he had a better plan.

'All boats in the mooring channel are in the custody of the Sailing Club and as I am in charge of this club, I guess that you could serve it on me. How long does it take to get a warrant?'

'My boss will have to get clearance, and then go to the Magistrate's Court, give evidence, and hopefully secure the warrant. We would probably not have one for a fortnight or so.'

'Oh, I thought that a constable could search immediately with only an inspector's authority?'

'That is only if the constable has already arrested a suspect, which is not our situation here.'

'But I suppose you want to search the yacht as soon as you get the warrant?'

'Yes, obviously, sir.'

'Well, I do have a responsibility to my members, and so I cannot really allow a search of the yacht without a warrant.'

' I appreciate that, commodore,' said Jo.

'I like to assist the police, because you never know when we might need you, as there is a lot of valuable property around here, so I will let you know if your suspect turns up here.'

'That is brilliant, thank you sir. If he does turn up, we will have to arrest him and hope we can get enough time to search his yacht before we have to charge him. I will also make sure that the custody sergeant understands that if a call comes in from the Sailing Club then it has to get priority. Here is my card, sir, so just ring me anytime,' said Jo as she wrote her mobile number on the back of her card.

'I presume that your CCTV footage from Easter would be erased by now, sir?'

'Oh yes. We only keep them for about forty-eight hours and then they are recorded over. Our system is to check out the premises each morning, and if there is a problem or issue, we will look at the tapes, but if not we just record over them. Data Protection is a problem, you see, detective. Often our camera will record car registrations, and images of people passing, including drivers, and as we do not have these people's consent to hold these images and details, we cannot store them. Also, if people think that we are holding images of them, they have the right to see them, and we really do not want that sort of hassle.'

'I quite understand, sir.'

'Was there anything that you were specifically looking for?'

'Yes, in fact we were hoping to locate information about a motorcycle and side-car that we believe was used in the commission of this murder. We have managed to spot it coming out of the road past the cemetery but nothing since.'

'Motorcycle and side-car? We have got one stored here. Come to think of it, it has been left here by your suspect, the owner of 'Eileen'. He asked if he could store it so he could come here by train, and then use it as his transport while here. Would you like me to show it to you?'

'Yes, please, sir. This is an unexpected bonus. I have been watching out to see if someone has been trying to sell it on ebay, but to actually find it now is fantastic. A real breakthrough.'

The commodore took Jo out of the club and around to the back area where there were more yachts stacked on sticks. Right down at the back fence there was the motorbike covered in a tarpaulin. The commodore removed the tarpaulin, and Jo looked inside. There were even two helmets in the side-car.

Jo said, 'I will have to get our forensic team down here. Could they come first light tomorrow please?'

'Yes, as it happens, we have a school group coming in tomorrow for sail training, and so I will be here at seven o'clock to open up for them.'

'I will try and get them here by then, or soon after. I will get you the warrant as soon as it is issued. I have just one further question please, commodore. Do your members have to sign in visitors?'

'Yes, they do. If your suspect had any, he will have had to sign them in, and so I'll get the register.'

The commodore returned and as he brought the register, he was flicking the pages over, then finding what he was looking for, he showed the open register to Jo and said, 'See here, the week before Easter, he signed in Josh Christopher and Simon Cheyney. Oh my God!' exclaimed the commodore. They are the two murder victims, aren't they? Well, that really does link your suspect with the case.'

'Yes definitely,' replied Jo. 'You have been a great help, thank you, commodore. But please absolute secrecy about this for now. We don't want our suspect to scarper. We still have a bit more research to do before we have the open and shut case that the Prosecution Service demand before we can arrest him.'

'Absolutely, detective. As I said, if he somehow gets wind of this and comes here to try and sail away, I will ring you, now that I have your number.'

'Yes, please. Day or night. I'll go and organise the forensic team. See you tomorrow commodore.'

Jo turned towards the gate, waved goodbye and headed off to her car. She immediately rang D.I. Bligh who was still in his office. 'Sir I have some important evidence in this case. Can you remain in your office until get there?'

'Where are you now?'

'Castle Sailing Club, sir. I will only be about five minutes.'

'Okay, Jo. I think that Matt is still here. Do you want him to sit in?'

'You could give him the choice, sir. It doesn't bother me. If Sergeant Munden is available, that would be good.'

'Okay, Jo. I will try and locate him. See you in five.'

It was more like fifteen minutes by the time Jo knocked on Spence's door. Jo entered and both Sergeants Oliver and Munden were there. Jo recapped her visit to the sailing club and her conversation with the commodore and when she mentioned that the yacht was there and the motorcycle and side-car, she saw that Matt was starting to look extremely uncomfortable, fidgeting and shifting about. She noticed that Spence saw it too.

She thought that she better say something to smooth things over, as she feared that Spence was really going to go for him for missing out on investigating the sailing club when he and his team were doing the neighbourhood door to door enquiries.

'I know Matt, that your not investigating the sailing club was an omission, but I doubt that it would have saved any of the other two victims, as by the time your team were doing the house to house, Simon was already dead, and our take at that time was the murder/suicide scenario until Salter's murder in the hotel. We might just have got to this point a bit earlier, that's all.'

Spence then spoke and said, 'It might have done, had I not been so eager to wrap up the case with the easy solution. Anyway, water under the bridge. Jo, you have saved the day. We now need to plan our next move.

Matt, can you please organise the search warrant and name Commodore Nicholas Massey as the person on whom we are serving the warrant. It will probably take about a fortnight but let me know when you have got it so we can serve it on the commodore as soon as possible.

Arthur, can you get SOCO together and get down to the sailing club just after seven tomorrow and search the side-car.

Get our pathologist there as well, as hopefully we will find Josh's blood in the side-car, and perhaps some DNA in one of the helmets. The suspect's fingerprints should be all over the show. They can then be compared with the fingerprints that Jo took off the ladder at the college, which are now on the database.

I will organise for the Portsmouth Police Launch to be at the Sailing Club when we get the warrant. Do those guys a bit of good to do something other than just motoring up and down past the 'Queen Elizabeth' aircraft carrier. When we search the yacht we will be looking for rope, a knife, and anything else, Jo?'

'Receipts or evidence of the purchase of the pulleys that we believe were used to haul Josh's body up onto the cross and all that we found in Simon's car.'

'Yes, of course.' said Spence. 'Well guys, if that is everything, see you all tomorrow. Sorry that it is a Saturday but that seems to be a bit of a characteristic of this case, doesn't it?'

As they went out of Spence's office, Jo went up to Matt, and said: 'If you need any info for the warrant application, let me know and I will get it to you.'

'Fine, Jo. And Jo?'

'Yes.'

'Thank for what you said in there. I was feeling pretty bad about not contacting the sailing club. Still do. I thought that Spence was going to go for me, until you spoke up.'

'That's fine, Matt. No need for a domestic at this stage. Remember, it was Spence who held out for the murder/suicide solution, so he has mucked up a bit on this case as well. Tomorrow should be a good day, and hopefully it will turn up more valuable evidence to nail this murderer.

Jo set off home and was surprised to see her front window open. She knew that she had never left it like that as she was

211

meticulous about locking and securing her home. The reason why soon appeared at the front door in the form of Chris holding a glass of red. 'You definitely don't work nine to five, do you, Jo? I have come down as I have a present for you.'

'Oh, I thought you had come to see me, but a present is next best, I suppose.'

'Of course, I have come to see you. Now, have a look at this.' He held out a pint beer glass in a cardboard box. 'What do you think this is?'

'A pint glass, you idiot.'

'Yes, and no. Yes, it is a pint glass, but it is also our suspect's fingerprints!'

'What!'

'Well, I thought that I would do some sleuthing on my own, and I remembered that you didn't have the killer's fingerprints. On my way home to my parents, I called in to Twickers where we are welcomed to drink at the bar, normally to give out gossip, but we usually collect more than we give out and our suspect was there drinking. I went over to his table and just started chatting about nothing in general but a bit about preparation for the All Blacks game and then I offered to buy him a beer.

He agreed, and I took his empty glass, and carefully placed it in my coat pocket which I was carrying and got him a pint in another glass. So here is his pint glass, and if you hold it up to the light you can see fingerprints there. I know that some will be bar staff, and I was careful to hold it by the base and so as not to disturb his prints. Hopefully, this will be your match.'

'Chris, that's tremendous. You deserve a big kiss for that.'

'Just a kiss. I thought it might be worth more than that.'

'Now, down boy. What's for dinner?'

'Pizza and salad.'

'Oh, healthy. Now I have got news for you.'

Jo told him about the day's events and her hopes for good solid evidence to be found by SOCO and the pathologist. Chris stayed the night but left by an early train on the Saturday to cover his rugby games. Jo was up early too and set off for the Sailing Club, hoping that it would be a good day.

And so, it was a good day. Not only did they find blood in the side-car that Peter Good, the pathologist later confirmed belonged to Josh, but they got a match with the fingerprints that both Jo had taken from the ladder and from the glass that Chris had taken from the Twickenham bar.

It was a fortnight to the day, when they got the warrant, and Matt served it on the commodore and the whole team were transported to the yacht by the Coastal Police, and they searched the yacht.

Amongst the evidence they gathered from the yacht, they found the knife that the pathologist later confirmed had been used to stab Josh's body, they found two dumbbells that would have been used to wind the victims and bring them to the ground. They also got a rope sample that matched the rope used to tie Josh to the cross, and to suspend Simon's body from the crossbar at the college.

Jo found a box of paperwork, which when she methodically went through it, she found receipts for the pulleys and a receipt from Kleeneze for the small collapsible ladder that was on the ground below Simon's body.

Jo was able to take the pulley receipts to the marine hardware shop at Port Milton where the manager found a link to the original purchase as the company gave discount to sailing club members and noted their membership numbers on their receipts for audit purposes.

213

There was now no doubt that the suspect had purchased the pulleys. Jo now had all the evidence she needed to sit down and write her brief for the Crown Prosecutor. She would start that on the Monday.

.

CHAPTER SIXTEEN

Jo decided to start writing her brief in her office at the police station, so that she had everything to hand. Spence kept popping his head around her door to see if she needed anything, but generally she was left alone to get on with it. She had decided to take Spencer's advice and concentrate all the evidence around each victim in turn,

She started with Josh, the first victim. Correlating photos and potential court exhibits with her text she started with Josh on the cross at St. Mary's Church, the rope that tied him to the cross, the sailing knots used, the theory that the pulleys that were recovered from Simon's car were used to haul the body up onto the cross and the fact that there were receipts for those pulleys identifying the murderer had purchased them from a local marine supplier. She noted that the same rope used on the cross was found on the murderer's yacht.

Then there was the fire door in the tea room where the murderer had exited the church after the Good Friday service, and re-entered later with Josh's body. She then wrote about the evidence of the cycle and side-car tracks around the church and how CCTV had recorded the vehicle passing along the lane from the college field where there were more tracks from the point where Josh had been killed and knifed with the knife found on the murderer's yacht. She included the CCTV photos of the motorcycle and side-car filmed going along Cormorant Path, towards the church. She also included the photos of the bloodstained field where the body had been stabbed and hidden until later in the evening when the murderer returned to take it to the church.

She included the fact that the motorcycle and side-car had been located at the Castle Sailing Club where the murderer was a member. As she wrote the brief, she annotated points at which different experts would be able to provide evidence, such as SOCO and the pathologist. She also drew up a list of exhibits, where each was found, and what importance they had as evidence.

By the time that she had finished dealing with Josh, she gathered up her files and laptop and called into see Spence and told him she would be working from home the next day and so wished him goodnight.

The next day would be a Tuesday. Jo knew that until she had completed the brief the Crown Prosecution Service (CPS) would not be able to evaluate the facts and decide as to whether there was a definite chance of securing a conviction. As this case would be high profile, Jo knew that the CPS would not proceed unless a conviction was virtually one hundred percent a certainty. Only then would they authorise issuing a warrant to arrest the perpetrator.

On the Tuesday, after a cooked breakfast Jo disciplined herself into getting started straight away on her brief. She re-read what she had written about Josh, made a few amendments and then started on victim number two, Simon.

She followed the same format that she had done with Josh, starting with the caretaker finding the body suspended from the cross bar of the rugby goal posts. The set of steps lying on the ground under the body to simulate Simon hanging himself and kicking away the steps. She linked the purchase of the steps to the Kleeneze receipt found on the suspect's yacht. The finding of Simon's car with the incriminating pieces of evidence in it.

The finding of the seller of the motorcycle and side-car on ebay, and the vehicle being registered in Simon's name. She then related the decision of D.I. Bligh based on these findings that Simon killed Josh and hung himself. She detailed her account of her rope test on the cross bar with weights and the fact that there was no evidence that Simon had an ebay account or had spent any money that could not be accounted for by his father. Her consequent conclusion later shared by the Detective Inspector and the team that Simon was murdered and did not kill himself.

She then turned to Raymond Salter, the third victim. She recounted the birthday party as relayed to her by Chris and confirmed by the hotel manager and Anne and Sarah, including the ascertaining and locating of the guest, Mr Brown, who purchased the bedroom for Raymond. She included the pathologist's report on the alcohol levels and injection points. She detailed the CCTV coverage and the evidence that the cameras produced, especially that of Frank O'Glynn returning to the hotel early in the morning and that his room was next to the victim's and it had a connecting door. She reviewed her notes and realised that there was starting to build up quite a lot of witnesses! It would be a long trial if they all had to be called.

Finally, she outlined how she came to identify the suspect with Michael's revelation that Arthur O'Neill was adopted, getting the biological mother's name from the adoption agency, visiting her in Ireland and finally identifying the suspect.

Once finished, she re-read it and was really pleased with the result. As Chris had come down, she showed it to him. He read it through carefully and said,

'Jo, this is really comprehensive and thorough. You really have a knack for this sort of thing. The killer does not have a chance, you will get a conviction. I couldn't use this as a basis for my story, could I?'

'Not straight away, no. Sorry Chris. However, if and when he is charged, he happens to plead "Guilty" then you could use it but if he pleads "Not Guilty" you could not use it until the prosecution have made their opening statement to the jury. If they are then sequestered and so legally won't have access to TV and papers so you could probably print it then. Your editor should advise you on that as it is the editor who will get rebuked by the judge if the line is crossed.'

On the Thursday morning Jo gave her brief to Spence. He flicked through it while she stood there, and looked up and said this is good, exceptionally good. I will copy it myself so as to keep it confidential and personally deliver a copy to the CPS. We should hear back early next week which will give us plenty of time to take the next step. Are you sure you still want to make the arrest?'

'Oh, yes sir.'

'Very, well.'

It was Chief Constable Emily James, who contacted Jo on the Friday morning to say that the Crown Prosecutor was happy with the brief and they will authorise a warrant. The Chief Constable added that the CPS were so impressed with the brief that they have asked permission to use it as a training brief after the case is over to show others how a brief should be written. She also said that the Crown Prosecutor had shown it to a legal colleague who is a criminal defence barrister, and asked him if he had this suspect as a client and received this brief, how would he advise his client to plead?

'Do you want to know what he said, detective constable ?'

'Yes, please ma'am?' replied Jo.

'He said that he would advise his client to plead 'Guilty' to Voluntary Manslaughter and rely on his submissions for a reduced sentence based on diminished responsibility due to an over-arching obsession to see his son play for England against the All Blacks and win the Autumn internationals. He added that he could not see any loopholes in your case that could be exploited by defence. There is just one question that he has for you, detective constable?'

'Yes, chief constable,' said Jo.

'What he wants is a brief opening statement for his address to the jury, if he has to make one, or that he could give to the press if he pleads guilty. Could you do that?'

'I would say something like, this is a case where the accused originally thought that he could achieve his plan of engineering the player selection process for fly-halves so that his biological son would be selected to play in the England squad against the All Blacks in the Rugby Autumn Internationals by murdering two players who had already been selected to play at fly-half for the team.

These murders were carried out to look like a murder and a suicide. That one player murdered the other, then out of remorse took his own life. The context of these two murders was within the christian tradition of Christ's death on the cross and Judas Iscariot's death by hanging. When a third player was up for selection against the accused's son, the accused tried to buy off one of the selectors to ensure his son was selected and when that ruse failed, he then took the opportunity at a birthday party to

219

murder this third selection, thus leaving the way clear for his son to finally be selected.

That is why this third murder is not within the same context as the other two, as it was not the original intention of the accused to murder three players.'

'Thank you, detective constable. I have noted what you have said and will pass it on to the Crown Prosecutor. All in all, you have achieved a great result, and you are to be congratulated. Well done.'

'Thank you, ma'am,' replied Jo.

About an hour later, Spencer entered Jo's office and said,

'Jo, the Chief Constable has been in touch with me and she would like to meet with you, the CPS and myself. It is apparently to do with the timing of issuing the warrant and arresting our suspect. The rugby game is not for a couple of months yet, is it?'

'No, Spence, not until Saturday 10th November.'

'Ah well, we have plenty of time. The meeting is set up for tomorrow afternoon, at 2.00pm at HQ in Winchester. Can you attend please?'

'Yes, of course. I'll take the train so as not use up the car pool.'

'Okay, I will see you there.'

Jo could only remember three previous occasions when she had set foot inside the Hampshire Police Headquarters and they were all to do with interviews for her career as a police officer.

Spencer was there when she entered the conference room, and he introduced her to the Chief Constable and the Crown Prosecutor, a young looking dark-haired man who obviously had some disability as he used a cane.

Once the meeting started, The Chief Constable praised the Fareham Constabulary in general and Jo in particular for the solving of these murders. The Crown Prosecutor endorsed the chief's comments, and then the meeting got down to the subject matter of arresting the suspect.

The Chief Prosecutor said that he had two main concerns, one was to do with Arthur and the other to do with public relations regarding this high profile case. The concern about Arthur was that the arrest of his biological father would reveal Arthur's adoptive status, and he did not consider it appropriate that he should hear about that in such a public way.

'Time,' he said, 'should be given to his adoptive parents to tell him that he is adopted, even if they do not reveal who his natural parents are, straight away.'

The Crown Prosecutor then went on to talk about the public relations aspect. 'At this time all the Rugby Union Officials will be engrossed in preparing the squad for the Autumn Internationals.

As our suspect is probably considered to be a key person in all of that, it would be very upsetting to the whole team to remove him at this stage, and the rugby public would not forgive us, especially if an early arrest affected any of the game outcomes. I don't see that there is any hurry, as there is no need for any more murders as the perpetrator has got his wish, and our suspect is not likely to vanish. I propose that we wait until the last game of the season is being played until we make our arrest. Now, my secretary tells me that is the game against the All Blacks on 10th November. Is that right,' he said, looking at Jo.

'Yes, sir, that's the last match,' said Jo.

'Well, what do you all think?' said the prosecutor.

There was about fifteen minutes debate, and everybody seemed to agree with the proposal. The Chief Constable then said, 'Well, that's what we will do. Jo, I understand that you want to carry out the arrest?'

'Yes, please sir,' she replied.

'Very well, a warrant to arrest our suspect will be issued and will be executed during the England versus the All Blacks game at Twickenham on Saturday 10th November. This delay will also enable Arthur's parents sufficient time to disclose his adoption status to him.'

At that, he adjourned the meeting and Spencer approached Jo, and said, 'I hope, Jo, that you are not too disappointed in not being able to make an immediate arrest?'

'Oh no sir, I agree with the sentiments expressed at the meeting, especially giving time for Arthur to come to terms with being adopted, as he will probably be playing for England and will need to be in top form.'

'Fine, Jo. In relation to that, can you tell his parents that they need to tell him sooner, rather than later and before the games start.'

'Yes, sir, I will.'

'Well, Jo I know it will be difficult waiting until November, but I am sure that there is something in your in-tray that you can start working on. If not, then there is always studying for your Sergeant Board exams. Can I give you a lift back to Fareham, or do you want to go by train?'

'Thank you, Spence, a lift would be very welcome.'

Spencer was right, Jo found it hard to concentrate over the following two months, but she managed to do other work of a more menial nature and part of her wanted to work on another murder!

But October passed, and November came. Chris had got her tickets for all the Internationals and she had sat with him in the press box and got to know the other reporters. There was a fair bit of ribbing of Chris because he was going out with a copper, but it was all in good fun. Jo had really enjoyed watching the games with Chris and her relationship with him developed. England played well, and Jo was particularly interested in watching Arthur playing. He was playing well. She had not spoken with him and hoped that his parents had told him of his adoption and how well he had responded.

England had won all its games, and then the last game was on. New Zealand had won all their games too, and so the last game was going to be a real spectacle.

CHAPTER SEVENTEEN

Jo woke early on the Saturday morning, as she was meeting Chris at Twickenham station at eleven thirty. She had to get a train to Waterloo and change for the Strawberry Hill train to Twickenham. As she was staying over with Chris's family, she had a holdall with her as well as the arrest warrant.

Mrs. Charlotte Foley was at the station with Chris and they both came to meet her.

'I didn't realise that you liked rugby as well, Mrs. Foley,' said Jo.

'Charlotte, please, Jo. Yes, I like rugby, but I am not coming with you. I have just come down to collect your bag, as you won't be wanting to lug that around the ground.'

'Oh, thank you, Charlotte. That is truly kind of you.'

'Jo, I was wondering if you would care to join me tomorrow and do a bit of shopping together?'

Jo quickly realised that this was a great opportunity for her to get to know Chris's mother, and so she immediately said, 'Yes, I'd love to.'

As Jo and Chris made their way to the rugby ground, Chris said, 'Sorry to land Mum on you like that, but since I am an only child, she likes to take someone shopping with her. She will probably want to buy you a dress or something, so I would suggest, just let her.'

'That's fine Chris. I really don't mind. It should be fun, and it will be good for me to get to know your Mum.'

'Our seats are in the press box as usual, Jo, they got drinks at one of the many bars around the ground and soon they were in their seats waiting for the game to start. After the National Anthems, the All Blacks assembled to do the traditional *Haka*.

Originally the *Haka* was a ceremonial Maori war dance that involves chanting, but today it is a similar performance before a rugby game. Whether the *Haka* fazes the opposition or not is never really discussed. It is just what the All Blacks do.

The first half was deemed technically particularly good rugby by the purists, but as a spectator sport it was fairly boring. Both sides had excellent defence and there was a lot of forward rugby going into twenty phases on occasion without any breakthroughs, interceptions or running backs. Fortunately, there were very few penalties and so no chances for penalty goals to start off the scoring.

Jo was interested to see how Arthur played, and his play as the fly-half was business-like but no sign of any real brilliance, mainly through lack of openings. By the thirty-eighth minute, two minutes before half time, the score was nil all, and then the All Blacks knocked the ball forward and a scrum was awarded on the halfway line.

England put-in. Jo thought that this would probably be the last play before half-time. The scrum was set, the ball put in and hooked back to the England half-back, who looked for Arthur to pass the ball to, and Arthur was coming around the scrum to the blind side, and he received the ball from the half-back, and then sprinted off down the side-line. Towards him came the All Black winger, the number 11, a large, extremely fast man, who usually needed at least three players to bring him down, and against him was only one, Arthur.

225

It looked like it was going to be a massacre but then Arthur punted the ball high and long over the All Black's head, raced past him towards the goal line, and then caught the ball as it was descending, the All Black full back being too far away to catch it. Arthur raced with the ball to the line and scored just to the right of the goal posts. There was a deafening roar from the crowd, and Jo even felt a surge of pride. The score was now five nil to England. Arthur converted his own try and as the half time whistle blew, he was carried off the field by his teammates, with the scoreboard flashing seven–nil to England.

Jo turned to Chris and said, 'Brilliant try. That will make Arthur's Dad proud. Now we are on, so come on Chris, let's do it!'

'At that comment, one of the other reporters piped up and said, 'Off for a half-time one in the tack room, eh Chris?'

'We know that you work for a smutty tabloid, Johnny, but you don't have to be smutty yourself!'

'Yes, Jo might arrest you!' piped up another.

'On what charge?' said Johnny,

'How about casting offensive matter, since you talk such excreta,' joined in Jo.

The group laughed, and Chris took Jo by the hand as they went towards the tunnel where the players entered and exited the ground. Both player and opposition dressing rooms were off this tunnel and Jo and Chris were headed for the English dressing room. As they neared the dressing room, Jo saw the two policemen standing at the car park end of the tunnel. She went up to them and said: 'Thanks for coming down, sergeant, and constable. Is the paddy wagon outside?'

'Yes, detective constable. We are all ready.'

'And are you going straight off to Fareham with the suspect?'

226

'No, we have orders to take him back to our nick, and he will be transported later along with some other remand prisoners on their way to Winchester.'

'Fine, said Jo. Well, let's do this.'

At that, Jo went and opened the door to the English squad dressing room. As soon as they all entered, somebody yelled out, 'Hey, this is private. No visitors allowed.'

Jo was expecting something like this so quick as a flash she replied: 'We are not visitors we are police, and we have come to make an arrest.

My name is Detective Constable Jo Fletcher, from Fareham Police, Hampshire, and we are here to arrest the person who killed Josh, Simon and Raymond.'

The cries of indignation that had been reverberating around the dressing room since they entered suddenly went quiet.

Jo broke the silence with, 'Great try, by the way Arthur. I have not seen one scored like that since watching our college first fifteen. Definitely the best way to avoid being brought down by their winger.' Jo then turned to the coach and said, 'You must be very proud of your protégé, coach. I hope that for your sake, you think that it has been worth the trouble to see him play against the All Blacks, and score the winning goal, at least for the first half.'

'What do you mean, worth the trouble?'

'Glen Francis, or should I say Frank O'Glynn, I am arresting you for the murders of Josh Christopher, Simon Cheyney and Raymond Salter. You do not have to say anything. But it may harm your defence if you do not mention when questioned something which you later rely on in court. Anything you do say may be given in evidence.'

'Could this not wait until the end of the game, detective?'

'Don't worry, sir, these guys...' Jo indicated the two policemen at the dressing room door, 'will take you to the Twickenham Police Station and I am sure there will be a television there for you to watch the second half. You may even be asked for your autograph!

I will see you on Monday at Fareham Police Station. Take him away please sergeant.'

As Jo turned to leave the dressing room, she called back, 'Good luck chaps for the second half,' and she was gone.

Once back in the Press Room, Jo turned to Chris and said, 'Well, at least that's done. I wonder how he will plead?'

'Once he hears what you have got on him, 'Guilty' I expect. Anyway Jo, now you can tell me. How did you know back in Ireland that it was the coach who changed his name from Frank O'Glynn?'

'Obvious really, most people who change their name usually change it to something that resembles a bit of their real name. I suppose it is a bit psychological, in that they do not want to lose their real persona completely. All he did, in effect, was swap his names around. First name to surname and vice versa. Frank O'Glynn became Glen Francis.

Now, Chris, I will have that pint that you were just about to offer me, and in view of the Irish connections in this case, I will have a Guinness.

CHAPTER EIGHTEEN

Jo woke on the following Monday to a ping on her mobile, which was a summons to Spencer's office. She quickly dressed and was soon knocking on his office door expecting high praise. 'Morning Jo, thanks for coming in. Please take a seat.'

'I would rather stand, sir, if that is okay.'

'No, Jo, I think you should sit for this.'

'Is something amiss, sir?'

'Well, I came in yesterday and Matt and I interviewed Coach Francis. Jo don't give me that look, it is part of my job. We are a team, here, a crime squad and we work together. It's not Jo Fletcher, Private Investigator!!'

'Point taken, sir, but I would like to talk to him too, if I may.'

' Firstly, there is no need, and secondly, you can't as he is not here.'

'What!'

'Well, you know that we can only hold a suspect for 36 hours, by which time we have to charge, release or apply for more time.'

'So I presume that Coach Francis has been charged?'

'No, I released him yesterday afternoon, as there were not enough grounds to hold him any longer.'

Looking dumbfounded, Jo blurted out, 'But the evidence I collected?'

'Ah, the evidence. Excellent in describing each murder, how they were committed and who was involved but it doesn't irrefutably link them to Coach Francis. That part is all circumstantial.'

Jo was about to interrupt, but Spencer raised his hand and said, 'Jo, you need to listen to the recording of our interview, and then we can talk. Okay?'

'Yes, of course, sir.'

D.I Blake went over to his desk and switched on a tape recorder. He turned up the speakers and sat down.

'This is a tape recording of an interview with murder suspect Frank O'Glynn, also known as Glen Francis. Present are the suspect, D.I.Blake and Sergeant M.Oliver. The time is 3:00pm on Sunday 11th November.

'How would like to be referred to, O'Glynn or Francis?'

'Coach will be just fine, thanks sir.'

'What are your immediate thoughts, coach, on being arrested for these three rugby related murders?' started Spence.

'Well, absolutely flabbergasted, really, sir, to think that anyone could even think that I am capable of this. I am the English Rugby National Coach and my job is to develop rugby throughout the land. My role is to bring in more talented players and develop them to premier standards or more, not kill them off.

Yes, these murders have enabled my own son to be selected to play for England, but that is not the way I do things. Further, my role is to help players like my son to improve to the point that they can be considered suitable for selection by their own merits, not by criminal queue-jumping.'

'Well, obviously we have collected a lot of evidence that brought us to the decision to arrest you, coach, so let us go through it. Okay?' continued Spence.

'Then I would like a lawyer present, please?'

'Sure, that is your right. At this point, would you be happy with the Duty Solicitor, or is there somebody you wish us to call?'

'Oh, I have already contacted my solicitor, he is over the road at *Freshcos* waiting for my call.'

'Right we will suspend this interview until he arrives. Interview suspended at 3:45pm.' announced Spencer. Once the solicitor arrived, he and the coach were given half an hour together and then the interview was resumed.

Spencer switched on the tape and followed the appropriate procedure and then launched into the specific evidence that he wanted the coach to respond to.

'Regarding the first murder, Josh O'Connor, the ropes used to bind him to the makeshift cross are identical to the rope found in the front locker of your yacht, the "Eileen", moored at the Castle Sailing Club, along with the knife used to stab Josh, the dumbells used to stun him and the receipts for the pulleys used to hoist his body onto the cross. How do you explain that please?'

'How did the police get into the locker, through the cockpit?'

'Yes, I think so,' replied Spence.

'Well the bow hatch on the deck is also an entry point into that locker and it isn't locked, but sits on the bow, so anybody could have access to the locker by merely lifting the hatch cover. That access is used for stowing away the spinnaker,' replied the coach.

'Regarding the murder of Simon Cheyney, your fingerprints were on the school's ladder that was used to hoist Simon's body and hang it from the cross-bar.'

'Is that the ladder that the caretaker leaves out for staff to use to retrieve balls from the school roof?'

'Yes, I believe it is,' replied Spence.

'The week before Easter, I was holding kicking practice with both Josh and Simon at the school and Josh kicked a ball onto the gym roof. It rolled down the valley and lodged in the guttering and hopper. I used the ladder to retrieve it, so yes, my prints would be all over it.

We train with proper competition balls which are very expensive and so I am not likely to leave them on the roof when they can be so easily retrieved, am I?'

By this time, Spencer was starting to think that perhaps the wrong man had been arrested and the coach should have been interviewed before he was so summarily arrested in so public a manner.

The answer to Spence's next question sort of clinched that for him. 'We believe that the murder of Josh O'Connor involved a motorcycle and side-car, purchased on ebay and this vehicle was found, stored at the back of the Castle Sailing Club. The commodore confirmed that it belonged to you and we found your fingerprints on it and a crash helmet with Josh's DNA on it.'

'Yes, the motorbike and side-car are mine. I have only had them a short time and store it at the club so that I have transport when I come down from from London by train. I bought it together with the helmets off a journalist friend, Chris Foley, who said he had no further need for it.'

At the mention of Chris's name, Jo emitted an audible gasp and Spencer stopped the tape and said, 'This is why I wanted to see you Jo, as soon as possible, and for you to sit down and listen to it. I'm afraid that there is more to come. Would you like a drink of anything?'

'No thank you, Spence, let's keep listening.'

'Okay,' said Spence as he turned the tape back on.

'How do you know Chris Foley?' asked Matt.

'Well, naturally I know him professionally in his role as the senior rugby correspondent for the *Sportsman Daily* but we

232

became friendly after he did a bio on me when I was appointed coach. He was the person who found out the name of the family who had adopted my biological son, Arthur.

On information that I gave him he travelled with his wife to Ireland and met Arthur's mother, Eileen. Then working through adoption contacts he located Arthur. I was really chuffed to find out that Arthur was such a good rugby player and now I coach him.'

Jo exclaimed, 'Wife?' and Spencer nodded. Jo sank back into her seat as the tape rolled on.

'Did, you tell Foley your real name?' asked Matt.

'Yes, I did. He needed to know that to find my son's biological mother. I have trusted him. At least up until now.'

On hearing this Jo now realised that the reason why Chris did not want to meet Eileen with her in Ireland was because she would have recognised him and know that he already knew what they had gone to Ireland to find out.

Jo really started to feel that in falling for Chris she had made a massive mistake. To think she would have probably said "yes" if he had asked her to marry him!

Spence then asked the coach. 'Do you know the Whiteley Hotel, coach?'

'Is that where Ray Salter was killed?'

'Yes.'

'Well, I have never been there, and I did not attend the birthday party. Perhaps I should have, to keep an eye on things, and then the outcome might have been very different.'

At this point, the solicitor cut in and said, 'Well, detective inspector, my client seems to have satisfactorily answered all your questions and his time since his arrest is approaching the limit of your authority. Are you going to charge my client or

233

release him, please?'

Spencer turned to Matt, and asked, 'Do you have any more questions, sergeant?'

'No sir.'

'In that case coach, you are free to go, but I would appreciate it if you don't talk to anyone about the evidence we have discussed, especially not to Chris Foley, as we still have to find our murderer.'

'No, of course I won't. I want you to find him too you know.'

Spencer then switched off the tape and he turned to Jo and said, 'I am sorry that you had to hear all that. but you can see now why we could not charge the coach for these murders. There was sufficient evidence to arrest him on Saturday, but in hindsight we should have brought him in under caution and interviewed him before we sought the warrant.

Now, Jo, since that interview Matt has been making further enquiries and so over to you Matt.'

'I have been following two lines of enquiry. One is a full background check on Chris Foley. Sorry Jo but you will by now appreciate that he is not whom you thought he was. The second is to get Sergeant Munden and his team to reconsider the fingerprint evidence, on the school ladder, the yacht and the motorbike and side-car.

With regards to Chris Foley his real date of birth is April Fool's Day 1976 and so he is 42. As you heard from the coach he is married and has three children. He met his wife some twenty-five years ago and they have a son aged 22 who was seven when his parents married. He is registered under his mother's maiden name which is Maidment. He is also a good rugby player who plays for the Wasps.

Spence and I think it would be a good idea for you to interview Foley's wife before you see Chris again. I have spoken to her by telephone and she would like to meet you. She did know about you as Chris had kept her informed. A strange set up, I think.'

'How could I get it so wrong, sir' asked Jo tearfully. To think I would have happily married him, if he had asked me?

Yes, I will arrange to meet her today. I am meant to be meeting Chris again this evening after work but that is not going to happen now.'

'Jo,' said Spencer, 'I do not think that you should meet Chris without some back-up support. We have a decision to make after we hear Sergeant Munden's account of his team's work yesterday and today.'

Spencer then rang the SOCO line and announced, 'He is now on his way here.'

As if on cue, there was a knock on the door and Sergeant Munden came in. He noticed Jo and nodded, mouthing the words "very sorry" to her.

Addressing the room he began, 'My team have reviewed all the fingerprints and using the prints that Jo gathered from the coach's pint glass, and from Chris Foley from the prints Jo took when they were doing the re-enactment at the school, Chris Foley's prints show up on the school ladder, the yacht hatch cover, and the motorbike and side-car. We presumed that it was quite probable that he was the one who checked into the Whiteley Hotel and took the room next to Salter's and checked in using the coach's real name.

Graham enlarged a photo of Chris from his *Sportsman Daily* by-line and we showed it to staff at the hotel, one of whom recognised him as the person registering as O'Glynn.

235

Consequently, I am pretty sure we can link him to all three murders, but his motive seems unclear, as his rugby playing son is nowhere near England squad standard. Perhaps Jo you can glean something there from his wife. That does seem a bit of a strange set-up.'

'My God, I have been sleeping with a triple murderer,' moaned Jo.

Spence got up and put his arm around Jo's shoulders and she burst into tears. Matt and Arthur quietly left the office.

Jo then took out her Hampshire Police warrant card and said, 'I suppose that you would like my resignation, sir?'

'No, Jo, I don't bloody well want your resignation. You are a good detective. You have just learned a valuable lesson, that in this game, you cannot trust anybody until you have checked them out.

Chris Foley needed to keep tabs on the investigation, for his own freedom, and he used you as his source of information. It is fortunate that he did not twig on how it was proceeding after Francis's arrest on Saturday, otherwise he could have turned against you, Jo.

I feel that I must take responsibility for this, due to a domestic situation I have taken my eye off the ball. I have left you to do all the work without my checking. I should have gone through the evidence and in hindsight interviewed Francis under caution before just approving his arrest during the game.

We have also come under fire for making the arrest during half-time and not waiting until the final whistle. It is thought that if we had waited, then the English squad might not have lost the match due to being upset at having their coach arrested for killing their former fellow rugby pals.

My eyes have been off the ball due to my daughter taking up with a known drug dealer. I am in the brown stuff with Abbotsford for pulling his rap sheet and even though I showed them his convictions my daughter and her mother think he should have a second chance. In my book, drug dealers don't get second chances.'

'Thank you, sir, for your frankness and support. I think I would welcome being in the brown stuff, if I could have found out about the type of scumbag Chris is before I allowed him into my life. I shall get the address from Matt and see Mrs. Foley and get back to you.'

Mrs. Foley looked more her age of 42 than Chris did and as soon as she introduced herself, she said, 'I know who you are, as Chris has kept me posted.'

'So you knew that he was sleeping with me?'

'Oh yes. He'll do anything for a story and good ratings. You see, Jo, if I may call you that, my husband has the happy knack of passing himself off as being 10 to 12 years younger than he actually is, whereas, as you can see, I am definitely my 42 years. That's probably from putting up with him for these past 22 years.'

'Doesn't it bother you, his being unfaithful?'

'No, it's just sex to him and usually with a younger woman and as soon as he has what he wants he comes home to me.'

'What about his mother. She took me to her bosom, I thought as a prospective daughter-in-law, and bought me a lovely expensive dress.'

'Oh, I know his mum very well and she just lets him do what he wants and asks of her. He says it is to maintain credibility in

237

his journalistic investigations. We are not a conventional family, Jo. You are best well out of it.'

'Oh, do not worry on my account, I am well out of it now,' stated Jo, 'but please tell me, what is his motivation, especially in respect of these murders?'

'It's the challenge. To see if he can do it and get away with it. Finding the coach's biological son gave him the idea of killing off those ahead of him in the rankings and framing the coach. It nearly worked too. He would do it as research for a book. Moving in with you was also for research and to keep apace with how the investigation was going and whether he was in danger or not. I am sorry to say it Jo, but you were used.'

'Am I in danger now, that his cover has been blown?'

'I wouldn't have thought so, as for all his faults, Chris is not a violent man.'

'Except for killing people!!'

At that Mrs. Foley let out a laugh.

'Isn't he afraid of going to prison?'

'Not really, he would see that as an opportunity for more research and probably do an "Archer" and write books from prison. After all he is a journalist at heart.'

'Anything for a good yarn. Well if he writes a book about me, I will sue the pants off him,' Jo replied.

'That will not be difficult, they usually come off him pretty easily!'

Jo wondered if that comment was directed at her. She suddenly wanted to get out of that house and away from the Foleys and all they represented. She made her excuses, thanked Mrs. Foley for seeing her and left.

On her way back on the train, she checked that her secretly

hidden Dictaphone had recorded their conversation and once back at Fareham she went straight to Spencer's office. She gave him a brief account of her meeting with Mrs. Foley and handed over the Dictaphone. 'I know this cannot be used in evidence as it was obtained secretly and off the record, but it at least confirms that he did commit the murders and his wife knew about it. If she is called as a prosecution witness then it gives the CPS areas of questioning.'

'Well done Jo. That was brave as if she knew that she was being recorded she might have got nasty. They are obviously a strange set-up all round. You are well out of it!'

'Yes, I realise that. What's next, sir?'

'Well, I will drive you home with a couple of uniforms as backup and if Foley is there we will arrest him and take him back the station. Before you ask, Jo, no, you cannot sit in on our interview with him, as you may need to be called as a prosecution witness.'

'Yes, I understand, sir. Anyway I don't want to spend another moment more than I have to with him.'

That is exactly what transpired. When they arrived at her house, Chris opened the door with a glass of red as usual and Spencer and Jo went towards him. The two constables stayed out of sight as Spencer said, 'Chris, Jo has something to say to you.'

'Chris Foley, I am arresting you for the murders of Josh Christopher, Simon Cheyney and Raymond Salter. You do not have to say anything, but it may harm your defence if you do not mention when questioned something which you later rely on in court. Anything you do say may be given in evidence.

Good-bye Chris. It was good talking with your wife, this afternoon. Very enlightening. Take him away constables, and feel free to give him a massive kick in the goolies when you lock

239

him up. Oh also, please get my set of house keys off him. Bye Chris. You will enjoy prison. You will fit in well as it is full of arseholes like you.'

Printed in Poland
by Amazon Fulfillment
Poland Sp. z o.o., Wrocław

23486582R00139